# MURDER BY MUSIC

A QUILTED MYSTERY

# MURDER BY MUSIC

## THE WEDDING QUILT

# BARBARA GRAHAM

**WHEELER PUBLISHING**
*A part of Gale, Cengage Learning*

GALE
CENGAGE Learning·

Detroit • New York • San Francisco • New Haven, Conn • Waterville, Maine • London

## GALE
### CENGAGE Learning·

**LIBRARY OF CONGRESS CATALOGING-IN-PUBLICATION DATA**

Graham, Barbara, 1948–
  Murder by music : the wedding quilt, a quilted mystery / by Barbara Graham.
    p. cm. — (Wheeler Publishing large print cozy mystery)
    ISBN-13: 978-1-4104-4448-6 (softcover)
    ISBN-10: 1-4104-4448-1 (softcover)
    1. Sheriffs—Fiction. 2. Quilting—Fiction. 3. Tennessee—Fiction. 4. Large type books. I. Title.
PS3607.R336M86 2012
813'.6—dc23                                                2011040635

Published in 2012 by arrangement with Tekno Books and Ed Gorman.

Printed in the United States of America
  1 2 3 4 5      15 14 13 12 11
FD351

*For Denny*

# ACKNOWLEDGEMENTS

With grateful thanks to my confused but accepting friends and family. I know it can't be easy dealing with my failure to keep up with the real world.

Thanks again to Michelle Quick, who doesn't like to do mystery quilts, thereby becoming the best possible tester. (If there's a problem, it's all her fault.)

To companion dogs without equal — Max and Grace insist I not spend all my time with imaginary friends. We are often together at the lakes checking for ducks, herons, swans, swallows, pelicans, and their favorite — other people with dogs.

Last, but certainly not least, my editor Alice Duncan, who makes sense of my stories.

# Big as a Mountain Mystery Quilt

## FIRST SET OF CLUES

This quilt is a large wall hanging or over-sized lap quilt. Use flannel on the back and snuggle in for the winter season. Approximately 60″ by 70″.

All fabric requirements are generous and based on standard width fabric of approximately 40″ of usable fabric. The instructions assume familiarity with basic quilt construction and sewing an accurate 1/4″ seam. After cutting it out, be sure to save your scraps — just in case.

**Fabric requirements:**

Fabric #1 — the main fabric, 2 2/3 yards of a non-directional print with light or dark background and motifs including at least three additional colors.

Fabric #2 — 2 yards of a strong medium matching one of the colors in the motifs.

Fabric #3 — 1 1/8 yards of a medium matching another color from motifs.

Fabric #4 — 1/2 yard of contrasting medium — may be darker or lighter than the others.

**Cutting instructions:** As you cut, be sure to label pieces by color number and size cut.

From **Fabric #1** — Cut 6 strips 6 1/4" by WOF (width of fabric), subcut into 36 squares 6 1/4".

Cut 5 strips 4" by WOF and subcut into 48 squares 4".

Cut 3 strips 4 3/8" by WOF and subcut into 24 squares 4 3/8".

Cut 7 strips 2 3/8" by WOF.

Cut 4 squares 4 1/2" from the remainder.

From **Fabric #2** — Cut 4 strips 4 1/2" by LOF (length of fabric).

From remaining piece cut 8 strips 2 3/8 by WOF (approximately 22").

Cut 2 strips 4 3/8" WOF and subcut into 8 squares 4 3/8".

Cut 8 squares 4" from remainder.

From **Fabric #3** — Cut 5 strips 2 3/8" by WOF.

Cut 8 strips 2 1/2" by WOF.

Cut 8 squares 4" from remainder.

From **Fabric #4** — Cut 2 strips 4 3/8" by WOF. Subcut into 16 squares 4 3/8".

Cut 3 strips 2 3/8" by WOF.

# CHAPTER ONE

Theo Abernathy tried to massage some of the tightness out of her aching back without Tony noticing. Her husband was worried, which was sweet. She appreciated his concern, but she needed a break and she'd get it in three days. The quilting retreat had been planned longer than she'd been pregnant.

She watched as Tony frowned, pulling his forehead wrinkles down to his eyebrows. After a moment, he grinned. His bald scalp smoothed and his bright blue eyes twinkled. "Couldn't you have your quilting retreat in town for a change instead of going up to The Lodge?"

"No."

"That's it? No? What happened to discussion and negotiation?" Tony pointed to their wedding picture. "Wasn't it in the vows?"

"No." Theo shook her head. The expression of mock outrage on Tony's face gave her the giggles, and she collapsed onto the bed laughing. "We *are* discussing it. You won the driving prize. You get to drive me up the mountain on Friday, lug my suitcase inside, along with my project bags and boxes, and vanish. I promise to sit with my feet up and do hand appliqué or hand quilting and let the hotel staff wait on me."

Tony tried frowning again, but Theo ignored him.

"You and the boys can watch football and eat junk food all weekend. I talked to Edith, and she said for you to call her any time, and she will run right over and stay with the boys." Theo knew part of Tony's reluctance had to do with having his mom and aunt up at the retreat with her. As the sheriff of Park County, Tennessee, he could be called out at any time, day or night. If their next door neighbor wasn't a sweetheart who offered to stay with their two little boys, whenever needed, Theo wouldn't be going away. "I'll be home in time for Jamie's birthday celebration. I've already arranged for Blossom to deliver the cake. She's going to decorate it to look like a baseball field."

"Okay, okay, you win." Tony joined her on the bed. "Just to prove I'm not a sore loser, roll over and I'll massage your back."

"Now that sounds divine." Theo rolled as

12

well as she could, given the already enormous size of her belly. Twins. She patted the small bulge near her ribcage and the foot digging into her side moved. A sigh escaped her as Tony's big hands eased some of the soreness out of her back. "While I'm up there, I promise to call you only if someone gets killed."

Tony twisted around until he could look into her face. "Are you expecting homicide?"

"No. I'm being silly. Quilters are too obsessed with fabric and chocolate to indulge in much violence. No one wants to risk getting blood on the fabric. Sometimes there's the threat of fabric thievery." She poked his shoulder with one finger until he sat up. "Our guest teacher isn't a quilter though, maybe she'll be a problem."

"What's this about a guest teacher? I thought your group was all about doing your own thing."

"We are." Theo eased off the bed. "But Scarlet LaFleur is a world renowned expert in Armenian embroidery. She is coming into town early for the wedding of Celeste and Patrick. Coming to the quilt retreat was her idea."

"Why?"

"Why what?"

"Early," Tony muttered. "Why so early?"

"I have no idea." Theo shook her head. "Or why she wants to hang out with a bunch of quilters. We're usually a lot louder and messier than embroiderers. Kind of like magpies versus robins. Embroiderers tend to keep their threads in good order and never trail scraps all over the place."

"At least, no dead bodies. Please, promise me. Especially not on Saturday." Tony shuddered in mock fear. "All those spooks and goblins."

Theo stared at her husband for a moment, wondering what she had missed. He looked almost desperate. Then it came to her. "Saturday's not Halloween." She had to laugh. "It's a week from Saturday. I'll be back long before then. And even if it was, the boys have their costumes all planned and the candy is hidden in the kitchen. There are three bags in the bottom cabinet, behind the flour."

"One bag's empty."

"You didn't!" Theo stared. Her husband looked as guilty as either of their sons would have if caught in a similar situation. "Did you share with the boys?"

Tony's response was interrupted by the ringing of his cell phone, so he just shook his head. "Yes?" He listened to the caller's message and said, "On my way."

To Theo he said, "Call me if Gretchen can't take you to the shop." And, after giving her a quick kiss, he trotted down the stairs.

Tony opened the front door, stopped and swore softly. Thick, gray fog concealed everything below the top step. Somewhere under it should be a newspaper and three more steps. He explored each step with his foot until he located the newspaper, which he dropped just inside the front door. Cautiously, he continued down the rest of the steps and onto the sidewalk. His wariness was rewarded when he discovered a skateboard in his path. Tony tossed it into the yard.

Parked at the curb was his white Blazer with its green trim and insignia. The official Park County Sheriff's vehicle, complete with enough lights on the roof to cover the whole thing. Stopping in front of the Blazer, he whacked the hood with the palm of his hand twice, waited a couple of seconds and whacked it again. A pair of calico cats dropped to the street and shot up onto the grass. As soon as they were a safe distance from him, the smaller one turned and hissed at him, showing a lot of teeth and attitude.

Ignoring the cats, Tony climbed into the car, rolled down his window and listened. It was quiet enough to hear the gurgles of the tiny creek running through the park and along the side of his house. He could almost hear the leaves falling.

Driving along the fog shrouded streets of the little town he knew so well, he didn't see another moving vehicle and noticed very few lights. The traditional end of tourist season had arrived last weekend, and now the whole town seemed to be recovering, sleeping in. The place looked much like it had when he had first seen it. Not quite a native, his family relocated here when he was eight. While in high school, he had dreamed of escaping and living someplace exciting. First there had been the Navy, and then college and finally a job with the Chicago PD. The opportunity to run for sheriff had come while he was recovering from a near fatal shooting that had left him with a monster scar, permanent indigestion and a hope of raising his children in the more peaceful environment near family. Silersville was home. He loved it.

Unlike neighboring Blount and Sevier counties, which had towns large enough to support a local police department, Park County, Tennessee had only the sheriff's department. His office contracted with the town to supply local law enforcement. Park County itself was a tiny wedge-shape piece of land that had been the result of long ago blackmail by Amoes Siler, one of Theo's relatives.

As he drove down the silent street to the address given by Blossom Flowers, he radioed dispatch asking for his deputy, Wade's location and considered the reason he'd been called out. The Flowers family had only lived in the area for maybe five generations. Blossom was the youngest and the closest thing Tony had to a groupie. Her adoration did not make him feel like a rock star. This was not her house, but she was the person who'd called 911 to report a man had died.

Tony pulled to a stop next to the sidewalk. Wade Claybough, Tony's eager beaver deputy, arrived immediately afterwards and parked his vehicle behind Tony's. The impossibly handsome deputy wasn't smiling as he climbed out of his car. Tony joined him, and they stared at the small house sheltered by a pair of huge maple trees. Brilliant yellow and red leaves drifted onto the grass. A nod of Tony's head sent Wade toward the back door, clearly ajar, illuminated by the golden light coming from the kitchen.

The fog swirled as Tony made his way up the front sidewalk, allowing him to see first Blossom's orange hair glowing like a beacon, and then her bulky figure sitting on the front steps of the house. On closer inspection, he saw her chubby fingers clutching a large package of cream-filled chocolate cupcakes. A box of tissues sat next to her, the used ones lined up in a tidy row along the edge of the step. Her protruding blue eyes were red-rimmed and watery. A blob of cream filling stuck to her upper lip and he could see chocolate cake crumbs trapped in the crevice between her third and fourth chins. The navy blue, short sleeved plaid shirt was too tight and cut into the soft flesh of her upper arms. Her expression turned from woe to worship at the sight of Tony. For a second, he thought she was going to jump off the steps and into his arms and start licking his face.

"How are you doing, Blossom?" Unwilling to upset her more than necessary, he was careful to make his voice low and soothing.

Tears welled, magnifying her huge eyes. "Oh, it's just terrible. I came to work just like usual, and then I saw him there, and he was sitting in his favorite chair. And he's dead!" A choking sob rose in her throat. She set a half-eaten cupcake back in the package and dabbed at her eyes with another tissue.

"Did you see anyone on your way in?"

"Couldn't see nothin' for the fog." A gentle belch rolled out from behind the tissue.

A moment later, Wade appeared at the corner of the house, shaking his head in response to Tony's inquiring glance. It meant there was no reason to call for medical assistance, just for the coroner.

After one more shuddering sob, Blossom recovered sufficiently from her shock and grief to polish off the rest of the cupcake. A faint aroma of chocolate hung in the damp air. Tony's stomach rumbled with a combination of his constant indigestion and lack of breakfast. He searched his pockets until he found an antacid tablet. There was only a little lint on it, which he dusted off before popping it into his mouth.

"Are you working for Mr. Beasley now?" Wade moved toward them and glanced at the front door and Blossom.

"Sort of." Blossom sniffled. "I still work at Ruby's, but Mr. Beasley needed someone to cook for him and do laundry and such and I could use the money."

"What time did you get here, Blossom?" Tony said.

"A little after seven. I was a few minutes late 'cause I stopped to pick up a little snack. And some eggs for Mr. Beasley." She sniffled daintily. "Then I had to go slow 'cause of the fog. It ain't been this bad in months."

She paused, as if waiting for Tony to nod in agreement. He did.

"Mr. Beasley, he don't like much besides eggs for lunch. Said they made his hair shine, you know." Another shuddering sob worked its way out. "It must a worked, 'cause did you ever see prettier hair than his?" She was staring openly at Tony's bald scalp.

"Can you tell me anything else that happened recently? Anything unusual, that is."

She puckered her little lips. Then she furrowed her brow. Finally shrugging, she answered, "No. He was his regular self when I stopped by yesterday afternoon about four. I was on my way to get my hair done, since I work every morning but Sunday and you just try to get a beauty operator to work on Saturday afternoon."

Tony forced himself not to smile. One thing he liked about Blossom was her hair. She was one of the few people in town who had almost as little as he did. Where his remaining hairs were shaved away, hers grew in little tufts, which she dyed a remarkable shade of orange. The whole mess was then glued into an artful arrangement bearing a curious resemblance to rusted steel wool. "He didn't say anything about feeling unwell?"

She pursed her lips again and furrowed her brow, pressing her index finger against her chin. It was obviously the "thinking" look she preferred. He wondered if she practiced it in front of the mirror. Finally she made her decision. "No."

"Did you ever hear him arguing with anyone?"

"No." She wadded up her tissue and put it in the cupcake package. "Well, yes, lots of times. But not yesterday. I don't remember who it was either." Gathering the rest of the tissues and putting them in the package, she shifted back and forth on the step, avoiding eye contact. "I don't feel too good, Tony."

"Go on home, Blossom, and get some rest. I'll be in touch later on, but do me a favor?"

She nodded.

Tony doubted it would do any good, but he asked, "Don't talk much about this yet?

Okay? If something's happened to him, I'd like to notify the family first."

Bobbing her head in agreement, Blossom heaved herself to her feet and started down the sidewalk.

"Oh, Blossom, could I have the key so I can lock up here?"

"Don't need one." She didn't even pause. "Just push the little button thing before you shut the door."

Tony smiled. "Never mind then. I can handle that okay."

Still hiccupping, Blossom waddled toward her car until even the orange hair vanished into the milky fog.

Wade waited until Blossom was out of hearing. "He's dead, all right. Sitting in his recliner. The television is on, and he's still holding the remote control. It looks like he just fell asleep."

"That's the second senior citizen this week," Tony said.

"Weird how these things seem to happen in a series of three, isn't it?" As if hit by a delayed reaction, Wade dashed away and threw up into a bush.

Even as Tony wondered who might be number three, he nodded and called Doc Nash's number. Silersville's doctor and also Park County's coroner, Doc answered on the second ring. He promised to be right over and was as good as his word.

When the doctor arrived, he virtually ignored Tony and greeted Wade like a long lost friend, slapping him on the back and not giving the deputy any grief about his usual reaction to a dead body. Instead, he appeared in good spirits, humming a little tune under his breath as he walked up the sidewalk. Not Doc Nash's usual style at all. Tony was instantly suspicious. What was the man planning?

"Where's our body?" Doc's attitude teetered on the edge of jovial.

Tony led the way into Weevil Beasley's house, going through the side door into the kitchen. A glance at the pile of empty egg cartons stacked inside proved Blossom's assessment of the man's eating habits. The kitchen was clean and orderly.

Doc Nash's attitude underwent an immediate change. He went to the body and briefly examined it.

Tony noticed the message light blinking on the man's telephone answering machine. When he pressed play, a raspy male voice said, "I hope you're dead."

The doctor's eyebrows flew up. "I'm guessing I'll need to check a few more things, given the tone of his recent message, but I think everything is natural. The old guy probably just expired in his sleep."

"Until we know for sure, I'm treating this like a crime scene." Tony sent Wade for his camera and studied the dead man and his living room. Mr. Beasley looked like the tidiest corpse he'd even seen. His thick gray hair was neatly combed. His slacks and button down shirt looked freshly ironed. No cups or papers littered the room. Most importantly, no suicide note sat on the desk in the corner.

Tony put on latex gloves but used the little bottle opener hanging on his key chain to pull the desk drawer open. In case there were fingerprints on the drawer handles he didn't want to smudge them, but he wasn't wasting the time and man hours needed to fingerprint everything unless there was cause.

The pencil drawer was empty except for three pens and a roll of tape. The larger drawer held a hanging file system but no file folders. There were no bills or bank statements; nor was there a checkbook, will or any correspondence. If, as rumor held, he indulged in off-the-record loans, there was no evidence of it.

Wade led the way through the house, his camera shutter clicking.

On the nightstand next to the bed was a wallet. Tony opened it and found forty-eight dollars in cash, a few credit cards and the business card for attorney Carl Lee Cashdollar. "I trust he has a copy of the man's will."

In the bathroom, Tony opened the medicine chest. A toothbrush and toothpaste, a hairbrush and eye drops but no pill bottles.

Tony went back to the doctor. "He's eighty-something and didn't need to take any pills?"

"Of course he did." The doctor frowned. "He needed several just for his heart."

"Where do you suppose the trash is?" Tony backtracked to the kitchen. Sure enough, several empty pill bottles were on the top layer. Tony fished each one out with a table knife from a drawer, dropping each onto the counter.

The doctor studied them. "He just refilled these yesterday."

"And did he take enough to die from it?"

Doc Nash shook his head. "I don't know. I'll run a test during the autopsy. He's been depressed since his wife died."

"So, why have Blossom bring him eggs if he wasn't planning to eat them?" Tony didn't expect an answer. "Does he have relatives in the area?"

"His wife does, did I guess, since she's passed on now, it's did." Wade looked over the top of his camera. "Her brothers are Angus and Davy Farquhar."

"Now there's a stellar family tree. No wonder she never wanted them to visit her in the hospital." Doc Nash pulled himself upright. "She told me her brother Davy's in the penitentiary and his three sons, the 'darlin' boys' are headed that way and Angus isn't any better."

Tony was shocked. "Sweet Aileen Beasley was a Farquhar?" Tony remembered her as a genuine lady librarian. Her nephews were definitely working their way up the ladder of crimes.

"Yep." Doc Nash bobbed his head. "And was ashamed of them all."

The ambulance crew arrived, and Tony stepped back to let them take Mr. Beasley's body. "Too many questions, not enough answers." He looked at Wade. "Let's place seals on the doors until we know more about the cause and manner of his death."

# CHAPTER TWO

Tony stopped by his house to pick up Theo and take her to her quilt shop. Not only was she no longer able to reach both the steering wheel and the pedals in her minivan, but it rarely started on command. The post office truck was just pulling away from the curb, so he collected the mail and walked up the walk.

The fog had lifted and now it was a perfect autumn day, sunny and cool. Sunlight reflected off the surface of the creek beyond the house. The skateboard was nowhere to be seen.

When he got into the house, he found Theo in the kitchen, humming and wiping the counter. She gave him a brilliant smile and took the mail from him.

Theo lifted a bright pink envelope from the top of the stack and tore open the flap. "It looks like we've been invited to another wedding. We've got a solid two weeks of weddings and birthdays."

"Whose now?" Tony filled a mug with coffee, emptying the morning's carafe. "We've already got Mike marrying Ruby, and Celeste marrying Patrick, both next week. I half expect Wade to disappear some day and return with a wife."

"Wait." Theo sat down, her fingers inside the envelope. "Go back to the part about Wade. He's getting married? To whom?"

"I don't know anything for sure, but he's acting very odd: long phone calls, trips out of town on his days off."

"And you know this because?" Theo pulled a stiff card out of the pink envelope.

"Because we have so few deputies, I have to know when someone is not going to be available for emergency call out."

"Okay, so what else is Wade doing?"

"He and Doc Nash talk a lot, and our overworked doctor has turned almost jovial, and I don't know how or why but I think it's all connected to a female." Tony reached for the abandoned envelope. "I can't read the return address."

"It's from Katti." Theo stared at the card inscribed with bright pink ink. "Claude Marmot and Katti are announcing they got married last week. This is an invitation for a party. A reception." She continued to stare

28

at the card. "At the dump."

"No way." Only a month had passed since the Russian girl arrived to meet her American fiancé for the first time. Tony had seen her only from a distance and thought she was cute. He'd wondered what she thought of a trash hauler whose yard and house were filled with salvaged items. If she married Claude, Tony assumed all was fine.

"Okay, it's at their house. Same difference." She looked into Tony's eyes. Hers were sparkling with delight. "My quilting group better finish the wedding quilt this weekend."

Remembering Claude Marmot's one request when he had Tony relay a message to Theo and the quilters, Tony said, "Did you ladies find a way to make a pink quilt that doesn't look pink?"

"We're mixing in a lot of brown fabrics, but I'll bet it will still look pink."

At Theo's quilt shop, Tony went inside to help move her out of her second floor studio/office. The stairs had become too difficult for her, and she'd made a stack of things she would need. Theo watched her husband stare at the pile of boxes and plastic bags at his feet. A sewing machine sat to one side. Suddenly unsure of her selection, she said, "I hope this is all I need to move downstairs."

"I can always come back or you can get Gretchen to help. She's nearly as strong as I am." He frowned, studied her appearance. "Why don't you go over to the dress shop and buy a few maternity things to wear. You look like a plaid elephant wearing my old shirt." He frowned at Theo, making deep furrows in his bald scalp. "I can carry this stuff downstairs from your workshop to the classroom without your supervision."

Theo felt stung by her husband's cranky attitude; after all, she was trying to save money. "I won't need them in a couple of months. It's just a waste of money."

The creases in his face deepened. He narrowed his eyes and glared. "I don't think I can spend two more days, much less months watching you steal shirts from my closet. I half expect to see you in one of my uniform shirts waddling down the sidewalk."

"I do not waddle."

"You do. You have to. You can't help it." Suddenly Tony appeared relieved and laughed. "I think you're afraid."

Theo did not laugh. She was. There was a tiny part of her saying, "If you buy maternity clothes, you'll lose the babies." It was nonsense. She could feel them healthy, strong and growing more viable every day. Twins doing acrobatics in her belly. "You're right."

Her confession earned her a big hug and a kiss. "Now, go get yourself something pretty. You're starting to dress worse than Nellie Pearl Prigmore."

Not responding to his observation about her trailing the worst dressed woman in Park County, Theo gestured down her body like a show room model. "Maybe something in a nice blue tarp with fancy silver grommets. You could lace me into it with stretchy cords like furniture on a car roof."

"Nuh-uh, someone might steal you thinking they're getting six sleeping bags." His eyes twinkled. "We *could* use a new tent though. Maybe you could pick up something up at the camping/fishing store in a lovely camouflage. That way, when you're done wearing it, you could sew a patch over the hole you cut out for your head."

Feeling much better, Theo cautiously worked her way down the stairs, using the handrail. She hadn't seen her feet, much less the steps, in weeks. Once on the main floor of her quilt shop, she picked up speed. While not generally concerned by fashion, she was tired of stealing her oversized husband's clothes. A couple of maternity outfits would be a welcome change. Maybe she'd get a dress to wear to the various weddings set for the next two weeks and a few tops to wear to work. Now that she'd decided to buy some clothes, she couldn't wait.

Almost directly across the street from her shop was Lila's Clothing for Ladies. The owner, Lila Ware, was in her late thirties like Theo. She had grown up in Silersville, gone to school with Theo, married and moved away. About five years ago, she'd ditched the husband, returned to her home town, bought the shop, and settled back into to small town life. Moderate prices and impeccable taste kept her customers happy.

The end of tourist traffic made crossing the street a simple task, even at a slow pace. The tiny bell over the door rang when Theo went inside, but Lila didn't seem to be there. That wasn't unusual. Lila only had help in the busy months. So Theo glanced around, knowing Lila would appear soon. The store was divided into sections. One was makeup and accessories like purses and scarves. One was geared for the teenage shopper. One for older shoppers. Maternity was near the back door. Closest to the front door was a rack of souvenir T-shirts and gift items.

Theo began sorting through the items on the maternity rack. She grimaced. She might be ready to buy a few new things, but not a T-shirt with an arrow pointing to her belly and *Baby* written in sparkly big letters.

Theo heard the back door of the store open and close. She was preparing to call out to Lila when she heard Lila talking to someone else and stopped in mid-breath, eavesdropping without meaning to.

"I won't put up with it any more." Lila's voice was muffled but distinct.

Theo thought it sounded like her friend was crying.

"I'll get a divorce." A man's deep rumbling voice. "I promise."

"When? You've said that before."

"I know, my love, I know." He cleared his throat. "I swear it won't be much longer." He laughed, making a harsh sound, like a sea lion barking. "Soon, we'll be free of her and all her wretched family and life will be beautiful. I'll be able to marry you."

Not wanting to be caught listening, Theo started tiptoeing toward the front door when she heard the back door open and Lila and her beau exited, leaving her alone in the store. The conversation she'd overheard was none of her business, but, she admitted, it was intriguing anyway. She couldn't guess who the man might be. She hadn't seen him at all, although there was something familiar about the voice. When she ran through her mental list of men Lila might love, she found none to fill the gap.

Theo turned back to the clothes, pulled out a crisp green dress with vertical dark and light green stripes. Moving in front of the mirror, she held it up to see how it might look on her. Ghastly.

Lila came through the front door surprising Theo. She paused to look at Theo and started to laugh. "I don't think so, Theo, honey. It would make you look like a watermelon wearing glasses and a fuzzy yellow hat."

"It was the first thing I saw in my size." Theo returned the dress to the rack silently agreeing with Lila's comment. "Tony says I need new clothes."

"Tony's right." Lila studied her. "The stretchy pants are okay but otherwise you're a mess."

"Can you help?" Theo didn't mention her friend's red and watery eyes.

"Yes." Lila reached around Theo and plucked a sleeveless blue dress from its hanger. "Try this. You can wear any kind of shirt under it, like a jumper, or you can wear it without a shirt and make it look dressier by adding a scarf or some costume jewelry."

"Any kind of shirt?" Theo touched it. The fabric felt good. Not stiff and not sleazy.

"No." Lila tugged on the sleeve of Tony's plaid shirt. "Not any of your husband's clothes." She handed Theo a couple of maternity tops she approved of. "Try these."

With Lila's help, Theo managed to get them on. She was surprised by how much better she felt in her new clothes. She wore one of the new tops when she went back to her shop. It was comfortable and flattering.

Tony looked up from the array of things he'd carried from his wife's studio to the classroom just in time to see Theo coming back into the shop carrying a shopping bag and wearing a new top. Very nice. And she was smiling. Very nice indeed.

"You look beautiful."

Theo stood on her tiptoes and kissed him. "Thank you."

"I suppose I'll have to carry all this" — he waved to encompass the sewing machine and bags — "to your quilt retreat."

"Nope." Theo eased onto a chair. "Remember, I'm taking handwork. I'll be quilting one of the baby quilts and learning Armenian embroidery."

"Learning?"

Theo massaged her lower back. "Our guest teacher, Scarlet LaFleur, is the sister of the first mother of the groom."

"Excuse me? What?" Tony pasted on the expression he used when he pretended to have been paying attention and got caught. "Which groom?"

"Given the number of weddings this month, that's a fair question." Theo laughed. "Patrick. Scarlet is Patrick's birth mother's sister. You know Elf."

"The singer?"

"Yes, our very own famous country singer with the huge house out near the Cashdollar mansion, another in Nashville and, I hear, a fabulous beach house in Malibu."

"Okay," Tony nodded. "Yes, I know Elf." Tony was still considered a new arrival in Park County. He wasn't born there and only lived there ten years before he left. Returning as an adult left gaps in his knowledge of local events. He both hated Theo's little history lessons and found them fascinating. "What about Elf?"

"Well her sister is the former Christmas Poinsettia Flowers, now known as Scarlet LaFleur. She is a world renowned expert in Armenian embroidery techniques. She had her name changed."

"I guess." Tony pushed her hands off her

back and began massaging it for her. "It makes her sound like a stripper. She's not one of Blossom's sisters?"

"Nope. Blossom's father is Aut, you know, short for Autumn. She's their first cousin."

Tony frowned, trying to sort out the various members of the extensive family. "So who's Elf? Really?"

"Easter Lily Flowers." Theo snorted indelicately. "Her father is Summer Flowers."

"You're making this up." Tony's hands stopped moving. "That's not a real name."

"No. Yes. I'm trying to explain." Theo pointed to a spot on her back needing a bit more of Tony's care. "Elf uses her initials for a name. And she's tiny and pretty and looks like a woodland fairy, so the name fits. Anyway, she was maybe fourteen when she gave birth to Patrick and let the MacLeod family adopt him. It's always been a very open relationship."

Tony considered Patrick. The nice young man was not only a new teacher at the elementary school, but also the new high school football coach. His was one of the upcoming weddings they planned to attend. "And Aunt Christmas Poinsettia, now Scarlet?"

"Always a whiny pain in the neck."

"Patrick's father?"

"A tightly kept secret. As far as I know, Elf has never disclosed his identity."

Tony's cell phone rang, startling them both. He listened for a moment, muttered a response, then disconnected. He headed for the door, waving farewell.

Someone had called his office and suggested the culprit driving around the county shooting signs, whether public or a private business, was the trash hauler, Claude Marmot. The problem began a couple of weeks earlier with some bullet holes in the yellow "Curve Ahead" sign out past the new folk museum. The problem had escalated hourly.

Tony actually suspected the caller more than Marmot-the-Varmint, because the caller claimed a .22 caliber rifle was involved. Tony considered so much detail in an anonymous call to be somewhat suspicious. It wouldn't hurt to ask. If nothing else, maybe Claude had an idea who might want him to take the blame. Plus, Claude's route took him all over the county. He might have seen something.

Tony collected Wade and took him along.

Claude's home was a former shack, set well off the road and behind a stand of immense old cucumber trees, about half way between the dump and town. With the recent large addition to his home, Claude had more than doubled his living space.

The television was loud enough to hear from the road, so Tony pounded on the frame of the warped screen door. He wanted Claude outside and downwind. The man wasn't famous for his aftershave. After several minutes he succeeded in rousing Claude.

A bleary-eyed Claude stepped carefully through the doorway. Clutching an empty jelly glass decorated with dinosaurs, he joined Tony in the center of the yard.

The midnight blue car/truck he had made from a 1989 Crown Victoria was the center-piece of his salvage display. What had once been the trunk was now the open bed, and the back seat was now a piece of lawn furniture sitting in the shade near the house. Somehow he had managed to cut the thing apart and then splice it together again, creating a functional car/truck.

Tony sniffed the air, expecting Claude's usual aroma of sweat and garbage. He was surprised when he smelled detergent and perfume. "Do you usually carry a gun with you on your travels around the county?"

"All the time in the dump truck." Claude's eyes rolled and he cleared his throat. "There's *ugly* things out at the landfill."

Tony smiled then, a real smile. He could imagine the truth in that statement. "What caliber?"

"Got me a twelve gauge and a .357 Magnum I take along with me. Don't want to take chances, ya know. Them skunks have rabies."

"How about a .22?" Wade asked.

"No way." Claude belched. "Then the rats would have bigger guns than me."

"Yeah, I know." Tony and Wade headed for the Blazer. "Talk to you later, Claude." Tony turned back, thinking he'd ask Claude to keep an eye out for the miscreants shooting holes in every sign in the county — with a .22 and hoping to frame Claude. The question died in his throat as he watched a stunning woman with short dark hair, dyed hot pink on top, join Claude in the yard. Her thin robe of bright pink flowers on a black background blew open just as she wrapped her arms around Claude and led him toward the house.

Next to him, he heard Wade exhale sharply. Tony grinned. "I'd say the mail order bride is working out just fine."

Tony took the whole family to Ruby's Café for dinner. On a good day, Theo wasn't much of a cook. After a long day at work, it was often much easier to eat out. Especially now, when standing for any period of time exhausted his wife.

"Why do you go to retreat?" Jamie began his interrogation.

"It's relaxing." Theo ran a hand over the boy's hair, smoothing the cowlick only to watch it spring up again. "It's like scout camp for quilters."

To an almost seven-year-old, camping was chasing squirrels and tossing rocks in the creek. Jamie was not seeing any connection to quilting. "What do you do all day?"

"Since it's a vacation for quilters, we don't have to do anything. There is no schedule, no housework, no husbands or kids, and the meals are provided. Everyone is free to concentrate on quilting, or sleeping or daydreaming or hiking, as long as they have brought a quilt for their bed."

"Are you teaching there?" Chris wasn't about to let his little brother hog the whole conversation, and he did understand Theo sometimes went out of town to teach.

"No. Some retreats have classes, but ours is just for relaxing. This one will have a short embroidery class, and I'll have the clues to a mystery quilt to hand out, but no one has to make one."

Jamie yawned and didn't cover his mouth.

"Sounds boring."

"I'm glad I don't have to go," said Chris. "I heard there isn't any television up there."

Jamie stopped scraping the meringue off his pie and looked at his brother. "I guess Dad's going to cook." His expression turned mournful and Chris's mirrored it.

"Is there something wrong?" said Tony. He wanted to laugh at their faces but managed to contain himself and pasted a wounded expression on his own face instead of a grin.

"W-ell," Chris looked uneasy. "I guess it's pretty good when you use a recipe."

"Okay, I promise I'll use a recipe. Now finish eating so I can drop you all off at the house. I've got work to do." He looked at Theo's raised eyebrows but didn't volunteer any information.

Tony drove to Mr. Beasley's home, hoping to find a neighbor who could answer some of his questions. His arrival startled three young men grouped on the porch, and he turned his spotlight on the trio. Davy Farquhar's three "darlin' boys." Boys no longer in Tony's mind. He spoke into his radio. "The Farquhar boys are at Beasley's house. I want extra patrols by here until further notice."

Although there was still some daylight, the shadows were lengthening, and he left the spotlight shining. The Farquhar boys turned and shaded their eyes with their hands. The three young men appeared interchangeable with similar unkempt dark hair, green eyes, medium build and zero work ethic. "What are you boys doing here?" He'd bet none of them was given a key by Mr. Beasley.

The one standing closest to the door stuffed something into his pocket while the other two moved to shield him. "We heard he's dead and we come by for our money."

Tony doubted the boys were owed anything. "You in the will?"

"Don't need one. We're kin — it comes to us automatic-like." The three shaggy heads bobbed in unison.

"Go home. All of you." Tony walked toward them. "If you get money, it will come later from his lawyer. In the meantime, you stay away from this house or I'll throw all of you in jail."

# CHAPTER THREE

The next morning, Tony opened the door to his office and froze. For a moment he thought it had been taken over by a giant canary wearing an orange wig, but quickly realized it was Blossom dressed in bright yellow sweatpants and sweatshirt. She waggled her fingers to catch his eye. Like that was necessary.

Tony had to smile at the sweet woman. She certainly didn't intend to be irritating as poison ivy. "Are you feeling better, Blossom?" He would have preferred to find her sitting out in the waiting area rather than in his office, but he knew why she was sitting there even before she said anything.

"Ruth Ann said I was to sit right here and not to touch nothing."

Her eyes were still watery, and she sniffled into her hand making Tony hope she had a tissue hidden in there. He glanced around but didn't see a pie sitting on his desk. She often brought him one, and he had to fight back a surge of disappointment. "Can I help you with something, Blossom?"

"What happened to Mr. Beasley?" Blossom reached into a frog-festooned shopping bag at her feet, extracted a roll of toilet paper, unwound a few feet of it and blew her nose. She dropped the roll in the neighborhood of her bag and missed. It rolled to Tony's feet.

Tony picked it up and handed it back to her. "Mr. Beasley probably died of old age, but all the tests aren't in."

"I don't suppose I'll get paid now."

Tony felt bad because he hadn't considered her finances. Blossom worked at Ruby's cooking desserts, and she did birthday and wedding cakes as well as light housekeeping and meals for several seniors, one less now. "You should. Just write up a bill and give it to whoever is in charge of settling his estate. He wasn't living on welfare."

"Will you take it to them?" Blossom's eyes overflowed. "His family ain't real friendly. I got a nasty call just this morning, like they thought I was helping him with his side business and keeping the money."

"Side business?" Tony paused, his curiosity piqued. "What's that?"

"Oh, it's like he's a bank, only not. He

lends money."

"Loan shark." Tony thought the information might explain the unpleasant message on his phone. "You do know it's not my job to deliver bills." He sighed. "Drop it off at the front desk when it's ready."

Thinking her cheery outfit wasn't making her feel better, he turned to the work stacked on his desk.

He called attorney Carl Lee Cashdollar's office and connected to voice mail. The message in Carl Lee's nasal twang indicated he and his staff were out of town and would the caller please leave a message. Knowing "the staff" was Carl Lee's wife, Tony called their home and received a similar recording. Tony did as requested, giving an array of telephone numbers and used the word "urgent" at least three times.

After a few more calls to people he thought might have additional information, he learned the couple had gone to Hawaii on holiday but were expected to be back in the office on Monday.

By the time he left for the day, he felt like he'd accomplished nothing at all.

Tony loved Theo's shop. And also, or so he was told, did every quilter who ever went inside. Light and airy, the main room was filled with thousands of bolts of cotton fabrics arranged by color, and there was every color imaginable. He'd seen fabrics with flowers and rocks and oriental fabrics and even some with dancing frogs and baseball playing geckos. To one side of the room was a long counter covered with protective mats. After the bolts were selected, this is where the fabric was cut. Behind it was a wall covered with packets of needles, templates, rotary cutters and rulers, marking pens, hoops and other toys and tools for quilters. One whole corner of the room was dedicated to threads — cotton threads, metallic threads and glossy rayon threads.

The man corner, just inside the front door, was reserved for husbands. A pair of comfortable chairs faced a television/DVD combination. A stack of sports magazines covered a small table. Tony had witnessed a couple of times the husband so involved in what he was watching, the wife had to wait for him.

The back room was a quilter's haven. Designed as a classroom, it was large enough to hold ten big tables and still have plenty of space to move around. There were enough electrical outlets wired into the walls and floors to accommodate lots of sewing machines and irons. Built into one wall was a bay window with a large, comfortable window seat. There was a window in the wall shared with the shop so both groups could see what was going on. The other walls were covered with flannel, creating large design spaces. In the corner were a sink, a small refrigerator, and a counter that held a coffeepot.

The regular patrons had their personal mugs hanging on hooks. Unless there was a class scheduled, a quilt on a frame always filled the center of the room. Various groups supplied the quilt tops and the finished quilts were usually given directly to the needy, sent to soldiers, or were raffled off to benefit a charity. Anyone who wished to work on the quilt could. The current quilt was going to be raffled to help pay for the restoration of the steeple on the oldest church in town. Tony knew that because a calendar hanging on the door listed the information.

He found Theo measuring and cutting fabric for a couple of young women. He thought their names were Susan and Melissa. The women didn't stop laughing and talking as they stacked more bolts on the table. Theo handed them each a sheet of paper. "You said you want to do the mystery quilt. Here is the first clue." Picking up her rotary cutter again, she grinned at them. "If I don't give it to you now, I'll forget."

"When do we get the next clue?" Careful to hold the paper out of the reach of the toddler in her arms, the one he thought was Melissa began reading right away.

"It's alright, Melissa, I'll take some up to the retreat on Friday, or you can pick one up here when you get back."

Tony was proud he'd guessed the woman's name.

"This looks like fun." The taller of the two, Susan, rocked a stroller and its passenger, a sleeping baby, as she read the paper. "I've never done a mystery quilt before." She hesitated, nervously fingering the macaroni necklace she wore with her red sweatshirt and jeans. "Can I ask you a couple of questions about it?"

"Sure." Theo grinned and pushed her glasses up. "Don't take it too seriously, though. It's not rocket science." She leaned forward to look at the paper. "What do you want to know?"

"You say that we need assorted fabrics that are lights, mediums and darks."

Theo nodded encouragingly and waited.

"I guess I'm uncertain how to categorize some of the prints."

"Okay." Theo pointed to a white fabric with black squiggles on it. "I would say that this is light. If you squint at it, it looks white. A black fabric with white lines would appear to be black. For this design, you don't need as much contrast between the dark and the mediums as you do between the mediums and the light. You can do it with either shade or color. Just remember some of your mediums will be darker or lighter than others. It gives the quilt texture. Like the different fabrics in a log cabin."

Melissa grinned. "I've got it. If I put this dark yellow against a light blue, it is still easy to see."

A wide smile softened the tall woman's face. "So if I want to, I could make it all shades of one color."

"Exactly," Theo said.

Susan's husband was one of the executives at the new fertilizer plant. Tony understood that sometimes new residents of Silersville felt alienated by the clannish society. He thought the ones who made their way into the quilt shop seemed to be assimilated more quickly.

With a gleam in her eyes, Susan began pulling blue fabrics and stacking them on the table. "Who's going on the retreat?"

Listening to his wife's list, he guessed

Theo wasn't ready to go home yet, so Tony settled into the man corner and caught up with his reading, studying the statistics of his favorite baseball players. He loved and hated the exciting end of the season. The winter, without baseball, loomed like the dark entrance to a long tunnel.

"The toilet in the downstairs bathroom doesn't work right," said Theo. "Do you want to fix it or should I call in the plumber?"

Tony watched Theo chase a puddle of milk with a rag, racing against Daisy's big pink tongue. The oversized golden retriever was winning. "I'll take a look at it later." Tony ducked as Theo's flying elbow came perilously close to his nose. "Since there's no baseball game tonight, I'm going to write for a while. Maybe I just need a mental break. An evening in the company of cowboys and buffalo and antelope sounds really good."

Tony's mood improved as soon as he entered his study. For a change, the boys were not playing on the computer. Although the room was actually a converted pantry, he considered it his space. Sharing the computer was a necessity, but it rankled a bit when he had to stand in line or throw someone out in order to do his writing. The expensive computer sat on a faux wood desk from one of the discount stores. A yard sale find, the chair was comfortable, if a bit worn, and one of the casters would fall off every time he leaned too far backwards. On the wall to his left was a small corkboard covered with magazine pictures of Montana and Wyoming. His inspiration.

He opened a file and read through his last typed words. His hero, the marshal, had just ridden out in pursuit of the bank robber when the bad guy circled around and rode back into town. Tony leaned back in the chair and closed his eyes, letting his thoughts drift through the scene. The smell of the sage and the heat of the sun mixed with the constant dust in his imaginary little town.

Unfortunately, no words made it from his mind to his fingers and, this time, the swirls on his screensaver went undisturbed.

# CHAPTER FOUR

Thursday morning when Tony arrived at his office, Ruth Ann was already at her desk just outside his office door. She smiled at him, not a good sign, when he walked in. She pointed to her companion, and Tony couldn't suppress a groan. Orvan Lundy.

Orvan was well known throughout Park County and beyond as a petty thief and part-time brewer of moonshine. He was suspected of many worse crimes. As far as Tony knew, the only crimes the man had never confessed to were the ones he actually committed. Tony was torn. He knew deep down this would be a waste of time, and he didn't anticipate learning anything he could use. On the other hand, there was often an element of truth hidden in Orvan's tall tales that led to the solution of minor problems.

"Mr. Lundy." Tony paused at the doorway, holding the door open with his shoulder.

"Would you care for a cup of coffee before we get started?"

The little man rose from his metal chair. "Why, that's right sociable of you to offer something like that, Sheriff." Licking his chapped lips in anticipation, he peered up at Tony. "I don't suppose you could add a bit of flavoring to it?" Since his faded blue eyes always had a glassy sheen, Tony couldn't be sure if the old man had already been in the moonshine.

Tony just shook his head and waited.

"Well, I didn't think so." Cocking his head to one side, Orvan appeared to be listening to something only he could hear. When, at length, he must have heard the end of the message, he said, "I'll take the coffee."

A nod from Tony sent Ruth Ann on the errand.

Tony let his office door close, and leading the little man down the hall to their interrogation room, he took the seat directly opposite from Orvan. The faded little man didn't look capable of crossing the street on his own, much less killing a man, but Tony knew inside the shrunken exterior was a man in his seventies who was as strong as hickory. Resting now on the surface of the inexpensive metal table, Orvan's gnarled hands looked crippled. Decades of outdoor labor had tanned his skin like cowhide and, although suffering from arthritis, he was still capable of caning the seats of the ladder-back chairs he made completely by hand. When he stood up straight, which he rarely did, he was about five foot eight. He might weigh a hundred and thirty pounds. Wearing his habitual denim overalls, he had spruced up for the interview by rubbing shoe polish on the top of his iron gray hair. Since he obviously hadn't consulted a mirror, the polish did not extend down the sides or back. The end result was he appeared to be wearing a very greasy black beret above a sunken-cheeked face as weathered as his hands.

Orvan was the first to speak. "I doubt you realize, Sheriff, but I dye my hair."

Startled, Tony pulled his eyes from the unusual hairstyle and back to Orvan's leathery face. "Why tell me?" What he wanted to ask was more along the line of wondering why their conversations almost always began the same way.

"I just want to be square with you, sir. You should know I'm an honest man."

Ruth Ann came in carrying three cups of black coffee and set them on the table in front of the men. Judging from the expression of disbelief Tony saw on her face, it

55

confirmed she had heard Orvan's statement and believed that while the hair was obvious, the claim to honesty was a lie. For the moment, she seemed to be too intrigued with the hair topic to even give Tony a mean look about delivering coffee. With her eyes still focused on Orvan's hair, she backed toward the door.

Wade came in right behind her, thanked Ruth Ann for the coffee and settled into the third chair. He cleared his throat as he pushed a paper across the table. "Orvan Lundy, do you remember me reading you your rights?"

"Yes." Orvan gripped his coffee cup with both hands.

"Would you like a lawyer?"

"Hell, no." The faded eyes seemed brighter. "Can't stand the mealy mouths. Never say what they mean. I wouldn't trust one of them with my trash."

Tony had to raise his hand, palm forward, to stop the tirade. The little man's lips slammed together, and he glared as if annoyed that he didn't get to finish his discourse.

Wade pressed on. "Are you making this confession voluntarily?"

"Yes."

"Are you currently under the influence of

alcohol?"

"Huh?"

Tony leaned forward, and handed him a pen. "Wade wants to know if you have been drinking today."

Orvan's lips pulled back in a wider grin. "Not yet."

"All right, Orvan," said Tony. "After you sign this paper that says you know your rights and don't want a lawyer, why don't you just start at the beginning and tell us in your own words why you are here today."

With painstaking care, the old man gripped the pen like he was holding an ax and made an X on the paper then wrapped his hand back around the cup. He looked at Tony and cleared his throat. "Well, you know I pretty much mind my own business. 'Live and let live,' that's my motto. Always has been." In his fervor to confess, he didn't seem to notice their silent disbelief as he continued. "Beasley and me use to be close back when we was in school together afore I left 'cause there wasn't much I didn't know by then." He shifted his skinny rump on the chair. "Beasley went on to high school and got him some high falutin' ideas like he was better'n everyone else in the area, and we didn't share much any more. But I've been watching him. I seen him turn into a real mean-hearted old bastard." He flexed his twisted fingers and stared into space. "It was the dog that did it though."

"Did what?" Tony asked blankly. Blaming Beasley's death on an animal was a new feature in Orvan's confessions. Plus, he was still having trouble believing Mr. Beasley and Orvan were ever classmates.

"You know, old Nem's dog, Sally. Old Nem loved that there dog, and someone ran over it apurpose. Old Nem ain't never recovered from her dyin'. Anyhow, it was on account of the dog I decided I couldn't stand him no more and I needed to do something to fix it. I snuck into his house and right there on the counter in his little kitchen, I found this here big knife and stuck it smack into his cold little heart. Didn't bleed at all." On his vigorously bobbing head, the polished hair did not move a fraction. "Can't get blood out of a durn stone."

Tony glanced at his deputy. Wade sat motionless, elbows on the table, his fists holding his chin up, apparently fascinated. Looking back at Orvan, Tony smiled. "Then what did you do?"

"I went outside and found a ladder and I propped it up against the house and used it to climb up onto the roof. Since I had gotten the job done so fast, I had to wait a few minutes for my ride." Orvan smoothed his hair and then wiped the excess polish on the bib of his overalls.

"You waited on the roof?" Wade encouraged him to continue. "Why?"

" 'Cause they was afeared of hitting the house in the fog, of course." Orvan's expression clearly indicated only a moron would have to ask such an obvious question.

"They?" The question came in unison. Tony and Wade leaned closer, breathed in, choked a bit and moved away again.

"You know." Orvan frowned at them. "The other world folk. It was their helicopter, after all. After they dropped me off on the roof of my place, they flew away and I ain't seen them since."

Several moments passed while Tony and Wade digested the confession, weighing the pros and cons of it. At length, Tony cleared his throat. "I do believe that your confessions are improving, Orvan. This one had lots of good detail. I would arrest you, you understand, but some of the details don't quite match the facts as I understand them."

"But Sheriff, you've got to. I've been a wicked sinner." Tears of frustration shimmered in Orvan's eyes. "I need to make things right." Pressing his wrists together, he held them out in front of his body.

"I don't doubt it." Tony massaged the back of his neck. "Maybe we can work out something." His chair screeched as it slid across the linoleum when he pushed away from the table. The sound drew the little man's attention. His was fairly vibrating with anticipation. "Wade, I want you to stay here and make sure that Mr. Lundy doesn't escape until we are finished with him."

"Yes, sir." Wade glowered at Orvan and patted his holster for effect.

It didn't take Tony long to find a file he had been reading the day before, but he deliberately delayed his return for a few minutes so Orvan would have a little time to wonder about his punishment. Taking the file with him, Tony returned to the interrogation room where he made a real production out of sitting down and reading through the file. The name Lundy was clearly printed on the file, but he doubted Orvan could read it.

Tony flipped the file shut, and lacing his fingers, rested his hands on the file. "I tell you what. We will make a deal. I am going to assign your punishment and if you help me out, I won't arrest you today."

"Anything, Sheriff." For a second it looked like he was going to salute, but he was just adjusting his hair. Orvan straightened his spine and gave Tony his full attention.

Tony's eyes held him still. "Even if it means turning in a relative?"

At those words, Orvan's face positively glowed. Evidently ratting out a relative was something to relish. "Sure thing. Which one? I got too many of them to keep track of."

"Jake Lundy. Isn't he one of your cousins?" The exact relationship was probably not even clear to the family. There were lots of Lundys and not much diversity in the gene pool.

Slack jawed, Orvan nodded. "It's Jake you want? What did he do?"

Given the nature of some of Orvan's relatives, Tony understood his confusion. Jake was certainly not the most rotten apple in the barrel. "He hasn't been making his child support payments, and the judge wants to see him."

"Why that's just awful!" Rubbing his whiskered chin, Orvan frowned again. "At least it must be, whatever that child thing is."

Tired of the game, Tony flattened his hands, palms down on the file and leaned forward. "Where is he?"

"Last I heard he was planning on passing

some time up at his pa's old place up near Pigeon Forge." Orvan's words tumbled out one on top of the other.

Wade cleared his throat to draw Tony's attention. "I know where the house is."

Tony grinned so hard, it made his cheeks ache as he regarded his new favorite deputy. "Are you volunteering to go get him?"

"Yes, sir!" A dark flush spread up Wade's thick neck. "I want to be a good deputy."

"Fine." Tony patted the file on the table. "The warrant is in here, and I'll call the sheriff over there and tell him you are coming to collect some garbage. He might even send one of his deputies to help out. Just to be on the safe side, why don't you take Mike along? And don't forget Jake never goes anywhere without a shotgun." Tony turned to Orvan. "I wonder if you'd mind visiting with Ruth Ann until Jake is in custody. I'd sure hate for him to accidentally hear about Wade being on his way."

"Why sure, Sheriff." Orvan stood up and straightened his clothes, ran his forearm over his hair, removing most of the shoe polish on the left side of his head. He managed to leave a strip of greasy black from his right eyebrow to the nape of his neck.

Tony decided it was not a style everyone could wear.

"That Ruth Ann, she is a gem."

Orvan was still singing her praises as Tony opened the door and led him out, ushering Orvan to a chair right next to Ruth Ann's desk. Knowing she wouldn't be delighted to be assigned the job of being the old sinner's sitter, he was careful not to make eye contact with her.

While he refilled Orvan and Ruth Ann's coffee cups, he told Mike what was happening and sent him off with Wade.

"Well now, Orvan, I'll just leave you here to enjoy your visit with Ruth Ann until Wade calls in. I'm going to make a call about Jake." It was difficult, but he managed to keep his grin to himself until his office door closed behind him. After his call, he worked briefly on his paperwork. "I'm going over to the Beasley house." This time he used the intercom to update Ruth Ann.

"Fine, Sheriff." The words were civil enough, but her tone held a definite threat. The nasal tones of Orvan's voice were clearly heard droning in the background.

Ruth Ann deserved a raise.

Tony knew Blossom was the youngest of Autumn Flower's girls. By the time she was born, their branch of the Flowers family had already produced Daffodil, Rose, Lily,

Daisy, Sunflower, Marigold, Zinnia, Azalea, Pansy and Tulip. There probably had never been a day when Blossom hadn't been told exactly what to do and where to go. He stopped by the Flowers home and picked up the handwritten bill for Blossom's services. Not even close to being part of his job.

The envelope was ready, sitting on a large paper plate of cookies. He inhaled the scents of butter and spice. Okay, so he didn't mind doing a few little extras. He thought about just leaving the bill with someone in the Beasley family and heading to his home office carrying his food reward. After all, this was officially his morning off, although he always went to the office for a few minutes.

In two recent conversations, the suggestion of Mr. Beasley's side business had raised his curiosity. He called Doc Nash from his car. "I don't suppose —"

The busy doctor interrupted him. "I don't know. Mr. Beasley might not have died of natural causes after all."

Tony groaned, pulled a cookie from under the plastic wrap and began eating it. "How?" He mumbled.

"Don't know." Doc Nash muttered. "I have to go. We have emergencies up the ying yang."

Tony stared at the silent phone. He pulled another cookie off the plate and chewed slowly, wondering about his next move. Wade was the only one of them with fingerprint training, and he wouldn't be back for a while, so Tony drove by Mr. Beasley's house, checked seals on the doors. While he stood there, the next door neighbor, a man about fifty wandered over. "I saw him chase them nephews of his away from his house with a shotgun."

Tony could believe it. "When was this?"

"There's been several times but the last one was maybe a month ago."

Tony thanked him and went home to write.

He settled right down at the keyboard.

# CHAPTER FIVE

For a change, Tony felt like he was making progress on his book. The mental slowdown plaguing him was gone, and his fingers fairly flew across the keyboard as his words appeared on the screen in front of him. The marshal was going to save the town and win the heart of the schoolteacher. It was glorious!

Surfacing from the Old West, Tony became aware the doorbell had been ringing for some time. The flow of words stopped abruptly. He didn't get up but poked his head into the hallway and shouted, "Who is it?"

The ringing doorbell was the only response.

Lunging from his chair, Tony stormed to the front door and jerked it open. It took him a full five seconds to realize the diminutive man still pressing on the button was someone he knew, DuWayne Cozzens, the plumber.

The ringing continued even after the door opened. "Lay off the bell, DuWayne!" It came out much louder than Tony intended.

"Holy Moly! Don't yell." The little man jumped away from the button and nearly tumbled off the top step. "Theo said you might be hard to rouse. I've been ringing for quite a while. Have you considered getting a hearing aid? My Aunt Sally got one, and she says now she can hear the grass growing."

"I don't need a hearing aid." Still half in the sage and heat of the West, Tony was not completely tracking this conversation. "Did you say Theo sent you?"

"Yep." DuWayne patted the large red toolbox by his feet. The metal was dented in places but the paint was still attached. "Said you've got a problem with the downstairs toilet."

"That's right. I told her I'd take a look at it." Tony stepped back to let DuWayne and his toolbox inside. "I admit I had forgotten all about it."

"I understand, yes I do." DuWayne vigorously nodded his head as he picked up the heavy box. "But you know one thing I have learned in my business is women just won't put up with toilet troubles. It's like an obsession with them."

"It's right down here." Tony led the way down the hall. Having DuWayne Cozzens walking right behind him made Tony feel like a giant lumbering along with his knuckles dragging on the ground.

It wasn't just because Tony was a big man, although he was. It was more because DuWayne had not grown an inch since he was in the fifth grade. But pound for pound and inch for inch, he was close to the strongest man around Silersville. He carried pipes and a heavy toolbox on a constant basis. With apparent ease, he wrestled hot water tanks that dwarfed him. In fact, his diminutive stature was a bonus when it came to working in a crawlspace.

Tony knew DuWayne liked big women. Evidently his self-esteem was not tied to being physically more imposing than his women. It was common knowledge he had been trying to court Blossom for several months and had failed to win her heart, or at least failed as far as anyone knew. Local wags suggested if they married, Blossom would have to lift DuWayne into the air for their kiss at the altar. Now there was a second suitor vying for Blossom's affection. The carpenter, Kenny Baines, was about the same size as DuWayne and possessed the same type of strength.

The citizens of Silersville were quietly watching the two men's courtship. A few bets were placed by the men who congregated at the Okay Bar and Bait Shop. In fact, a chalkboard tally detailed where Blossom went, with whom. Only Blossom seemed unaware of the intense interest in her love life.

"Much obliged for showing me the way, Sheriff." DuWayne's face glowed with pleasure as he viewed his latest challenge. "This shouldn't take too long at all."

Tony got back into his chair and was just reaching for the keyboard when the first question came down the hall.

"Oh, Sheriff, can you show me where the shutoff valve is for your water?"

Tony was sure the little man knew its location, but he led the way into the cellar. He left the plumber bemoaning the poor location of the valve and headed back to his study.

Minutes later, he heard DuWayne's voice again. "Oh, Sheriff, I think you better come take a look at this." DuWayne didn't sound happy. His tone made the muscles in Tony's shoulders tighten. He forced an expression he hoped displayed both intelligence and curiosity onto his face and trudged back down the hall.

DuWayne was frowning at something in the waterless tank. "This is just in awful shape. I'm surprised it has lasted this long. I can't imagine why a part like this was used in the first place. Do you have any idea when it was installed?" His expression appeared baleful and accusatory.

Feeling a bit guilty for taking the smile from DuWayne's face, Tony looked where he was pointing. The thing was nondescript, looked a bit rusty, and was totally out of Tony's realm. "Since I don't even know what it is or what it does, I'm sure that I couldn't say, but you know this house has been overhauled a lot in the last hundred or so years. I'm sure it hasn't always had professionals working on it."

"That's right. This is the oldest house in town, isn't it?" DuWayne looked somewhat mollified, evidently satisfied the Abernathy family had not set out to intentionally destroy the plumbing, thereby causing grief and hardship for the plumbing industry in general and misery for him specifically.

"The oldest brick house," Tony corrected him. According to the town's historians, the original homes had been log homes. Over time, they had been replaced by more sophisticated wooden ones and finally brick.

DuWayne settled his skinny rear end on the edge of the sink and crossed his arms over his chest. "Which one came next?"

Alarmed by the way DuWayne was settling in, Tony began backing away. "The house next door is the second oldest." He checked his watch. "Oops, eleven-thirty. I better be getting on down to the station. You call Theo if you have any more questions and just lock up when you finish with whatever it is you are fixing."

DuWayne looked crestfallen. It was the only way to describe the little man's expression. Tony felt like scum. He ran away, telling himself it was time to do some work. Maybe Wade was back.

Tony expected another call from Doc Nash which might include a definite decision about the cause of Mr. Beasley's death. Tony wasn't getting any younger and Beasley needed burying. But, according to a quick telephone message relayed by Nurse Foxx, it might be a long wait. The doctor was overrun with emergencies.

Tony set the receiver in its cradle when he heard the sound of a muffled sneeze behind him and turned to glance at his deputy. Wade's eyes had turned pink and watery. "You okay?"

"No." Wade pulled a handkerchief from his pocket and covered his nose with it. He didn't seem to notice it was decorated with lace and embroidered violets. "I'm allergic to cats." The strangled voice did not resemble Wade's usual baritone. "I didn't realize she had so many."

"Who?"

"Your favorite citizen, Portia Osgood." Wade sneezed again. "Since you refuse to answer any calls from her house, I no more than got back here with Jake Lundy when I had to go over and listen to her litany of complaints about you, your aunt, your salary, which, by the way, she thinks should be no more than ten dollars a month, and all of her neighbors who are taking photographs of her to send to trashy magazines." Wade waved the handkerchief in a parody of the old lady's favorite mannerism.

Letting the insults roll past him, Tony grinned at his hulking deputy. While not quite as tall as Tony, the former Marine was heavily muscled and had a face the angels must envy. Not pretty, but handsome enough to stop traffic. Tony did covet his hair — thick, dark and glossy as mink fur. The picture he presented with his pink rimmed eyes and the dainty hanky was just too much. "Go on back to the car or home or wherever you have to go to get rid of the sniffles." Then he added in a laughter-tinged voice meant for only Wade to hear, "And get yourself a handkerchief with fewer frills. This one clashes with your uniform."

Wade looked at the piece of cloth he had pressed against his face. "What *is* this?" He held it at arm's length and frowned.

"Been near Miss Flossie today?" Tony guessed. Miss Flossie Lewis was as gentle and genteel a soul as ever lived, but she did have her ways. She liked to take things, but she would always replace what she took with another item. If the person realized what had happened before Flossie traded it with another person's belongings, she was always amenable to a direct exchange. If she traded it away, she wouldn't have any idea what had happened or even whom she had been near. Sunday dinner at the River View Motel Coffee Shop was the unofficial place and time to make the appropriate trades.

"I carried her groceries into her kitchen this morning." Wade lightly touched the embroidered violets with his fingertip as if making sure they wouldn't break. "I'll wash this before Sunday." Cautiously he lowered his hand and patted his holstered gun before exhaling a sigh of relief. "I'll just wait in the car for you." His own handkerchief was in his pocket. As he walked away, sneezing and checking his handcuffs, his pockets, and the tools of his trade, he was mumbling, "I wonder what she took from me?"

By the time Tony got home, Theo had been there for a couple of hours. The boys had walked to the shop, and Gretchen drove them all to the house on her way home. Theo watched, from her spot in the kitchen, as her husband stopped just inside the front door and stood as if he was absorbing being there. Tony looked beat.

The house was filled with pleasant sounds. Behind her, Chris was giving his brother advice as Jamie played some computer game. Theo enjoyed the sounds of the game itself. It had a bright little tune. Daisy dashed up to greet him, and he rubbed the golden retriever's ears between his fingers and dodged her doggy kisses.

He looked up. "She smells like she's been playing in the creek."

"She has." Theo adjusted the frilly pink apron his mom had given her. It contrasted with the worn sweatpants and the oversized red and gray flannel shirt she'd stolen from his closet, still saving her new clothes for work. She sat at the kitchen table working on her lists. The main list, along with the master calendar, was in the full-sized note-book recycled from college. Other lists of varying sizes were written on an assortment of colored sticky notes.

"What's all this?" Tony leaned over her shoulder and picked up a sticky note designed to look like a miniature yellow legal pad. "I doubt the Allies preparing for the Normandy invasion required this much paperwork."

"That's because all they had to contend with was the weather and the Nazis, whereas I will have some strong personalities under the same roof all weekend long."

"Nobody says whereas." Tony kissed the back of her neck. "You could always stay here with me."

"No, I'm an adult. I can do this." She reached around him and tugged at the snap holding the handcuffs on his belt. "But just in case, do you have a couple of extra pairs that I could borrow?"

"Just use the old whip and chair trick. If it works on lions and tigers, it should work on a couple of middle-aged women."

"Hah! Wild animals are wimps compared to these women." She stood up and gave him a kiss. "Why don't you go and change and I'll get dinner finished. Then you can give me all of the details."

Tony nodded and left the room.

A minute later she heard the sound of him locking his gun in the safe. She put her lists away and set the table.

Tony barely sat down to eat when his cell phone rang. A glance at the screen sent him into the hall, away from the dinner commotion. A call from Doc Nash at this hour could not be a good thing.

"Tony, we've got a real problem." The doctor cleared his throat. "Weevil Beasley died from an overdose of medications."

"Tell me it was an accident."

"Nope. I'm afraid Mr. Beasley was in complete control of his mental faculties. In short, he knew how and when to take his medications."

"So we're left with . . ." Tony's words slowed to a stop.

"Yep, homicide or suicide." The doctor cleared his throat. "I don't suppose you found a note of any kind?"

"No. There was an unpleasant phone message from someone hoping he'd die."

"Weevil was never interested in being popular." The doctor sighed. "I'm afraid I need more information before I can finish the death certificate."

Tony headed for his antacid stash. It

wasn't what he wanted for dinner. "Was Weevil his real name?"

"Yep. I'd guess it was part of the reason he was such a cranky old soul. How'd you like to be named for a bad bug?"

As he disconnected the call, Tony thought his being named Marc Antony for an ancient Roman sounded just dandy. As he climbed the stairs to put his uniform back on, he called dispatch and asked for Wade, Mike, and Sheila to meet him at Mr. Beasley's house. Maybe the four of them could find the truth.

Theo handed him a sandwich as he left the house.

By the time he reached the Beasley house, he'd eaten half of the sandwich. He finished the rest, standing in the tidy front yard, staring at the house. It was a red brick rectangle. The narrow end faced the street. Three steps led up to a white front door. A row of small windows ran across the top of the door. Larger windows, covered with miniblinds, flanked the door.

The door they'd used before was actually a side door opening into a utility area. He knew that next came the kitchen, dining room and living room. The other side of the house contained two bedrooms, a bathroom, and a closet-sized library. Upstairs a single room ran the length of the house.

A detached garage sat back from the street. Ruts worn into the grass made up the driveway.

When his deputies arrived, he sighed heavily. "Sheila and Mike, I want you to talk to the neighbors. Wade, grab your fingerprint case. I'll get the camera."

He didn't expect to find much, and they didn't. When they gathered around Mr. Beasley's table, Tony flipped through his notes. "Anyone find anything?"

"I did learn," Sheila began, "that he argued publicly with some of his relatives after his wife died last year. Nothing specific."

"What did the neighbors think of him?" Tony thought of Orvan's complaints.

Mike said, "He was crusty and cranky but not too bad. He didn't mind if kids used his yard for football games. Not Mr. Sunshine, but an okay guy."

"Wade?" Tony knew it would take fair amount of time and energy for Wade to identify the fingerprints.

"Oddly, not much to do." He twirled his best brush. "I found some smudges on the pill bottles. None on the glasses. The dishwasher was filled with clean dishes. There were smudges on the television remote and nothing else but a few partials. I'd say Blossom is a good housekeeper."

# CHAPTER SIX

"Where's Dad?" said Jamie at breakfast. He sat at the opposite end of the table from Chris. Theo poured milk on Chris's cereal and headed for Jamie's bowl.

"You remember he got called out last night? He got home late, so try to hold down the noise when you go back upstairs, okay?"

"Okay." Daisy sat next to Chris staring at him as he shoved a spoonful of cereal in on top of the one already in his mouth. The big dog didn't blink. "You leave today?" Milk seeped between his lips and dripped back into the bowl.

"Don't talk with food in your mouth. And the answer is yes." Theo sipped her coffee. "I'll leave about noon, so after school just walk to the shop. Miss Edith will pick you up, and she'll come over in case your Dad gets called out in the night."

"Dad's cooking, isn't he?" Jamie blew

80

bubbles in his orange juice.

Theo took the glass from him and set it on the table. "You know he is. We talked about it the other day."

"Well, you know, Mom," Chris started, then swallowed before continuing, "it's good Dad can cook 'cause Miss Edith is the worst cook in town."

Jamie joined in. "Maybe in the whole world."

Theo smiled. "Then I suggest you encourage your dad's efforts. Edith might have to cook if you hurt his feelings." She stood and checked a newspaper clipping attached to the refrigerator with a magnet cleverly disguised as a butterfly made from a magazine page. "Hot lunch today is tuna salad with crackers, broccoli casserole, black eyed peas and a cake square."

"What kind of cake?" Jamie looked interested.

"It doesn't matter," said Chris. "It's not worth eating if you have to look at their broccoli casserole. It's totally gross." He made a melodramatic gagging sound until Theo glared at him. "I'm taking my lunch."

"Me too. Can I fix my own, Mom?"

"Sure." Theo handed Jamie a brown paper lunch bag. "Just remember to put in something more nutritious than chips and crackers. I'll be checking."

Chris jumped to his feet. "I'm first in the shower." As soon as he was out of the chair, Daisy began mopping up the milk and cereal with her tongue.

"He'll hog all the hot water, Mom." Jamie starting moaning as he dried the apple Theo washed and handed to him.

"Go ahead, Chris, and leave some hot water."

"Yeah, yeah."

Tony still wasn't up by the time both boys were showered, dressed and ready for school. The boys groaned out of habit when Theo posted their lists of chores to take care of until she got home Sunday afternoon. "Both of you check Daisy's water bowl several times a day and make sure she isn't running low. Last time when I got home from a trip, her bowl was almost dry." She gave them her best stern mother look and then gave them big hugs and kisses. "I'll see you Sunday."

"What time?" Jamie said.

Her younger son's worried expression made her smile. "I'll be back in time to celebrate your birthday, Jamie."

"Okay. Bye, Mom." And they were off, letting the front door slam behind them.

Enjoying the peace, Theo cleaned the

kitchen. It was a long, narrow kitchen with a fireplace at the far end and walls made of brick. It had only been partially modernized. It ran the width of the house, and even though it was too dark, it was her favorite room in the house. On lazy days, when she and the boys made cookies, she could almost swear she could feel her grandfather's presence. He had taught her to bake in the old wood burning stove. She had lived in this old house every year of her life except the college years and the Chicago years, as she thought of them, but even then it had been this house she called "home."

She scribbled a short list of things they would need from the store. At nine o'clock, she slowly made her way upstairs to wake Tony. Sprawled on his stomach, he covered the whole bed. He looked so comfortable that it seemed cruel to awaken him. "Tony?" She touched his shoulder. He flopped onto his back and clutched the quilt with both hands, pulling it up to his nose. He didn't open his eyes.

Theo had to smile. Jamie slept the same way. "Tony, it's nine. You asked me to wake you."

"Can't be." His voice was muffled. "I just got to bed."

"I know, but Ruth Ann will be calling any

minute now."

"Um." He opened one eye and reached for her hand. "So, are you are scared of her too?" The other eye opened. "What did she ever do to you?"

"Are you kidding?" She tugged on his hand but he didn't budge. "I've been interrogated by her for years. If I'm ever arrested, I'll be able to fool the polygraph and withstand countless good cop-bad cop routines." She couldn't keep a straight face because she and Ruth Ann were good friends.

"Think so?" Moving like lightning, Tony gently flipped her onto the bed and started kissing her neck. "Am I the good cop or bad cop?"

The telephone's shrill ring pierced the moment.

"Hell's bells!" Tony jumped out of bed. "I'll be in the shower."

"Coward!" Theo called to his back and grabbed the telephone. "Good morning, Ruth Ann." She warbled into the receiver. If a silence could be anything, Theo mused, this one was surprised.

"Theo, it's Jane, not Ruth Ann." Her mother-in-law always insisted on identifying herself as if Theo hadn't known her for years. Today was no different.

"Sorry, Jane. I was sure that you were Ruth Ann calling to check on Tony." The second the words were out of her mouth, she wanted to stuff them back in.

"Is something wrong with him?" Jane still worried as if her children were all two years old. Tony's job in law enforcement didn't put him any higher on the worry list than any of his siblings.

"No. He's fine." Glad Jane couldn't see her, Theo rolled her eyes. "He's just running a little late. Did you call for him or me?"

"You. What time are you going up to The Lodge?"

"About noon." Theo tucked the receiver between her ear and shoulder and started making the bed. Almost immediately she had to stop and rest. "Do you need something before I go?"

"Would you stop by the shop and pick up the birthday present for Martha? I left it there last night because I don't want her to see me carrying it in." Jane chuckled. "I left it in the classroom."

"Oh, thanks, I almost forgot. I need to call The Lodge and remind them about the birthday cake they're making for her." Theo sat on the bed and leaned into the pillows. Daisy jumped up on the bed next to her and rested her big shaggy face on what was left of Theo's lap, staring up with her sad, golden retriever eyes. Obligingly, Theo began scratching her ears. Jane was a sweetheart, but sometimes she made Theo nuts. What Theo really wanted to tell Jane was she could come early and carry her own package. Jane's driving was a frequent topic of conversation. She had become so paranoid about hitting animals on the road that when the reintroduction of elk into the Smokies was discussed, she fussed around, convinced that they would attack her car. At least she would be arriving at The Lodge with Martha. "When are you two coming up?"

"About five I think. Anything special going on at your house this weekend?" Jane used her inquisition voice. It took Theo a minute to understand what she was asking. As Tony wandered back into the room, a towel wrapped around his waist, she covered the receiver with her hand and mouthed, "Your mother" and grinned when he backed away.

"It should be pretty quiet around here. The boys will entertain themselves for the most part. Tony and Chris have a special scout thing to go to this evening, and Jamie can either go with them or stay with Edith."

Daisy rolled onto her back so Theo could scratch her stomach. The dog's lips fell back, exposing a fierce looking set of teeth.

Tony lifted a questioning eyebrow. Theo was able to answer both their questions. "It's at the church at seven o'clock. Other than that, it's the same old thing around here."

As she was hanging up the telephone, Tony asked, "What's this special scout thing?"

"You remember. They asked if you would do it since you were in the Navy and they figured you would know all about knots."

"I forgot all about it. It's a good thing you reminded me." He was pulling on his shirt. "Do they know I was just a cook?"

"I don't think they care, and you did agree to do it." Planting her hands on her hips, she glared at him. "Chris is all excited to have you there, so I guess you'd better practice during the day."

"I will, I will." He grinned at her. "I will be the best knot teacher they've ever had. Who all is going today?"

Abandoning Daisy, Theo scooted back against the headboard. As she gave each name, she ticked off a finger. "There's Martha and Jane, Melissa and Susan, Lucinda, Freddie, Ruth and Holly." She looked at her fingers and shook her head. "There's more than that."

"Doesn't Nina usually go?"

"Yes, she was planning to be there, but she's in Paris until Sunday."

"Paris, France?"

"Yes, that Paris. It's some special one week trip for language teachers she won." Theo sighed, only a little envious. "I don't know how she can think it's going to be more fun than retreat."

"Don't forget Eleanor," said Tony. "Didn't you tell me she's going?"

"I'm trying very hard to forget her." Theo went through the names and fingers again. "Oh, of course. Dottie and Betty."

"Betty?"

Theo could tell Tony was amazed and with good reason. Betty was almost blind, and osteoporosis was shrinking her at an alarming rate. She resembled a gnome more and more each day.

"How can she quilt?"

"She never goes anywhere without Dottie. Dottie's eyes are okay so she threads the needles for both of them. As long as the light is good and you don't care how even the stitches turn out, she can quilt up a storm."

"Good for Betty." He bent over and gave

Theo a kiss. "I'll take you up at noon, and for heaven's sake take your cell phone with you. Last time, I called your phone six times, only to find out you left it in your workshop."

"Okay, okay."

By mid-morning Theo was ready to leave the house. She checked her to-do list. There were plenty of clean clothes for Tony and the boys. Plenty of food. Today was a beautiful day, and she always enjoyed the fall retreat. It was a time for her to concentrate on her own projects and not on teaching. She stacked her retreat bound bags by the front door. Her bag of clothes weighed almost nothing: pajamas, slippers, T-shirts. The most weight was in the jar of prenatal vitamins. She added a large, extra strong garbage bag filled with one quilt in progress, the large wooden hoop she used while working on it and a small fabric bag holding her thread, thimble and extra needles. Thinking she might want to rest and read for a while, she added a book. Realizing she almost forgot the box holding the embroidery supplies required by Scarlet LaFleur for her mini-class in Armenian embroidery, she waddled off to get it.

Just in case she ran out of projects, she added the bag holding Tony's Christmas present. She was making him a new lap quilt and still had a couple of months until the deadline. Even so she hoped to get the binding done this weekend. Once the twins arrived, she might never have another free moment. The top was alternating stars and snowball shapes pieced with fabrics printed with cowboy, and the back was a flannel barbed wire print. Theo had sewn it extra long so it would cover him from nose to toes when he napped in his recliner.

Needing a little rest, Theo sat and propped her feet up. She closed her eyes and immediately fell asleep.

# CHAPTER SEVEN

Theo relaxed in the Blazer's passenger seat, relieved to let Tony deal with the drive. The road to The Lodge was ten miles of inclines and switchbacks. At night the dangerous drive seemed much farther. At noon, even at this time of year, it was a beautiful drive. In the protected valley where Silersville sat, the fall foliage was fading, but some colorful leaves remained on the trees. Not up here. The Lodge was not only at a much higher elevation but perched on the side of the mountain overlooking the national park. Up here, all of the deciduous trees were stripped of their leaves, leaving stark gray or brown limbs twisted against the dark of the evergreens. The even higher peaks of the Smokies were swathed in a deep blue haze.

After next weekend, when The Lodge would be filled with wedding guests coming for Patrick's wedding, The Lodge would close for the season. Because the quilters normally came on the last weekend of the season, they were charged only a minimal rate for their rooms and meals. This would be the third year for their event, and while some of the ladies were repeats, it would be the first year for Melissa, Susan and Eleanor. Fresh young faces and a harpy. What a combination!

The tiny sign reading "The Lodge" with its faded red arrow pointing toward a gravel road was almost hidden under the drooping foliage of an overgrown mountain laurel. If she had not been up here many times, Theo would have hesitated to make the turn, unsure if this was really the correct road. As Tony guided the car around the sharp bend, she wondered how many first-time visitors either missed the sign or didn't believe it. Heavily wooded on both sides, the road could lead anywhere. A fanciful imagination could see a witch's house through the trees. Theo anticipated the end of the driveway, and Tony slowed the Blazer even more.

Suddenly, The Lodge was directly in front of them. Its native stone edifice fitted onto the side of the mountain as if it had grown there, much like lichen on a rock. Shaped in a V, the point aimed at the bigger mountain to the south. The lobby filled the ground floor in the point of the V. A covered veranda, open from front to back, made up the upper level point. Peeled log rails prevented tourists from leaning out too far while admiring the various magnificent views. The veranda was designed and decorated to be a wonderful area for relaxing. The flowers in the whiskey-barrel planters were faded, but there were still evergreen topiaries and clusters of locally made ladder-back chairs arranged around small tables, forming conversational groupings.

On the ground level, a flagstone terrace surrounded the whole hotel. Except for a postage stamp–sized grassy area near the front, shrubs and trees — rhododendron, dogwood, mountain laurel and balsam fir — grew right up to the edge of the terrace. Concrete benches had been placed in niches, giving the occupants privacy.

The small parking lot was actually a little past The Lodge and hidden from view by more trees. Tony turned into the semicircular drive and stopped in front of the big hotel door. Several empty luggage carts stood waiting.

As Theo climbed out of the Blazer and glanced around, she shivered. Although she knew The Lodge was staffed with good people, for just a moment she felt threatened. Swallowing back a bubble of panic coming from nowhere and threatening her peace of mind, she watched Tony stack her things on one of the luggage carts. She couldn't shake the feeling someone was watching her.

The feeling vanished the second Tony dragged her luggage cart into the lobby. Immediately, two-able bodied men jumped to help. Art Trimble, the owner of The Lodge, beat his young assistant to the cart by inches. "Do you have more in the car, Theo?" Art took the handle of the cart.

"Not this time." She had to laugh as much in relief as in amusement. "You've seen us arrive with truckloads of stuff before."

Art smiled widely. "Just testing." He indicated his assistant. "This is Gavin Thompson. He's Beth's nephew."

Theo extended her hand to the young man who looked big enough to carry a small truck up the flight of stairs without breaking a sweat. "Nice to meet you." Theo had to tug a little to get her hand free. "Have you been working up here for very long?"

"I started this summer after I finished at the university." He grinned at his brother-in-law. "Working for Art and Beth, I get to save just about everything I make so I will start grad school after Christmas." Ignoring Tony, he grasped the cart. "Which stuff do you want in the sewing area?"

Thinking the young man looked familiar and older than most college students, Theo pointed to the small bag. "Everything except this."

Without another word, Gavin picked up the two largest items and dashed away.

"Thank you." Theo said to his vanishing back. She turned to face Art. "Do I need to check in?"

"Let me get Beth for you. She wanted to go over the room assignments and other arrangements with you." He headed for the back of the hotel at a near run.

"You have fun. I'll be back for you on Sunday about noon." Tony bent and gave her a kiss. "I'd better move the Blazer before one of your group decides it's in the way and pushes it off the mountain."

Theo waved goodbye and wandered toward the sunken lounge. A low stone wall kept the unwary safe. The lounge area was about four feet lower than the lobby, gift shop, game room and restaurant. Beth had once explained the builders designed the enormous fireplace at the far end of the lounge before the rest of the building. When it had become apparent that the fireplace, as designed, would not fit the hotel, the builder had the area around it excavated so the fireplace would fit perfectly.

"Theo?" The cadence of the soft female voice behind her was a pleasing drawl.

"I'm down here admiring your fireplace."

With only a little clicking of her customary three inch high-heeled shoes, Beth Trimble made her entrance. Theo grinned at her, admiring her dedication to her own fashion sense. Theo probably only noticed it because it was so far from her own lack of it. Beth Trimble believed in being noticed. Today's high heels were red, matching her red leather mini-skirt. Theo wondered if she had borrowed her flowered tank top from a child, a small child. Topping it all was a hairdo requiring lots of hairspray and time.

"Welcome." Beth approached Theo, arms wide. Running a hotel was the perfect occupation for Beth. She never met a stranger, and everyone was her best friend.

After the brief hug, Theo stepped away. "Thanks, Beth. Are you ready to do this again?"

"Absolutely! We love having the quilters." She glanced at her heavily-laden nephew standing at the top of the steps like a beast of burden. "Hey there, Gavin. Anything you don't need to bring down here, take to her room. I'm putting her in room seven."

Theo pointed to her small bag. "I can take

it myself. That's the only thing for my room." She smiled at Beth when the large young man ignored her and dashed off with the little bag. "What about your other guests? Have they been warned that there will be lots of laughter coming from the lobby?"

"There's only a few of them, and we explained the lounge area will not be available. They all seemed fine with it. If not," she said with a shrug, "they don't have to come back."

"Well, I doubt any of us would mind if they just wander through and look, as long as they don't stay too long."

"Come see how we've set up for you." Beth led the way through the comfortable seating area to an open space. "We have lots of extension cords and power strips in there." She pointed to a cardboard box in one corner. "Several folding tables. Just tell Gavin or Art where you want them set up."

"It looks great, as always, Beth. The only thing that comes to mind right now is that we'll need more light."

"Of course. I know some of your group will bring their own, but we have eight floor lamps in this little closet. If you need more, we'll just bring them down from the empty rooms." Beth pulled a note from her pocket.

"We'll put out snacks this evening, but not dinner. You are welcome to use the kitchen any time." She grinned. "I know you ladies love to eat at odd times up here. We are cooking three meals tomorrow and brunch on Sunday. Is that right?"

"Perfect." Theo pulled out a list of her own. "We need seven rooms."

"Seven? Last I heard, there were only going to be twelve of you this year."

"There are, but no one, including me, wants to share with Eleanor."

"Eleanor Liston is coming here?" Beth's look of horror was almost comic. "I'll put her next to the stairs on the second floor. The wind howls through there and makes horrible shrieking sounds. She should feel right at home." Opening the drawer in the desk, Beth pulled out a roll of tape and a pen.

"As long as you are prepared to listen to her bitching about it, it doesn't bother me." Theo handed her the list. "I have bracketed the ones who are sharing. Except for Eleanor, we should be a merry group. Although I don't know much about our guest teacher, Scarlet LaFleur. She also booked a private room."

"I'll put her upstairs next to Eleanor." Beth paused. "Speaking of upstairs, the rail ing on the verandah is being repaired. There's a temporary barrier, but you might want to warn your ladies."

Theo nodded and watched as Beth taped the list onto the desktop.

"I'll just leave the key drawer open until everyone arrives. That way they can just check this and not have to wait." Beth wrote room numbers on the paper using a red marking pen. Her numbers were practically big enough to read across the room. "We'll bring out Martha's birthday cake whenever you want."

"I brought up some champagne. Do you think you could serve it with the cake? Tea too, for those of us not imbibing."

Beth chewed on the side of one finger, careful not to chip the nail polish that matched her skirt. "Sure, we can."

Theo dug two bottles out of one of the bags stacked in the lounge and handed them to Beth.

As Beth turned to leave, she paused and pointed to a button under the counter. "Ring the bell if you need help at any time, day or night. It rings in our apartment."

"Thanks for your help."

"No, problem." High heels clicking, Beth headed for the kitchen.

■ ■ ■ ■

Tony made it back to his office in record time in spite of a quick stop at the library. He carried with him a book about knots and several cords for practice. As long as he was waiting for phone calls, he might as well hone his skills.

Tony was working with his knots and cords when Wade arrived, bleary eyed but reasonably alert. He had worked long hours at the house looking for fingerprints.

"I can tell you Blossom turned on the dishwasher. Her prints matched exactly." He yawned. "Some partial prints on the medicine bottles look like hers, but I can't say for sure."

Tony frowned.

"But, partial prints most likely belonging to Mr. Beasley were on the bottles too."

"Telling us?" Tony untied his knots and picked up his pen.

"Well, it tells us either or both of them could have supplied the overdose."

"And?"

"And maybe because of the smudges, someone else wore gloves and handled the bottles."

"Fabulous." Tony tossed the pen acros

the room and reached for the antacids.

Theo wasn't surprised the first arrivals were Susan and Melissa. The young women drove up at about three o'clock, laughing and dragging bag after bag into the lobby. Giddy from escaping their preschool children, they explored every nook and cranny of the hotel, laughing the whole time. Melissa finally insisted they sit for a while and talk to Theo.

About the time they settled down in the lobby, a vintage Ford pulled up in front and Dottie and Betty climbed out. The driver, a thin, freckle-faced boy with shocking purple hair, jumped out and started unloading their gear. Gavin was soon lending a hand, looking a bit surprised by the weight of the bags. Linking arms, the ladies strolled into the hotel like a pair of queens with two serfs behind them staggering under the volume of luggage. The boy stacked his load by the desk, kissed Dottie's wrinkled cheek and bolted for the door. "Have fun, Grandma. I'll be back on Sunday about noon." And he was gone.

Four of them came together. Lucinda, Freddie, Ruth and Holly were inseparable. This weekend, they planned to work on a quilt in a frame. They sent their luggage to the rooms with Gavin. "Just stack it all in one of the rooms, sugar," said Freddie, the spokeswoman. "We'll sort it out later."

"Do you need any help?" Beth Trimble stood at the top of the stairs. It looked like her hair had grown even bigger. "I can send Gavin and Art in to help."

"Thanks, Beth, but we do this all the time. We can arrange it ourselves." Theo sent her away.

The older ladies, Dottie and Betty, made their way into the lobby, carefully negotiating the stairs, and headed for the corner where Susan, Melissa and Theo were sitting. Melissa and Susan jumped up and began moving chairs into an open U. Once they had everything arranged they were able to sit and chat.

"Who else is coming?" asked Holly.

"Martha and Jane will come up together sometime later. They have to wait until Jane gets off work. With Martha teaching, Jane seems to feel she has to be at the museum all the time. Even if they aren't open to visitors yet." Theo paused. "Eleanor will show up whenever it suits her, I guess."

Someone whispered, "I wish that witch would drop dead."

"What about Scarlet LaFleur?" said Susan. "I'm excited to learn her embroidery techniques. Wouldn't it be gorgeous on an appliqué project?"

"You know who she was before she changed her name, don't you?" One of the older ladies muttered as she settled at the frame. She announced the answer to the woman next to her.

Theo thought everyone looked stunned, which surprised her. She thought it was common knowledge. Scarlet was the former Christmas Poinsettia Flowers. Country music star Elf's older sister.

Tony had just about tied himself to his desk chair with a very complicated series of knots when Ruth Ann interrupted him. Stepping into the doorway of his office, she said, "You'll be interested to know, Sheriff, Mike just called in from Ruby's Café."

Tony had a step-by-step instruction book about knots open on his desk. If he had known anything about these knots before, he had forgotten it, and he had only a few hours left to learn them. "And?" Tony didn't look up from his project. When Ruth Ann didn't say more, he was forced to move his eyes away from the end of the recalcitrant cord to look at her. "So, now he can operate the phone?" Acid dripped from each syllable.

Ruth Ann waved her fingers, drying the latest shade of polish. It looked purple to him. "There was an altercation on the premises. It's under control."

"What?" Tony went back to work on his project.

"You know. A fight." She didn't flinch when a paper clip sailed within inches of her nose, but a look of disdain curled her lip.

"I know what one is, and you know it." He narrowed his eyes and glared at her. "Dammit Ruth Ann, just tell me what's going on." Tony had neatly tied himself to his desk while practicing his knot-tying for Chris's scout meeting. He was sure the boys would do a better job if he just handed out photocopies of the instructions and sat off to the side and offered encouraging words.

His phone rang.

"Ruth Ann! Will you get that please?" When she actually answered the phone and identified herself, he decided she needed a raise. "Thank you."

She put the caller on hold. "Blossom wants to know if you've got her money."

"Her what?" Tony stared at the Gordian knot at his ankles.

"Money. As in paycheck." Ruth Ann studied him. "Put the end through there and then push it through this hole." She pointed to a small space near his ankle bone with a glistening wet fingernail.

It worked. The knot was transformed into a neat, useable piece of string art. "How'd you know to do that?"

"I practice on my mother-in-law all the time." Ruth Ann waved her hand again, sending the aroma of polish into his nostrils. "If I don't tie her up from time to time, I'll have to kill her."

Tony glanced up. He couldn't tell from her expression if she was kidding or not. "What's the latest with Walter? Any change?" Ruth Ann's husband had been injured over a year previous, and her mother-in-law had moved in to "help out."

Ruth Ann's smile illuminated the room. "After months of therapy, he suddenly seems to be making great progress. It's like the message has finally gotten to his brain, and he's making clay figures."

For a man whose hands had been lying useless in his lap for months, it *was* a miracle. "So is his mama leaving any time soon?"

"I sincerely hope so." Ruth Ann sighed. "Oh-oh. I left Blossom on hold."

"I am hopelessly tied up." Tony released the knot. "Tell her I can't do anything until

Carl Lee gets back into town. Thanks to you I'm ready to be the entertainment at tonight's meeting."

Ruth Ann used the telephone on his desk then turned and strolled away. She smiled at him over her shoulder. "Have a fun weekend with the boys."

"You have a fun one too. Maybe you can find your mother-in-law's suitcase."

"Not a problem." Ruth Ann paused at the door. "I put it under her bed the day she arrived."

"Wait, you didn't tell me about Mike." Tony began working on the next knot in the book.

"He said that Elmer Smith and Dudley Thomas got into a knockdown, drag out fight at the counter in Ruby's. Elmer evidently told Dudley if he didn't mend his ways and become a better person he was going to end up dead, just like Mr. Beasley." Ruth Ann walked closer, leaned forward and pointed to the loose end of the cord. "It needs to come back up through here."

"Thanks." Tony did as she indicated and the new knot slid perfectly into place. "Does Mike need any help?" When Ruth Ann shook her head in negation, Tony relaxed. "What else happened?"

"I guess Dudley didn't feel like improving

himself, although I wish he would. His nickname isn't Dud because he's so ambitious. Anyway, he tossed Elmer onto the floor along with a considerable number of dishes, and Ruby flipped out and called it in and Mike answered the call. When Mike arrived, Elmer was unconscious on the floor in the middle of the café and Dudley was holding a piece of a broken plate against Elmer's throat."

Tony started untying the knots as Ruth Ann continued. "To make a long story short, Mike is bringing Dudley in now. Doc Nash is fixing Elmer up, and Ruby won't let either man back into her café." She touched the edge of her fingernail checking it for dryness. Smiling with satisfaction, she sauntered out of his office.

Still holding the cord, Tony leaned back in his chair, his thoughts on Dudley Thomas. Dudley had spent some time in the county jail and was certainly no saint. His main crimes were usually drunk and disorderly behavior, public intoxication and car theft. The car theft charges were what Dudley preferred to think of as borrowing what he couldn't afford to buy. His target victims were almost always tourists from out of state who parked in Ruby's parking lot. It was strictly a matter of convenience for him.

Dudley worked sporadically at his brothers' gas station. The station next door to Ruby's. On the occasions when he did work, he was the best auto mechanic in three states. Even though he failed to fix Theo's minivan.

Tony knew when Mike arrived with Dudley. He could hear Dudley swearing in the back seat of the patrol car as it pulled into the parking bay. Tony met them in the interrogation room. "Did Mike read you your rights?" From across the room, he could smell Dudley. His odor was an unpleasant combination of sweat, grease and beer. The navy blue jumpsuit he wore had enough grease on the front of it to lubricate every hinge in Park County.

"Yeah, he did, like I'm not smart enough to know what they are without him going on and on about it. I got me a terrible headache." Dud whined. "Can I leave now?"

"No." Tony hooked his foot around the nearest chair and dragged it towards him.

Mike just smiled at the screeching sounds it made as it crossed the linoleum, but Dudley covered his ears with both hands and moaned.

Tony said, "Have a seat, Dudley."

Dudley did as he was told. He crossed his arms on the table and rested his head on them. Seconds later he was snoring.

Tony looked at his deputy. "Ruth Ann gave me her version of the story. What's yours? You think he meant to harm Elmer?"

"Yeah. I think he was just drunk enough and just mad enough about something Elmer said that he would have killed him if the others hadn't gotten involved. I don't know how long you can lock up someone on 'would have.' "

Tony shrugged. "What started it? Ruth Ann said something about a threat."

"From what I gathered at the scene, Elmer accused Dudley of running up a lot of extra miles on his car when he was supposed to be checking the transmission. Evidently he billed Elmer for several hours when he was just driving around in Elmer's car. Elmer called it gouging and claimed Dudley was using his car for a personal trip. Dudley called it fair business practice." Mike consulted his notes. "Five witnesses saw him slam Elmer in the face with a plate, knocking him off the stool, and then Elmer started fighting back. All of the diners jumped in then. I was only about a mile away when I got the call, but by the time I arrived Dudley had knocked Elmer unconscious and was threatening to kill him to keep everyone back. The piece of plate he was using as a weapon was sharp enough to have done a lot of damage. I have it in the car."

"How is Elmer?" Elmer was in his early sixties and was fit enough to walk eighteen holes, carrying his golf clubs but Dudley was in his thirties and had an advantage of fifty pounds of muscle.

"Right now he is pretty dizzy and sick to his stomach. Doc says he'll have a headache for a couple of days. Lucky thing for him that Doc was having lunch there. Doc might have thrown a couple of punches himself." Mike looked at Dudley, whose snores were increasingly loud. "How long are you going to let him sleep there?"

"His time's up." Tony pounded on the metal table. The combination of the sound and vibrations had Dudley on his feet in seconds. As he pulled his arm back, his hand tightened into a fist and he snarled at Tony, his teeth gleamed white in his dirty face.

Mike had the handcuffs on him in the blink of an eye. "I think I'll just take this garbage on down to the jail."

"Good plan." Tony opened the door. "Let's call in Archie Campbell at the county attorney's office. I'll bet they charge him with assault, and Ruby will press charges over the damages to her café."

# CHAPTER EIGHT

Friday evening, The Lodge was a happy place. Theo and her friends laughed and caught up with the news as they worked on their various projects. The older ladies had their frame set up and were busy hand quilting. Melissa and Susan were near enough to converse with, working with their sewing machines. Conversation covered topics from the best brand of needles to recent events.

Eleanor Liston entered the lobby with all of the dramatic flair she could muster. She had her current project clamped under one arm, and it dragged on the floor behind her like a train. One hand was filled with the special thirty-two ounce covered plastic coffee mug she always had with her. Her purse hung halfway off her shoulder, and she clutched an old shoebox, splitting open at the corners. "I don't know why we have to come all the way out to this godforsaken place. Surely there is a nicer place we could use." She lost her grip on the shoebox and it dropped at her feet at the top of the lobby steps. The lid fell off and her spools of thread, scissors, and assorted notions spilled out and went in all directions.

No one offered to help gather up her belongings. Instead there was a series of muttered comments, one of which sounded like, "She's got more money than sense, so why won't she get something better to carry her stuff in than a twenty-year-old shoebox."

Even as Eleanor harangued everyone within earshot about their lack of assistance, the sound of laughter announced the arrival of Martha and Jane. The pair came through the front doors like a pair of tornadoes. Only the tops of their heads were visible; Martha's gray curls were on the left and Jane's not quite natural brown on the right. Art Trimble rushed forward and rescued the bags and boxes they carried and sent Gavin out for another load.

Jane issued a command to the younger man's back. "Better take the cart. There's lots more."

While they were arranging their possessions and finding the chairs they wanted to use, Theo waved to Beth and pantomimed blowing out the candles. Beth nodded and headed toward the kitchen. Art took her place behind the counter. After a quick check of the rooming list, he picked a pair of keys out of the open key drawer. As he handed one to Jane, he smiled at her, using his best innkeeper smile. "I hope you have a pleasant stay."

When Martha reached for hers, he held on to the key and cleared his throat. "Um, Martha, I'm, um, I hope you enjoy your stay too."

He headed for the kitchen, but the sound of his laughter caught Theo's attention. He sounded just like a barking seal. She wondered if he was Lila's married lover.

Scarlet LaFleur's entrance distracted her. The embroiderer swept through the doorway, descending onto the hotel like a queen returning from a long, long exile. She dropped a small bag near the front desk and glanced around. "Where's the help in this dump?"

Gavin's arms were filled with bags as he stopped in mid-step, automatically moving away from the elegant woman in a swirling red cape. Her jet black hair and large violet eyes did nothing to dispel his surprise. "I'm the help." He finally managed to speak. "I'll be right with you." He bolted down the hallway.

"Idiot." Scarlet glanced around. "Is he the only employee?"

Theo opened her mouth to reply, but Martha beat her to it. "No, but the others are occupied at the moment." She hustled to the front desk and checked the list. "Here you are." She handed Scarlet a room key. "Up to the second floor, then go left."

"And my bags?"

"Gavin will take them up as soon as he can." Martha's teacher voice took over. She might work part-time at the folk museum now, Theo thought, but she could still command a crowd.

Theo managed to work her way out of her chair and stood at last. "Come down and meet everyone." She gestured for Scarlet to join everyone in the work area. "We're just setting up a wedding quilt for one of our friends."

With a haughty sniff and an elegant toss of her cape, Scarlet LaFleur condescended to join the apparent riffraff. Her lip curled. "Quilters are such a messy group."

Having watched almost all of the women around her before, Theo could only grin and nod. Some of her friends were messier than others, but none of them could sew without creating a nest of thread bits. She found herself even more intrigued by Scarlet's presence among them. And why was she here a full week before the wedding?

Scarlet swept into the work space, commandeered the best chair, the best lamp and arranged them to suit herself. She managed to whack several quilters with her oversized purse without offering the slightest hint of apology. Flinging off her red velvet cape with a flourish, she uncovered a cream-colored cashmere sweater and a heavy gold necklace set with a large ruby.

She did not greet anyone, not even making eye contact. Instead, she reached into her large handbag and a moment later had on a headset, like a hands-free phone. Since most of the quilters were determined not to be disturbed by families calling on cell phones, a few eyebrows raised, but no one said anything.

Next Scarlet extracted an emery board and proceeded to work on her fingernails. The myriad lights around her caught on her ruby earrings, bracelet, and ring. She inhaled through her mouth, making a loud "Ah" sound, then released it in four short "ahs" descending the musical scale. As bored sighs went, it was a twelve on the melodrama scale of ten.

Theo saw some physical resemblance between Scarlet and her more famous sister, singing star Elf. Scarlet was about five years older and several inches taller than her sister, who was close to Theo's height. Very short.

Scarlet went through the sighs again. By the fifth time through, Theo considered sticking something in her mouth to stop the sounds.

As the last quilters settled down with their projects, their chatter almost drowned out the sounds of Scarlet sighing. With a sour expression on her face, Scarlet glanced at the woman to her left. "You're doing that wrong."

Theo leaned forward, believing Scarlet picked the wrong person to criticize. Eleanor had never been known for her good behavior. The quilters tolerated her, mostly because they felt sorry for her, but Scarlet wouldn't know or care.

Eleanor glanced up. "I think you're a bitch."

The clear case of the pot calling the kettle black made the chatter level around the room increase as the quilters left the pair to fight it out.

Scarlet stood, then stalked away when Gavin reappeared. The beleaguered young man had retrieved her multitude of bags from her car and now offered to show her to her room.

During Scarlet's absence, Theo was assailed by complaints from her friends. She had no defense. "It's not my fault. She asked to come here."

A few minutes later, Scarlet was back. Her list of complaints had grown to include the size and decor of her room, Silersville, the world in general, her famous sister, and her unpleasant assessments of meals not yet served. "If the food is not up to my standards, I may not be eating here." She glared at Theo. "I will not pay for mediocre meals, and you can't make me."

Theo glanced over Scarlet's shoulder and saw obviously angry Art and Beth Trimble glaring at the woman's back. Luckily for Scarlet, neither of them held a knife.

Hoping a little genial conversation on a different subject would loosen up the woman, Theo said, "How did you get interested in Armenian embroidery?"

Scarlet smiled, clearly reveling in the attention. It might have been the first real smile any of them had seen on her face. "I learned from my mother-in-law."

"I didn't realize you're married," Theo blurted. The expression on Scarlet's face was not encouraging.

"I'm not." There was no smile now. "There

117

were too many 'cultural' differences. My husband and I parted ways after less than a year."

Hoping to move the conversation to a happier path, Theo said, "Will you show us some of your embroidery pieces?"

Reaching into a large, expensive tapestry bag, Scarlet pulled out a piece of black velvet about three feet square. As she unfolded it, the room fell silent. The stunning, intricate needlework done in silver thread looked like something from a dream.

"Oh, my."

"That's gorgeous."

"Is that what we're learning to do? It's much prettier than the photograph."

A pair of machine quilting wizards studied it. One said, "Maybe I could do it with an embroidery machine."

"If I can't do it with my machine, I'm stuck." Her sidekick's voice was a mere whisper. "I don't do anything by hand."

"Tomorrow," said Scarlet. She began her sigh down the scales again.

Martha and Jane were still sorting out their projects when Beth wheeled out a service cart bearing the sheet cake. The cake had been cleverly decorated to resemble a patchwork quilt, and there was a candle in each square. Fifty of them. The shelf below the cake held plates, silverware, napkins and champagne glasses. The waitress from the hotel coffee shop carried the two chilled bottles of champagne. The party officially began with the ritual singing of "Happy Birthday."

Martha's expression of surprise and delight was unfeigned.

The fifty candles gave off a lot of light and heat. "That's a real fire hazard, Martha. If you don't blow those out soon, we'll have to cover it with a quilt," quipped Dottie.

"Not one of mine." Martha took a deep breath and managed to get most of the candles with the first blow. The second one finished the fire. "Okay, let's eat."

Theo had her mouth full of sinfully rich chocolate cake when Eleanor attacked. "If that husband of yours comes by to ask me any more questions, I'll have him thrown out of office. There must be something more important for the sheriff to do than harass a poor defenseless woman."

Theo had no idea what she was talking about and wasn't sure she'd survive a weekend with Eleanor and Scarlet.

Martha whirled around. "You? Defenseless? That's a laugh. You are as defenseless as a copperhead slithering through the grass. It wouldn't surprise me if you killed

Mr. Beasley." She balled her hands into fists and took a step closer to Eleanor. Before she could move again, her friends pulled her to the other side of the room and pushed her into a chair and handed her a glass of champagne.

Eleanor glanced around the room as if seeking support, but none was forthcoming so she didn't say more but settled into a comfortable chair on the fringe of the group. For most of the rest of the evening, she held her tongue. Soon the group settled down to work, and the festive atmosphere returned.

"When do we get the next clue for the mystery quilt?" Jane asked as she parted her bangs and clipped them to her scalp with little butterfly clips. Theo thought it was not a becoming hairstyle on her mother-in-law, but it did allow her to see what she was doing.

"I have it right here." Theo reached into her big bag and pulled out a sheaf of papers. "Who needs one?" Several hands went up. "I have news, too. Katti and Claude already tied the knot."

"We'd better get busy on their wedding quilt." Jane clapped her hands to call them to attention. "Who brought their pink and brown fabrics?"

The project had been discussed at the shop. Katti Marmot loved colors. Lots of colors. All happened to be shades of pink. Rose pink. Baby pink. Hot pink. Pale pink. Pink stripes. Pink dots. So, when the quilters decided to make her a wedding quilt, the only real discussion was what color to add to the pink to tone it down a bit and let Claude feel like not everything in his masculine decor was disappearing. The quilters decided on brown.

Lots of hands went into bags, dragging out piles of pink and brown fabrics. When they added it together, there was probably enough to make three complete king-sized quilts.

"So, what should we make with all this?" Theo stared at the mountain of fabric.

Susan said, "We could make a sampler quilt. If we each make two twelve inch blocks, it should go pretty fast and use lots of different browns and pinks."

The others nodded.

Betty, who was legally blind, piped up. "That's still going to be a very pink quilt."

Martha's voice came from the doorway. "I'd pay a hundred dollars to see Marmot-the-Varmint's head on a pink pillowcase, covered with all those pinks in the quilt, and maybe a heart-shaped satin pillow of

121

hot pink."

"Wait until you see the backing fabric I found." Theo dragged a large piece from one of her bags. "Look. It's chocolate brown with big pink hearts all over it. Kind of like Valentine's Day dragged through the mud."

"It's perfect," said Jane. "Let's get to work."

# Big as a Mountain Mystery Quilt

**Block A** — Using 8 of the 4 3/8″ squares of both fabrics #1 and #2, place one 4 3/8″ square fabric #1 on a 4 3/8″ square of fabric #2, right sides together. Draw a diagonal line corner to corner on the wrong side of one. Sew scant seam 1/4″ away from drawn line on each side. Cut on line. Press to darker fabric. Repeat with remaining 7 squares, creating total of 16 half-square triangle blocks measuring 4″ square.

**Layout** — Place one 4″ square of fabric #3 right side up. Place four 4″ squares of fabric #1 on each side of it. In the corners, add a half-square triangle block with the 90 degree point of the triangle of fabric #2 touching fabric #3. Sew block together.

Make 4. Square to 11″ and Label — Block A.

**Block B** — Using 16 of the 4 3/8″ squares of fabric #1 and of fabric #4, use the same technique as in block A to create 32 half-square triangle blocks. Press to the darker fabric.

**Layout** — Place a 4″ square of fabric #2, right side up. Place a 4″ square of fabric #1 so each has one corner touching a corner of fabric #2. Place one half-square triangle block in each space created, with one edge of #4 touching the right edge of square #1 and the top edge of center square #2. Working around the block, place the remaining three half-square triangles to form a star. Check to make sure as you rotate the block, the top star point should always look the same. Sew. Press to solid squares and away from center row.

Make 8. Square to 11″ and Label — Block B.

# CHAPTER NINE

"I just love doing a mystery quilt." Susan tucked her feet up under her while she studied the instructions.

"Me too." Jane dug through the large green plastic box at her feet until she found her stack of precut fabrics. "Even if I guess right away what it is going to look like. I find it very freeing to work on something without having a preconceived notion about what it should look like when it is finished."

"Well, I think it is silly." Eleanor snapped. The expressions on the others' faces encouraged her to soften her words. "I just mean I already have more than enough to do."

Realizing those words for Eleanor were a true apology, everyone nodded and went back to work.

"How are things at the museum?" Susan shifted the conversation back to Martha and Jane. "I heard the grand opening is next Friday at Celeste and Patrick's wedding reception."

"That's the unofficial opening. Everyone in the county, plus the out of town guests will be free to explore the museum, but we won't actually open to the public then." Martha massaged one eyebrow. "We hope to have most of the kinks worked out by Thanksgiving."

"What's wrong?" Several voices asked in unison.

"Oh, nothing serious. The barn and display building are completely ready." Jane waved her hands in a big circle. "Wait until you see the quilts we have. They are gorgeous. And lots of hands-on exhibits too, like spinning."

Martha chimed in. "We're waiting for one of the new ovens for the snack bar."

"A snack bar?" Holly stuffed a bite of cake into her mouth. "Who's going to cook?"

"Sally Calhoun."

"Really?" Eleanor set her mug down and clapped her hands. "I think that's wonderful!"

Theo turned to Eleanor, surprised the cranky woman was so enthusiastic. "Have you eaten her cooking before?"

"Yes. I hope she hasn't lost her touch. Her pie crust was even better than Blossom's." She frowned. "Of course, that was before

Possum married her and dragged her away to be his prisoner."

As melodramatic as she made it sound, Theo agreed with the basic story. The abusive man had married Sally and kept her isolated from her family and life in town. "What about her baby?"

"Oh, she's so precious." Jane cooed. "We have set up a nursery room next to the snack bar and Celeste has promised to help out when she can."

Eleanor picked up her mug and took a couple of loud gulps of liquid. "Who's Celeste? I don't think I know her."

"Uhm." At that moment, Theo realized what Eleanor was drinking and fell silent. Pregnancy made her sensitive to certain aromas she might not notice otherwise. Rum. In her big travel mug, Eleanor had lots of rum and something coconut. No wonder she tended to get quiet in the evenings. She was intoxicated.

Giving Theo a confused look and picking up the story where she stopped, Jane explained. "Celeste is the nice young woman from Kentucky who's marrying Patrick MacLeod on Friday. You know, he's the new high school football coach."

"Patrick is *my* nephew." Scarlet LaFleur's

voice traveled through the room like an icy wind.

"The name's not familiar." Betty whispered to Dottie but loudly enough for all to hear. "Who are his people?"

"My sister, Easter Lily is his mother." Scarlet's expression did not invite further questions. "I am the only person besides her who knows the identity of his father. I will take her secret with me to the grave."

As melodramatic as it was, the statement managed to stop further, at least open, inquiry about the groom's complicated family tree.

Tony was a hit with the scouts. He'd arrived at the meeting with enough rope to bind all six of the boys, plus the scout leaders, and Jamie into total immobility. It had taken a bit longer than expected to release them all, but the laughter and jokes made it even more fun.

Chris and Jamie hadn't had any problem talking him into a stop at Ruby's Café for dessert on the way home.

He was surprised when Blossom came out of the kitchen, followed by Ruby. Neither of the women was usually there after the dinner rush. Blossom's eyes were watering and her normally smooth skin looked red and blotchy. She stopped at their table and sniffled.

"Hey Blossom, I didn't think you worked evenings." It was lame, but Tony was curious.

A shudder worked its way through her, jiggling her extra flesh. "I don't." She began crying in earnest, buried her face in a towel, and waddled toward the kitchen.

Ruby kept her eyes on Blossom even as she rattled off the desserts available. The moment Blossom disappeared, she turned to Tony. "Poor Blossom. She's hiding here."

"From what?"

"Some members of Mr. Beasley's family have called and accused her of murder." Ruby's beautiful brown eyes flashed with anger. "There's just no way."

Tony didn't dispute her assessment. He was curious, and not just about the identity of the callers. Why pick on Blossom? "Will you ask her if anyone told her their name? I'd really like to have a chat with these people, and as far as I know, none of his relatives live in the area."

The first quilter to go to bed was Melissa. The young mother stretched and yawned. "I'm going to soak in the tub, without having little hands coming under the door, and then slide into bed. I'll see you all when I see you."

Eleanor was the next to go to bed. Her room was upstairs and she staggered slightly before grabbing the handrail.

Mumbling complaints about the lack of an elevator and the drab décor, Scarlet followed Eleanor up the stairs to her own room.

The rest of the group worked on until about midnight. Most of the quilters, including Theo, went to bed then, leaving just a few night owls still working.

When Theo got into her room, it seemed stuffy, so she opened the window. Standing in the cool air, she yawned and stretched as she admired the stars and the crescent moon. Other than a few points of light in the hills across from the hotel, the only lights she saw came from the path lights lining the sidewalk around the building. Laughing so much was exhausting, she thought, and climbed into bed. Minutes later, she was sound asleep.

Only half conscious, it took Theo a little while to realize she was awake and shivering. Not stuffy any longer, the room was freezing cold. She smelled rain in the gentle breeze carried through the open window.

The breeze blew directly across her bed, so she snuggled under the blankets and listened to the drops hitting the ledge outside the window. The rain was welcome after weeks of unrelenting dry weather, and Theo relaxed back into the pillows, savoring the moment.

She couldn't remember the last time it rained. Tears rose and spilled from her eyes, sliding onto the pillow. She wasn't sad. She was so hormonal, so emotional, that a little rain brought her to this state.

As she lay there, teary and yet pleased by the cool rain scent drifting through the room, she felt one or both of her babies turn. Gently rubbing her belly, she smiled, her eyes drying as the rain dripped from the eaves and splashed on the vegetation outside.

Whipping one hand out of the warm shelter of blankets, Theo pulled her travel alarm off the table and into the bed, diving deeper into the covers with it. When she pressed on a bar at the top of the face a light came inside and she could read the time. Three o'clock. She groaned. It was too cold to sleep and too early to get up. "Why don't they have remote controls for windows? There is one for everything else." Grousing, she crawled out of bed and headed first to the bathroom then toward the window. She noticed the room was much darker without the glow of the moon and the stars.

Out of habit, she looked out the window. The only lights came from the path lighting, glowing upwards. Illuminated from below, the trees now had a menacing appearance. There was no color. Only shades of gray. The chill air carried the aromas of decaying leaves and damp earth to her. She shivered and reached up for the old-fashioned window sash. As she tugged on it, pulling it down, closing the window, she caught a glimpse of something odd in the shrubs below. It seemed much lighter in color than the bushes. Theo was sure it had not been there when she went to bed. Squinting made it clearer but not clear enough to identify. It looked like a white branch. She found her glasses on the nightstand and looked again.

A bare leg stuck out of the bushes. A woman's leg.

Wide awake now, Theo pulled on her robe and stuck her room key into the pocket. Without taking the time to think about what she was doing, she headed down the hall, across the lobby, past the Trimbles' apartment and out onto the back sidewalk. Not until she was standing on the wet flagstones did she realize her feet were bare and she was alone in the night with a corpse. Shivering uncontrollably, she backed toward the safety of The Lodge, even as she stared at the grotesque scene.

Draped backwards over a rhododendron bush was the very still body of Scarlet LaFleur. The leg Theo saw from her window pointed to the sky, the other one bent into the shrub. Scarlet's head was turned in an unnatural fashion, and rain droplets splashed into the water pooled in her open mouth. Theo thought something long and thin was tied around Scarlet's neck.

Some small creature moved in the vegetation, making Theo realize how vulnerable she was alone with a dead body in the dark. Sickened and terrified, she headed back into the hotel as quickly as she could. Almost to the owner's suite, she heard heavy footsteps coming behind her. Stepping into an alcove, she ducked down behind a potted plant and watched as Art Trimble, dressed in jeans and flannel shirt, walked past her hiding spot without stopping. His heavy hiking boots left a damp trail behind him.

As soon as she heard the apartment door close, Theo headed for her room. Close to panic, she waddled as quickly as she could.

It took several attempts before she managed to get the key into the lock. She kept glancing backwards over her shoulder. Not until she fastened the security bolt and chain did she start to calm down. Ignoring the hotel phone, her shaking hands trembled as she lifted her tiny cell phone from her purse. She pressed two, automatically dialing Tony's phone.

Tony's grumpy, mumbled greeting was the sweetest sound imaginable. It brought tears to her eyes. "Tony." The most sound she could produce was a bare whisper. With her heart pounding in her throat, she had to stop and catch her breath. She took huge gasps of air.

"Theo, honey, is that you?" Instantly, concern replaced the irritation in his voice. "Are you all right?"

"I am now." Gulping the air had given her the hiccups, and she waited until they subsided some. "Tony, Scarlet is dead."

"Dead how?" His voice was professional, the words clipped. Under control.

It calmed some of her panic, and she coughed a couple of times, clearing her throat. "I don't know how, but her body is outside in the bushes. It looks to me like her neck is broken. There's something around her throat and now it's raining on her." As Theo talked her voice rose to a wail and then the hiccups got louder. She kept seeing the gaping mouth. The splashes of water dropping into it. "I was going to wake the Trimbles and call from their apartment, when I saw Art walk by, and he laughs like a seal. He was dressed." She knew she wasn't making sense, but she couldn't seem to organize her thoughts at all. "Why was he outside at that hour? Did he call to report Scarlet's death?"

"Where are you now, sweetheart?" Tony's voice was calming and so dear. "Are you somewhere safe?"

A hiccup was her answer. "I'm in my room with the chain on. But, but I can see her body from my window." She felt like a ninny, but she couldn't stop crying.

"Okay, I'm on my way. Just keep watch from where you are and let me know if anyone gets near the body. I'll be there as soon as I can."

It didn't take Tony long to get ready. Even as he dressed, he called Edith to come over and stay with the boys. She answered on the second ring and arrived at the front door at the same time he did. It looked like she had pulled sweatpants and a sweatshirt on over her nightgown, but her eyes were bright

135

and calm.

"You're a great neighbor." He kissed her wrinkled cheek as he walked past.

As he drove, the Blazer's light bar was flashing but there was little need for it. He didn't see a single other vehicle on the road. Even keeping his speed down to a safe level as he maneuvered the twisting section, he was able to make good time. Luckily, the only animals he spotted were a couple of raccoons having a picnic next to the road. Their little masked faces made them look guilty as they sat there, immobilized by the bright headlights on his vehicle.

As he drove, he played back in his mind the conversation he'd had with Theo. He hadn't caught it all since he had been sleeping soundly when she started talking, and then when he was wide awake, she was dissolving into what he thought of as prehysterics. Why had she been so upset it was raining on the body? And what had she said about Art Trimble? She had seen him outside? She didn't say when, but assumed it was just before she had called. And what else? He slapped the steering wheel when it came to him. Of course, the barking seal. He'd told her about the odd message, delivered in a raspy voice, left on Mr. Beasley's telephone. Had Art Trimble made that telephone call? Had he left the message on the answering machine? And if so, why?

Tony pulled past the covered drive in front of The Lodge and parked the Blazer. He left the covered space for the ambulance. Doc Nash was already on his way up with it. Tony took the camera with him. If this was anything except an obvious accident, he'd get Wade out of his nice warm bed and let him stand out in the cold rain taking pictures.

The front door was locked, so Tony rang the night bell about six times in quick succession. Finally, the disembodied voice of Beth Trimble came through the speaker. "Yes?" She sounded really cranky about being disturbed.

"Beth? It's Sheriff Abernathy. Can you unlock the door please? It's official business."

"Tony? It's not even four-thirty in the morning. Okay, okay. Art's on his way to open the door for you." Even as she spoke, Tony saw the door to the owner's residence open. Art Trimble was pulling a dark plaid robe over his baby blue pajamas. His feet were bare as he padded toward Tony, yawning and stretching.

As he pushed the door open to let Tony inside, he mumbled, "Couldn't stay away

137

from Theo, huh?" He gave Tony a sly, leering look that made Tony want to punch him.

"Like I told Beth, it's official business." Tony noted Art's wardrobe and demeanor. He acted like he had just been rousted from a sound sleep, but Theo had seen him only a few minutes earlier. Had there been enough time for him to change and get to sleep? "I'll need you to wait here and let in Doc Nash."

"I can just unlock the door and go with you," Art bounced back. "You know, in case you need help."

Tony stared at him, and finally Art quit jumping around. Why hadn't he asked about the nature of the business? Unless he already knew what it was about. "Just wait here for the doctor."

Without lingering any longer, Tony strode down the hallway and out onto the walkway. The path lights were the only form of illumination in the back of The Lodge, but at least the rain had all but stopped. Fine drizzle like this wouldn't make the scene much worse. It had to have been almost destroyed already, thanks to the earlier heavy rain. He shone his flashlight on the shrubs. The sudden beam of light sent a pair of rabbits scurrying deeper into the bushes. When it came to rest on the still body, draped so obscenely over the bush, Tony understood why Theo had been so disturbed by the rain. It disturbed him too. It would also make the investigation more difficult.

He looked up, trying to see where Scarlet had fallen from. Theo waved from her window, almost directly above the body. He waved back, even as he noted part of the railing around the veranda on the floor above her room was down. He also noticed where the body lay in relation to the gap in the railing and decided the general scene was wrong for an accident. She hadn't fallen. There was no way the thing around her neck had come to be there accidentally.

Doc Nash trotted along the sidewalk holding a blue golf umbrella over his head as Tony started punching the buttons on his cell phone. "Got us another one, I see."

Doc Nash waited until Tony snapped a series of photographs before making a cursory examination of Scarlet. He stood for a long time, shining a light on the woman's neck before returning to the shelter of his umbrella.

From where they stood, Tony could see both the body and Art Trimble. Art stood in the doorway of The Lodge, shifting his weight from side to side, making his bathrobe sway. His eyes were moving constantly, never appearing to focus on anything. To Tony it looked like Art wanted to come outside and see what was going on and also wasn't sure he was up to the scene.

Doc's conversation was short and to the point. "I'd guess your killer strangled her upstairs and dropped her into the bush. It was murder."

"Why are you so sure?"

"There's a thin wire wrapped twice around her neck." The doctor shook his head, a silent commentary on the cruelties people inflict. "It's tight enough to dig into her skin."

# Chapter Ten

Tony saw Theo from the corner of his eye. She had changed from her pajamas and robe into warmer clothes. Tony knew she had kept her horrible vigil until he waved to her. Now dressed in sweatpants and one of his old sweatshirts, she stood motionless near the outside door, staring at Art Trimble's pajama covered legs and his bare feet. Her expression might have been confusion or surprise. With a shiver, she lifted her face and met Tony's gaze. Her head moved slightly from side to side.

Tony watched both of them. He was concerned about Theo and intensely curious about Art. Whatever the hotel owner was involved in, he had changed clothes since Theo had last seen him. "Well, Art," said Tony. "I think the best thing for you to do now would be to return to your apartment and stay there with your wife. I'll have some questions for you a bit later." As he watched the man vanish down the hallway, he knew Art was guilty. The question was: guilty of what? He might have been simply cheating on his wife, but he had definitely done something wrong tonight. Why hadn't he been more persistent about trying to determine what had brought Tony into his hotel at this hour? And with Doc Nash at his heels? Was the man completely devoid of curiosity, which Tony doubted, or did he already know why Tony and Doc were here so early in the morning?

He turned his attention to Theo, who stood so still and looked so forlorn. The lobby lights were dim, and she was almost part of a shadow. Tony stepped toward her, leaving the umbrella in the doctor's care. Only when he opened his arms for her did she finally leave her post and dash into their shelter. Pressing her chilled face into the warmth of his jacket covered chest, she clung to him. After a minute, she finally managed to ask, "Did she fall?" Her voice was a mere whisper and she was shaking all over.

"No. It doesn't look like it to me." He wondered how much to tell her. "Doc thinks she was dead for some time before she was dropped over the side. That's just his first impression and nothing I want spread around." Theo nodded her understanding. Her shivers increased, and he pulled her even closer. "While we wait, I need for you to answer a couple of questions." He led her over to where he could still see the body but kept her face turned away from it. "Wade will be here in a few minutes, and then we can go inside."

"Okay." Her shivering lessened a bit.

"Did anything unusual happen last night? What time did everyone go to bed?"

Theo thought for a minute and pulled back so she could look up at Tony's face. "Melissa went to bed first. I'm not sure of the time, but I think it was about ten-thirty. Then Eleanor went to bed about eleven-thirty and Scarlet was right behind her." Theo's eyes searched his. Hers were glistening with unshed tears as she answered his unspoken question. "As expected, I guess, Eleanor was pretty obnoxious at the start and then, after Martha blew up at her, Eleanor shut up and just sat there quietly working on her quilt. When she went up to bed, she said she was going to read for a while. Do you know she drinks? The big travel mug she always carries was filled with some rum concoction."

Tony watched as Theo repeatedly ran a hand through her tangled curls until her hair formed a ball around her head like a wad of dandelion fluff. He waited for her to finish her story.

"Most of us went to bed at about midnight, I think. When I went up, Susan and Martha and your mom were the only ones still working. I have no idea what time they called it a night."

"Do you know what rooms everyone is in?"

"Sure. I have a list Beth gave me when we checked in, but there is also a master list taped onto the counter in the front. Anyone could check it and know where to find the others."

"Hell's bells, that will certainly help narrow the field, now won't it?" Tony felt something between incredulous and appalled.

"Going back to last night." Theo ignored his bluster. "The evening was normal for a retreat. We worked. We snacked. We got caught up on current events. We had birthday cake. Scarlet was pretty aloof, but she showed us her embroidery, which is beautiful." She took a deep breath. "When I went to my room, it was stuffy so I opened the window before I went to bed. I stood there for a while and enjoyed the fresh air, so I know she wasn't down there then. I had on my glasses, and I would have seen her."

"Did you see or hear anything that seemed to be out of place? At any time?"

"No." She paused with her fingers still entangled in her hair. "Not then." She glanced up and Tony waited patiently. "It didn't seem important at the time, but . . ." When she stopped talking and didn't start again, Tony squeezed her side, encouraging her. "I thought I woke up because I was cold. Now I think something else woke me up, and it was only then I realized I was cold. Does that make sense?"

"Absolutely." He pulled her fingers out of her hair and tried to fix the curls for her. "What woke you?" He managed to keep his tone even, but it was taking all of his self-control to just stand there playing with her hair. Sweet little Theo could have witnessed the killing and become a target herself. What he really wanted to do was to hit something. Hard.

Theo turned away from Tony and faced the corpse. "Give me your flashlight." He did. When the bright light hit Scarlet's face, Theo's arm jerked, and she quickly moved the beam to illuminate the bushes and small trees growing right up to the stones of the building. Theo appeared to be listening to something. "It wasn't her landing there."

Her focus turned upwards. The light showed a space where a rail was missing from the veranda. "It was a wooden sound, like a board was being scraped against something. I'll bet it was someone moving that rail. We were all warned about there being a temporary barrier on the veranda. Now it's not there."

Doc Nash ushered Wade into the area.

The deputy was already taking photographs as he came through the hotel. He smiled at Theo but did not speak. Tony pointed up to the area where the rail was missing. "After you finish photographing the scene down here, I want you to be sure and focus on the missing rail, the area all around it and her room. Check for footprints and fingerprints if you can." The rain began falling again in earnest. "That's not going to help. You'd better snap those as quickly as possible." Tony pushed Theo back into the hotel. "Show me the list."

Theo did. As described, the list was posted where anyone could read it. The drawer where the keys were kept was ajar. Tony felt anger surge through him. "I'm going to get Art. You want to stay here or go to your room?" He was already headed for the Trimbles' apartment.

"I'll wait over there." Theo pointed into

the lounge. "I'm still cold, but I can wrap up in my unfinished quilt. There is one more thing I think you should know." Theo glanced up, looking into Tony's eyes. "Art was dressed in hiking boots and warm clothes when he came in behind me and not in the robe he was wearing just now."

"Really? How interesting." Tony's lips lifted into a parody of a smile. "Do you think he saw you?"

"No." Theo pointed to the plant in the alcove. "I was in my pajamas and ducked down behind that." She walked away as Tony approached the owners' suite.

Art Trimble was neatly dressed in slacks and a sweater when he answered the knock on his door. "You haven't told me what's going on, Tony. Can I help?"

"Yes." Fascinated by the man's costume changes, Tony waved toward the lobby. "I need you to come out and answer a couple of questions about the front desk." He slipped his notebook out of his pocket. "To start with, what time do you lock the doors?"

"Usually, it is eight, but last night we locked them at seven-thirty. We weren't expecting any other guests. The guest keys will unlock the outside doors, you know."

"Is this drawer with the keys always open?"

Tony hoped not. It would be an open invitation to a building-wide crime wave.

Art shook his head. "It is almost always locked. Beth and I have keys and so does Gavin, her nephew, but that's all."

Tony nodded. "Don't touch it. It will need to be checked for fingerprints." He rubbed the side of his nose and cocked his head. "Do you know how many keys should be in there for each room?"

"No. As far as being locked," Art cleared his throat, "it was left open for the quilters because they all know us and each other. We're going to redo all of the locks and get the magnetic strip keys this winter. We haven't been replacing lost keys for a while, so we don't have as many as we used to and each room is different. I'll have to get into the computer to tell you how many are left for each room." Stopping his nervous monologue at last, Art took a deep breath and rested his fists on his hips. "Now will you tell me what is going on? If someone was robbed in my hotel, I have a right to know."

"I guess that's fair," said Tony. He watched Art carefully. "It looks like Scarlet LaFleur was murdered some time last night or early this morning either in her room or on the veranda. Then the body was dropped or pushed into the shrubbery."

"Not in my hotel!" A vein on the innkeeper's forehead throbbed, and his complexion went pale, then red and then chalk-white. "I won't have it."

Tony was impressed. If Art was acting, he was doing a fantastic job. "Well, we are going to have to determine where she was killed for sure, but her corpse is in your flowerbed decorating one of your bushes. I know this is very disturbing, but we have to cordon off the area and question your staff and guests. All of them." As he spoke, Tony kept wondering where Art had been during the night. Not for a second did he doubt Theo's account of what she had seen.

While Art Trimble was still staring glassy-eyed at him, Doc Nash came inside through the back door. The raincoat he had tented over his head was not enough to keep him dry, and he wasn't carrying the umbrella any longer. He shook the excess water from the coat and held it away from his body as he tipped his head, calling Tony over.

"I'm not going to do this autopsy. I'm just not set up for something like this, but I'm pretty sure the cause of death is a broken neck and a sophisticated autopsy might turn up fibers or skin fragments I could miss." He started putting his jacket back on. "It was a deliberate homicide."

"I appreciate you coming out, Doc." Tony said as he dodged droplets of water flying off the doctor's jacket. "I'll send Wade along to deliver the body." Doc's basset hound expression stopped him. "Oh, no, don't tell me he's sick again? There isn't even any blood."

"He's out there with his head in a bush." The doctor shook his head. "I've got a patient who is bulimic who spends less time barfing than Wade does. Send him along. Maybe a good autopsy is just what he needs."

"Along with a bag and some smelling salts," Tony added.

The doctor was halfway down the corridor when he stopped and turned. "I just remembered. I came up on the ambulance. I guess I'll have to wait for them so they can drop me off." He plopped into a comfortable chair across from the front desk and yawned widely without bothering to cover his mouth. He began to rub his eyes with the heels of his hands and paused to yawn again.

Tony turned back. He wished he hadn't because standing there next to the doctor was Winifred, the newspaper reporter from hell. From the expression on her face, Tony assumed she had heard every word Doc Nash had muttered. Heaven only knew what kind of story she would be able to concoct. At that moment, Tony wasn't too sure the first amendment had been such a good idea. Without another word, he stalked back out into the rain.

Tony watched Wade begin stringing lights and setting out a stack of scene markers, ready to start his photographs and evidence collection. The Tennessee Bureau of Investigation was on its way to lend a hand with the evidence collection and investigation. He'd have some help inside and outside. Without the TBI, he had no idea how he would be able to conduct an investigation of this nature.

"How'd you find her?" said Doc Nash. The doctor reappeared at Tony's side.

Wade shook his head.

"Theo did." Tony zipped his jacket up, staring at the doctor. "And she called me. I thought you went inside to wait for a ride."

"I'm hiding from Winifred." The doctor confessed, paused and then confronted Tony. "Are you saying Theo was outside in this weather? Tonight? When she should have been sleeping?" Doc Nash's voice rose in pitch and volume with each unanswered question. "Where is she?"

Tony nodded toward the lobby and

stepped back to let the doctor storm past.

"Oh-oh," Wade shook his head. "Your little wife's in trouble now."

"I wish him luck. She won't listen to me." Tony pointed to Wade's camera. "Start clicking."

Theo was comfortably ensconced in the chair with her feet on an ottoman. She was covered from nose to toes with unfinished quilts, making her toasty and drowsy when Doc Nash charged into the room and yelled at her.

"What in thunder do you think you're doing, woman?"

"Getting warm and resting, like I'm supposed to." Theo barely clamped her teeth down before she said something really sassy she was bound to regret.

"Go to bed." Furious brown eyes stared at her. "Now."

"I'm fine here." No way was she going to admit she wasn't sure she could make it back to her room. She was too exhausted to walk or to argue.

Doc Nash picked up the imaginary gauntlet and tossed it back. "Okay, here's my offer." He rubbed the back of his neck and dragged a chair around and sat on it, facing her.

His obvious fatigue and concern made Theo feel guilty. "I promise to be good. Just let me sit here for a bit longer."

The doctor pretended he didn't hear her. "I'm getting you a wheelchair and an aide. You are going to bed. When you're not in bed, you'll sit and have your aide push you in a wheelchair. If you're hungry, she'll get you food. If you're sulky, she'll throw water in your face. If you argue with me, I'll put you in the hospital until you deliver those babies."

Theo glanced up and saw Tony walk in just in time to overhear the doctor's diatribe. He paused in mid step. His frown deepened. "Doc?"

Doc Nash stared at Theo until she nodded her acquiescence.

"I won." The doctor smiled as he stood and faced her husband. "Theo lost the battle." He walked away from Theo, telling Tony about his plans for her and what he needed.

Truth to tell, Theo wasn't all that sorry to lose. She was tired constantly, and the weight of the babies seemed to increase on an hourly basis.

Tony studied the floor plan of the hotel printed on one of the little black and white information sheets from the front desk. It was the kind a clerk would give a guest after circling the room number.

Scarlet's room was near the stairs on the upper level. No rooms were in the point of the V, just a large veranda. Unlike the lower level rooms, each upper level room had a sliding door instead of a sash window. The door did not open onto a true balcony, but the ledge was wide enough for someone to stand outside and admire the view. An agile person might be able to climb from the veranda onto a ledge and then onto the next ledge.

According to his notes, Eleanor Liston was assigned the room next to Scarlet's. Tony knew he'd better talk to her. He considered several other options he'd prefer, like a nap, or a root canal. Just then he saw her coming toward him. As he waved for her to join him, there was a spot of hope. She might ignore him.

He would classify her response to his gesture as "reluctant" but reasonably timely. She moved smoothly onto the chair he'd indicated and settled her travel mug on the floor near her feet. Unlike most of the quilters, she had combed her hair and applied makeup. Her clothes were finer than those of the other ladies.

"I didn't kill her." Eleanor's expression gave no clue to her emotions. "What else can I tell you?"

"Well, for starters, did you hear anything coming from her room?" At Eleanor's silent stare, he continued. "A conversation, noises, a shout or scream?"

"Oh. Let's see." She took several big gulps from her mug and closed her eyes. "There was a squeak, like a desk chair that needs oiling."

Tony jotted he comment down and waited.

"No scream. No voices." Eleanor shook her head. "But I took a shower before I went to bed. Oh, wait. I was awakened by something bumping — at first I thought it was thunder, you know, because it kind of echoed and then it went all quiet."

It wasn't much, Tony thought, but it was something. "Did you check the time?"

"No."

"Were you acquainted with Scarlet?"

"Knew her all her life."

"And?"

"She was always a cold-hearted, small-minded tramp." Eleanor's lips pinched together. "I try not to speak ill of the dead."

Eleanor's animosity jiggled a faint memory in his brain. "Rumor once suggested your husband and . . ."

"It's true." The lines around Eleanor's mouth deepened. "He was faithless. I'm sure she, like all his paramours, thought he'd leave me and my money for her. She was just another name on his list."

Tony didn't understand why she seemed so pleased to keep the man. Her husband had been lower than a worm, and she put up with it. He was thinking about other couples who continued in the same manner.

"It was your aunt who threatened to kill her. Not me."

"Did you really threaten to kill her?" Tony waved his Aunt Martha into the alcove where he set up his temporary interview station. He had commandeered a couple of chairs, a supply of cups and coffee and a big box of tissues. Theo was near enough to overhear the conversations, but she appeared to be sleeping. After the hours of questioning the staff, the quilters and what he thought of as "normal guests," his stomach was killing him. It was definitely time for the emergency bottle of liquid antacid he kept in the Blazer. Should he drink it from the bottle or sip it from a coffee cup?

The lobby was filled. Everyone in the

hotel seemed to have gathered together of their own accord. The conversations were muted. Tony and Wade had talked briefly with each of them. For the most part, there was not much information, but a few common threads about Scarlet's unsociable behavior emerged. He handed Martha a cup of coffee.

"Well, yes." Accepting the cup, his aunt settled into the comfortable chair. This morning she wore a lavender sweatshirt bearing the slogan "Quilters keep you in Stitches." Her curls were standing straight up in the air on one side and were smashed close to her head on the other side. The hairdo gave her a comical appearance, but Tony wasn't smiling. "It was a joke."

Tony glared at her in response. "No one's laughing."

Martha sighed. "I said something like if she saddled me with another UFO I'd have to kill her."

"UFO?" Tony thought he should know what it meant.

"Unfinished object." His aunt lifted an eyebrow. "Are you sure you live with a quilter? I know Theo has at least twenty UFOs. I meant nothing by it. It was just, you know, the kind of comment everyone makes from time to time." When he didn't respond, she sipped her coffee and watched him. "You look awful, kid. Can't you take a break?"

Tony flipped back in his notebook. "When did you go to bed?"

"It was a little after midnight. I told you that already." She tried to squirm around until she could read what he had written but to no avail. "Us late ones went up at the same time."

Tony nodded. "And did you leave again?" His eyes met hers. If he was a decent judge of anything, she was telling the truth, but he knew she was lying to him.

"No." Setting the empty cup on the floor, she crossed her arms over her chest and sank deeper into the chair.

"No?" Tony's eyebrows jumped and he leaned closer to her and lowered his voice. "Are you sure?"

"Of course, I'm sure." Her tone no longer seemed so certain. "You don't believe me. Why don't you believe me?"

Leaning back in his chair, he frowned at her. "I want to. I really do, but the facts are just not lining up." He looked in his notebook and sat fanning the pages. "You're sharing a room with Mom?" She nodded, and he asked, "Did she leave the room at any time after the two of you went up?"

"No. We talked for a little while and then we went to bed. If she left, it was after I fell asleep, and I didn't hear her go out, and besides, she barely knew Scarlet. I can't see her pushing her off the veranda."

Tony's felt his frown deepen. He did not correct her assumption about the cause of death. Even he wasn't sure if it was the fall or strangulation that killed the woman. Everyone in the hotel had seen the investigators combing the area around the railing and also knew Scarlet had been found in the bushes underneath. "Did you go to sleep right away?"

Martha glared at him and snapped, "Yes. And just for your information, I didn't hear anything but Jane snoring. She makes a world class racket when she gets rolling, so I know she was in there."

Tony glanced at his notes again and looked up. "Mom said she woke in the night and went to the bathroom." He stopped talking and adjusted his watch and pulled his shirt cuff down. Then he flipped through the notebook. Exhaling loudly, he leaned forward. "She says you were not in the room. Would you like to tell me where you were?"

"What?" Martha jumped to her feet. "Why would she say such a thing?"

He just stared at her. Finally, Martha plopped back into her chair. Running her hands through her gray hair, eyes closed, she mumbled to herself. "I don't understand. We went up to the room. I put on my pajamas and brushed my teeth. We talked for a little while about this and that. I read a few pages in my book while Jane was doing her thing — you know, brushing her teeth and slathering cream on her face. I turned out the reading light just minutes later and fell asleep right away and slept until I was awakened by the commotion in the hall this morning." She stopped suddenly and frowned. Her eyes squeezed even more tightly closed. "No, that's not right."

"What do you mean?" Tony shifted in his chair.

"I mean, I did get up." Martha's eyes flew open and she bounced on her chair. "I thought I dreamed it, but I woke up and thought maybe I hadn't unplugged my iron downstairs. It really wouldn't do to burn down The Lodge, certainly not before the retreat is over." She flashed a smile at him. "Anyway, I didn't bring a robe so I tiptoed into the lobby in my pajamas, checked the iron, and was back in bed and asleep without ever fully waking up."

Somewhat relieved, Tony made note of her

story. "I really wish you had remembered to tell me that before I found an error in your story."

A light touch of her hand on his arm drew his eyes back up to meet hers. "I know it sounds improbable, Tony, but I really did forget it. It was so brief, and I was sleeping so soundly. This past week has been so busy I hardly know my own name anymore."

Tony sighed. It was a great exhalation of air with a hesitation in the middle. "I don't suppose you suddenly remember seeing someone else on your excursion." His tone and expression both felt sour.

Martha rubbed her eyes behind her glasses. "I got up." She paused, her fingertips still pressed against her closed eyes. "I didn't put my glasses on. I went downstairs. I heard something." She held her hand up, demanding silence. "It sounded like a door opening, and then something thumped like it was dropped or bumped against a wall, and then the door closed. I don't know if it was upstairs or at ground level."

Tony scribbled a doodle that was shaped somewhat like a cowboy boot in his notebook then looked up. "What time was it then?" Pencil poised, he watched her thinking. He didn't actually suspect his aunt of any wrongdoing, but having the facts and a clear timeline would be very helpful.

"I have no idea. Did Jane give you a time?" At Tony's answering nod, she smiled. "Since I don't know, I'll go along with Jane. I couldn't have been gone for more than five minutes."

By the time Tony worked his way through the quilters, he was ready for a nap. A duller group to question would be unimaginable. They were all very nice. They were all clean, if not neat. Almost every one of them had loose threads stuck to some article of clothing. They were all sober, at least at this hour, law-abiding, comfortable women with whom he had little professional contact. They didn't even run stop signs, at least not as a rule. If he knew them personally, it was from living in Silersville for most of his life, or he saw them at church or the school or in Theo's shop. None of them was on first name basis with the jail staff.

Tony's conversation with Gavin, Beth's nephew, was only marginally more interesting than the ladies. "Had you met Scarlet before?"

"No, not really." Tony thought Gavin's expression seemed at bit defensive but many people are uneasy talking to the police. "I think I've seen her, you know."

"I understand she was somewhat demanding?"

"You can say that again, Sheriff. I'm running my backside off carrying bags and boxes for all the ladies, and she swoops in looking like a portable jewelry store and her spy toy and wants me to carry her stuff first."

"Spy toy?"

"You know, one of those amplifying headsets." Gavin growled. "There was nothing wrong with her hearing. I'm sure of it."

Although Gavin was disgruntled, it wasn't criminal. The only thing Tony could think to do was just let the hotel guests and staff continue with the weekend as planned.

After a while, Tony realized he'd been simply staring out the tall windows. The rain had stopped about the same time the ambulance bearing Scarlet's body and Wade as her escort left. They had been gone for hours. The sky was bright blue now, and there was little haze on the mountains.

His eyes crossed with fatigue, and he let them drift shut as he leaned back in his chair, thinking. It would be less surprising if someone had done away with Eleanor. Even as intensely annoying as she was, they didn't have the nerve to tell her she couldn't join their quilting group, much less kill her. It seemed unlikely, therefore, that one of the quilters would resort to killing a virtual stranger like Scarlet. If anything, they would have slipped poison into her coffee and gone on quilting. He knew these women, and they had definite priorities — fabric and chocolate.

# CHAPTER ELEVEN

True to his word, Doc Nash returned to The Lodge with a wheelchair. He opened it and waved Theo into the seat with a courtly bow. "This is your best friend for the next few weeks. You will not walk more than three feet. You will not stand for more than three minutes. Take fast showers. You will spend more time in bed than in the chair."

Theo nodded her acquiescence and sat. "I'll be good."

"I know you will, Theo." The doctor patted her shoulder. "Just as I know this is very difficult for you. I've seen the way you live and work. You're a cute little tornado, but you can't keep it up."

Theo relaxed into the seat, quietly relieved to be off her feet. "Do I walk up the steps into the house or does Tony have to carry me?"

"I'll talk to Gus and see what he can throw together. You can't walk, and not even your oversized husband can carry you up and down all the time. No stairs in the house. You'll live on the main floor. We'll find a hospital bed for you."

"Thank you." Theo knew he had gone out of his way to deliver the chair and the lecture. The poor man probably got less sleep than anyone she knew.

The doctor's eyes twinkled behind his glasses. "You're going to love your assistant."

"Who?" Theo's curiosity was piqued.

"Just wait and see." The doctor's cell phone rang, and he had it pressed to his ear as he trotted away, leaving her parked in the lobby.

Tony's cell phone ringing jolted him back awake. He didn't realize he'd fallen asleep. Wade's name appeared on the phone's screen. "What's up?"

"I'm still in Knoxville."

"And?"

"They haven't determined the actual cause of death, but it's most likely strangulation. There was a single wire tightly wrapped, twice, around her neck. It looks like something from a musical instrument." Wade's voice took on an even more somber tone. "Or, it's possible her neck was snapped. The odd thing is there were some smudges of grease on the back of Scarlet's clothes. Only on the back. You know, like the heavy stuff off equipment or car engines. The clothes have gone to the lab."

"So maybe her killer, wearing dirty clothes, caught her from behind and killed her."

"Yep. Probably brought the wire along. But here's the second odd part." Wade's voice faded out for a second. "The body wasn't dropped over the railing until at least three hours after death, something to do with lividity. Don't you think that's weird? Why not just leave her where she died?"

Tony wanted to hit his head against a brick wall. Instead, he congratulated his deputy and asked him to stay in touch.

Just then he spied Art making his way through the lobby. Tony called him over and waved in the direction of the chair recently vacated by his Aunt Martha. "You are just the man I needed to see." Tony deliberately kept silent, watching the man.

Art did not seem at all pleased to be there and fidgeted like a five-year-old in church during a long sermon. First he crossed one ankle on his knee. Then the other. He sat back in the chair. He moved to the very edge of the seat. Finally his patience snapped. "Did you have something to ask, Sheriff? I do have work to do. And my guests to take care of."

"I sympathize. I do. But it's hard to rush through an investigation of this nature, you understand." Tony pasted on his best artificial smile, knowing Theo would probably kick him in the shins if he used it on her. Art didn't know him well and seemed to find the smile reassuring. "Why don't you just start with yesterday afternoon and tell me what you did between the time the ladies arrived and the time I arrived." Resting his elbows on the chair arms and lacing his fingers over his stomach, he leaned back comfortably, trying to look relaxed. The open notebook lay on his left thigh and his pencil was tucked into the spiral. It might appear to be a simple man to man chat.

Art finally quit squirming around on his chair. "Well, it was pretty busy for a while. We were trying to get everyone checked in and the luggage delivered while we attended to our few non-quilting guests. People coming and going." Art helped himself to a cup of coffee. "Let's see. I guess by then it was time for dinner. I worked in the dining room. Except for the birthday cake and singing, it was pretty quiet in the lobby. After everyone was settled in and since there

168

were no more reservations, I locked the outside doors and went to our apartment. Beth and I watched television until I made a last door check before I went to bed about midnight. There was still a group of quilters down here doing their thing."

Tony looked around. The quilters had moved back into their work area and appeared to be talking normally among themselves. He saw Theo experimenting with her new wheelchair. "How did you handle room assignments?"

For some reason, that question seemed to please Art. Waving his arms expansively, he gestured toward the front desk. "Normally, of course, we assign the rooms and hand out the keys individually. With this group though, since they are old friends, we let them check the rooming sheet and get a key so they wouldn't have to wait if we were busy."

"So anyone could look at the list, see what room everyone is in, take a key to any room and wander off with it?" Tony's eyes narrowed, and his expression grew hard. His hands tightened into fists. "That's the worst security I ever heard of," he growled and leaned forward. "My wife was in one of those rooms."

The skin on Art's neck and cheeks reddened, then paled, and his mouth dropped open but only a bubble of air came out and as he leaned away. His hands rose to shield his face.

They sat staring at each other for a full minute before Tony exhaled and relaxed his fists. "Answer me this then. What time did you go to bed?"

"It was about eleven-thirty. The news was just ending, and I watched the sports with Beth and fell asleep. I slept soundly until you arrived and rang the bell."

Tony glanced at Theo. She had parked her wheelchair in a shadow, holding a quilt in her lap. She shook her head at Tony after hearing Art's story, but she didn't say a word.

"Are you sure about that?" Tony watched the man's eyes. Even if Theo hadn't told him what time she had seen Art, Tony would have known he was lying. He really wasn't very good at it. In the past two minutes, his story had shifted from bed at midnight to sleep at eleven-thirty. Tony was puzzled. What possible innocent reason could the man have for being out at that hour and then lie about it? Tony couldn't come up with a single one, but his reaction to hearing of Scarlet's death didn't fit either. Only a fool would kill someone staying under his own roof. A fool or a very desperate man.

"Yes, of course, I'm sure. So." Art jumped to his feet. "That's all?"

"Sit." Tony picked up his notebook and leaned back into the chair. He made his notes. "I have a few more questions for you."

"Really?"

Tony noticed a definite quaver in Art's voice. He perched on the very edge of the chair and squeezed his hands between his knees, but Tony could see them shaking. "Do you do any of the mechanical repairs around here?"

"Mechanical repairs?" Art blinked rapidly and his face went blank. "What kind of repairs?"

"I don't know, maybe changing the oil in the car, mowing the lawn. Something like that?"

"Sheriff, I can barely change a light bulb." Amusement lightened his expression. "My wife would kill me if I so much as threatened to change the oil in the car. We always take it to the Thomas brothers when it needs work."

"Well, then, would you like to tell me why you were outside about three this morning and why you are pretending to have been in your bed the whole time?" Tony would love to connect him to some greasy work clothes.

"Oh, I must have gone jogging." Art's eyes opened wider, like a man who just remembered where he left his wallet. "Sometimes I jog when I can't sleep."

"Really?"

"Oh yes. You can ask anyone. When I remembered, I thought I shouldn't tell you about it because I know I already said I was somewhere else and you would probably think I'm a liar." Art stopped for breath.

Tony could see he wasn't going to get any kind of rational statement out of the man and waved him away. The next time he talked to Art, he wanted the man in the interrogation room at the law enforcement center.

Art scuttled out of the room like a crab headed for water.

Theo rolled her chair to his side. "Do you believe him?"

Tony lifted one eyebrow in her direction and grinned, but he wasn't amused. "Are you saying you think he could possibly make up a statement more inane than that? If I heard him correctly, he just told me he is in the habit of running in the middle of the night, in the dark, and forgot he had been doing it. And then, when he did remember, he hesitated to change his story because he knew I would think he'd been lying?"

"Absolutely not." Theo pulled her curls away from her face. "I think he was lying through his teeth the whole time, and not just because he wasn't panting and sweating like he'd been running. It is pitch black in these woods at night, and he didn't even have a flashlight, at least not one that I could see. I think he is covering up something." She hesitated. "It might be personal. I wonder if he is Lila Ware's married boyfriend."

"Boyfriend, hmm?" Tony thought it might fit. "He's not a good liar, but he could be a bad husband. I don't see him killing Scarlet, at least not in his own hotel. As provoking as the woman might have been, I just don't see him losing control and killing her."

He spotted Beth across the lobby and waved to attract her attention. As she began making her way toward him, she was not smiling.

"You think she'll tell the same story?" Theo whispered.

Tony watched as Beth stopped to talk to Dottie and Jane. He rolled his shoulders until they loosened up enough to stop cracking.

"Don't forget about Mr. Beasley." Releasing her hair, Theo waved her hands for emphasis. "Didn't you say the voice on the message sounded like Art's?"

"There is no evidence the two deaths are connected." Tony dodged her hands. "Certainly, the causes of death are not similar. I intend to investigate them separately." He flipped back in his notes. "Now then, assuming she was the intended victim and not a random one, who besides the quilters would know Scarlet was going to be up here?"

"Well, everyone who knows her, probably." Theo stopped and her eyes widened. "And everyone who reads the paper."

"The paper? It was in the paper?" There was as close to a squeak in his voice as his rumbling bass was able to produce. "When? Why?"

"It was in the community calendar stuff in the latest edition. You know, like when AA meets and where the garage sale will be held to benefit the scouts." She closed her eyes. "I'm trying to see the piece. I'm sure it listed all of the names of the participants and the location of the retreat and invited anyone interested to call me for more information about the retreat or Scarlet's class." Opening her eyes again, she straightened her glasses and peered at him. "Now that I think about it, it was unusual. I don't remember Winifred ever doing an advance notice before."

A sensation of dawning horror twisted Tony's gut. "I'm going to have to talk to Winifred. She should know better than to put that kind of information in the paper before it happens. It's an invitation to burglars. Why not just say that Mrs. So and So will be out of town for the weekend, so take your time and steal everything including the wallpaper?"

"Uh, Sheriff?" From the shadows came a quiet, seemingly disembodied voice.

Tony focused on the origin. One of the younger investigators from the TBI was headed toward him. "What is it?" Tony could hear Vince, the lead investigator, bellowing something in the distance.

"We're ready to leave." Casting a worried look over his shoulder, he clutched his clipboard to his chest with both hands.

Frankly relieved, Tony reached for his pen. "So you have a few hundred papers for me to sign?"

"Yes, sir." Ramrod straight, the boy looked like he was ready to click his heels and salute. He handled the clipboard of papers like it was the Holy Grail. Tony could tell Vince hadn't trained him. Vince could slouch in any position and thought paperwork was a communist plot. His idea of a salute was lifting a can of beer to eye level before attaching his lips to it. Luckily for law enforcement, Vince was able to overcome his prejudice against paperwork long enough to keep the lawyers happy. He was one of the best. The man could find flea footprints on an Old English sheepdog.

Beth arrived at the alcove after the young man left. "Do you need something, Tony?"

"I need to get a statement from you about last night. Just routine." He waved her into the chair. Beth complied, but she sat on the very edge of the seat as if poised for action. "Can you tell me about last night?"

Theo rolled her chair back to rejoin the quilters.

"I . . . that is, we went to bed when the news was over. I watched some old movie for a while and turned the TV off. Midnight, I guess." She toyed with a paper napkin in her lap.

Tony watched. At the rate she was going, there would be nothing but confetti in a few more seconds.

"Art was already asleep. It didn't take me long to fall asleep and I didn't hear anything."

Her eyes moved constantly and never seemed to focus on him at all. She, like everyone he had talked with so far, looked exhausted. Freshly applied, her heavy makeup did not conceal the dark circles under her eyes but instead seemed to emphasize them.

"Did you awaken when Art left or when he returned?" Tony tried a trick question.

"I think I remember him returning but it is not real clear." Apparently fascinated by what she had done to the paper napkin, she focused on the scraps and with painstaking precision, rolled them into a ball. "I'm kind of used to it by now."

"But you're sure he left? Do you know what time?" Tony sensed her whole story was a fabrication. Why?

"Oh, but I'm not sure he left. He might have because he does sometimes, but I just don't know." Tears slipped down her face, leaving tracks of mascara on her cheeks. "I don't remember."

The one thing Tony felt positive about was Beth was not any better at lying than her husband was. They were covering something up together and hadn't had time to get the story straight. But what? Tony had no idea. "I'll probably have more questions for you later, but for now, you can go." Beth jumped off the chair and headed away from him before he finished his sentence.

Tony was staring at her rapidly departing

back when his cell phone rang. The call came in from dispatch. "I just thought you'd want to know, Sheriff, there's been some disturbance or shooting or something going on at the Oak Lawn Trailer Courts. Roscoe Morris called it in, and I sent a unit over to investigate."

Tony recognized the voice, Flavio Weems, the new dispatcher. "And you called me because?" Tony made a mental note to talk to Rex about his dispatch team. Most of them were highly qualified and, if not as eerily calm as Rex himself, managed to do the job well. But Flavio was the exception. His conscientiousness and his skills were okay, but his judgment could use a lot of improvement. Still, all in all, he did a decent job and showed way more astuteness than any of the other member of the Weems clan.

"Well, just in case it's connected to the business up at The Lodge." Flavio sounded a bit less confident that he'd done the right thing by calling.

"What kind of disturbance?" Tony wasn't sure he wanted to hear the answer. With the murder of Scarlet LaFleur, sister to a worldwide celebrity, Tony felt he had as much on his plate as he could handle. The ordinary crimes of Park County were sounding more controllable than usual.

"Well, Roscoe was screaming into the phone so loudly I couldn't understand, but I clearly heard 'gun' and 'shooting' and Quentin. Sheriff, I can believe someone would take a couple of shots at Quentin Mize."

"Okay, okay, I've got the picture." He disconnected without another word. Then he watched Theo practicing her wheelchair turns. He winced when she almost ran over an elderly woman in the lobby. She rammed into a huge flowerpot instead. When she glanced at him, he walked over to tell her he had to go.

"I'm leaving. I'm done here, and Roscoe Morris has reported gunshots at the trailer court involving Quentin."

"At this hour? Isn't it a bit late for the Friday night crowd? Or is it early for Saturday night?"

"I doubt if Quentin knows if it is day or night. He's fallen off the wagon and is drinking again." Brains not being Quentin's strong suit, Tony seriously doubted someone was shooting at him unless he had provoked the incident and knew exactly who was working the trigger. It wouldn't be the first time someone had shot at Quentin. When he drank, his belligerence factor was followed closely by sheer stupidity. His home

179

away from home was the Okay Bar and Bait Shop. Tony simply couldn't imagine what was going on. Why was Roscoe involved? Quentin had a home up on the mountain.

"Maybe he has a girlfriend." Theo yawned into her hand.

Not listening carefully to his wife, he answered the wrong question. "Roscoe? Sure he does. She's a vending machine, remember? Quentin, I'm not as sure of." Tony's focus was on the group by the front door. Art held the door open, but his attention was on his own wife. Beth stood by his side. The couple was involved in a serious conversation. Beth glanced in Tony's direction several times during the course of it, and each time she looked back to her husband he shook his head. Finally, Beth headed toward Tony, but Art released his hold on the door and reached for her instead. Something he said to her stopped her completely. After a long moment, she moved slowly away from her husband and went back into their apartment without looking at any of them.

"Now what do you suppose?" Theo said.

"Whatever he said to her was a surprise, wouldn't you agree?" Tony continued to watch the action.

"Yes, but at least he didn't tell her he has

a girlfriend."

Her words brought Tony's attention around to her. "He has a girlfriend? Art? How do you know?" Fascination and surprise were written all over his face.

Theo's toes connected with his leg. "Isn't that what we were talking about?"

"No." Tony rubbed the back of his neck and then his stomach. "You asked if Roscoe had a girlfriend, and then you said something about Art having a girlfriend." Tony grinned. He couldn't help himself. Sometimes he would just wind his wife up for the fun of it. He tried to mask his amusement, but she realized what he'd done.

She began to laugh. "Does anybody have a girlfriend?"

Tony gave the question serious thought. "No one I can think of."

Before Theo could respond, the lobby suddenly became a busy place. Beth came from the kitchen area pushing a wheeled table. She maneuvered it down the ramp to the quilters' area and spread a white damask cloth over it. Like the wise men bearing gifts, three teenaged girls carrying baskets of rolls, stacks of plates and pump-style coffee dispensers followed her. Unlike the wise men, they chattered about the discovery of Scarlet's body, and one girl all but fainted from the excitement. Some of the guests, who must have been watching for the food, arrived before they were completely set up. Beth issued directives like a general. The girls hurried to do their jobs.

"How did she get into the kitchen? Didn't we just watch her go into the apartment?" Theo peered down the hallway. The kitchen was on the opposite side of the building from the apartment and business offices.

"Good question." Tony started walking toward the kitchen. It seemed as if they would have spotted her if she'd used the hallway. He stopped one of the girls. "Is there a shortcut from the kitchen to the Trimbles' apartment?"

The girl started to shake her head and then stopped. "Oh, yeah, I forgot for a minute." Her eyes widened, and Tony saw she wore contact lenses designed to make her eyes look like cats' eyes. "There is some kind of a hallway in the basement. I think it's used for storage, but I've never been down there." Noticing Tony was staring at her eyes, she blinked a couple of times for effect. "The stairs are behind the door right next to the outside door from the kitchen." With what sounded like a "meow," she vanished through the kitchen's swinging doors.

# CHAPTER TWELVE

Feeling like he had covered what he could at The Lodge, which seemed insignificant, Tony decided to drop by the Oak Lawn Trailer Court on his way back to town.

The turnoff to the Oak Lawn was halfway between Silersville and The Lodge. At one time there had been a decorative sign pointing the way. Now, however, there was just a slab of weather-beaten plywood with crudely painted letters that read Oak Traile Par.

Thirty years ago when it was first constructed, the Oak Lawn had been nicely landscaped and all of the residents lived in new mobile homes with their own small yards. But now, after years of neglect, accumulated garbage and kudzu, it was little better than an open cesspool. By all accounts, Roscoe loved it there. His home had once been white with red trim and decorative shutters and had an attached covered porch. The shutters were gone now, except for one, and it dangled from a single bolt. Instead of the steps, an aluminum stepladder provided access.

When Tony arrived, there were two patrol cars parked in the center. Roscoe stood in front of his trailer, talking to Deputy Sheila Teffeteller. Deputy Darren Holt stood nearby talking with a couple who shared an old RV across the way from Roscoe. The woman, dressed in a red tube top and lime green pajama bottoms, was shaking violently. For support, she seemed to be depending on the overgrown honeysuckle vine growing where there once had been an engine and hood of the RV. A couple of chickens wandered loose in the yard. A spotted hound of mixed breeding was sound asleep on an old backseat of some car. Every eye was focused on a rifle propped next to the door.

Roscoe's skinny white torso gleamed in the morning light. Dressed only in filthy jeans and a beer hat, Roscoe was smiling when he faced Sheila. His smile exposed more teeth than his mouth could hold. When Sheila pointed to the group by the RV and said something to him, Roscoe laughed so hard that he dropped to the ground. Sheila left him there and went to Tony's window.

"What's happening here?" Tony was relieved to see everything was apparently under control.

"A rifle shot passed through the trailer, just above Roscoe's bed. If he was fat, it would have hit him." Sheila dug at the dirt with her heel. "Mrs. Smith over there claims she was having a fit of jealousy and fired the rifle for emphasis. We think the bullet passed through the Smiths' wall and then continued on through Roscoe's wall." Her smile lifted some of the fatigue from her face. "Roscoe is claiming 'no harm, no foul.' "

"And what do you think?" Tony half-wondered where the other residents of the trailer park were.

"I'm going to get the bullet from Roscoe's trailer and bring in that .22." She nodded to the rifle. "Their stories don't quite match up. I want to know if the bullets do, or if this is related to the other .22 shootings."

"Speaking of stories," Tony said. "I got a call from Flavio saying someone here was shooting at Quentin."

"Quentin?" Sheila looked confused. "I haven't seen him around, but I'll certainly check it out. I know he and Roscoe have become buddies lately."

Tony nodded, thankful the call had turned out to be nothing more serious.

"Uh, sir, I did hear something maybe related to the death up at The Lodge." Sheila cleared her throat again. "I'm not sure how information travels around here, but it seems to get around. Was Art Trimble at home last night?"

Tony smiled, sensing he was about to learn something good. "Funny you should ask. I'm not sure one way or the other, but Theo claims she saw him fully dressed and returning to the hotel about three in the morning. About the same time she found the body. Why?"

"Because I was told Art, Claude and Prudence were making mischief together."

"Mischief?" Tony studied her expression. He wondered what connection the hotel owner and the trash hauler could have with the hairdresser/fortune teller. The same woman who was married to his deputy Darren Holt, who stood only twenty feet away. "Who says mischief?"

"So true. I heard it from Pops Ogle. You know he can't use strong language. He about choked saying 'mischief.' He'd pass out cold if he heard some of the things I hear every day." Sheila laughed. "I think he's a gentleman. Anyway, he said he was on his way home from a late night music session with Dan-the-Dulcimer Man when he saw Art, Claude and Prudence all clustered around some of the highway department equipment. They were over by the turnoff to the possible ancient burial ground."

"Did you notify the highway department to check their equipment?" Tony reached into his pocket for the last of his antacids before remembering he'd chewed them hours earlier. "If they've tampered with the machinery and someone gets hurt . . ." He didn't have to finish his statement.

Sheila was already nodding. "I called Flavio. He said he'd notify them."

Satisfied, Tony left her to deal with the paperwork and headed back to town, thinking about her words.

Theo could barely work on her project and keep her ears open to the conversations around her. Most were focused on the death of Scarlet. All of the ladies had taken a turn at being interviewed about what they had seen and heard during the night. In the case of the most elderly ladies, their stories hadn't been worth talking about, but the experience was thrilling for them. A couple of them were already looking forward to sharing the excitement with their friends and the ladies at church.

The Trimbles were acting very peculiar. Theo witnessed lots of whispered conversations between the two of them and what looked like, from across the lobby, an intense and prolonged argument culminated by Beth Trimble stalking into the apartment and slamming the door behind her. Seconds later, she left the apartment, slamming the door behind her again, disappeared into the kitchen for a couple of minutes and returned to the apartment, carrying a heavy tray that held two bottles of wine along with a platter of something like nachos. After the door slammed the third time, Theo was sure everyone heard the lock clicking into place.

Art watched his wife from his perch near the front desk. When the last sound died, he turned to the gathering of quilters and smiled — a half-hearted smile to be sure — and announced that lunch would be served in about fifteen minutes. He went on to comment about how welcome the rain had been after so many days of sunshine. He pulled a paperback book out of a drawer and settled into a comfortable position and began to read, ignoring their curious faces.

As if realizing the argument between hotel proprietors followed a pattern well known by the players involved, it didn't receive any comment from the women.

Theo watched Martha pace in the lobby until Theo finally snapped at her. "They are going to have to arrest me for killing you if you don't settle down somewhere." Theo paused to thread her needle. "You're wearing me and the carpet out." She glanced over the top of her glasses at Tony's aunt. "No one thinks you've done anything wrong. Do you think you killed the woman in your sleep?"

Susan winked and pointed to an empty chair near her. "If you will sit and relax a while, I promise to bake you a cake with a hacksaw in it if you get arrested."

"Even better would be a small appliqué project," Dottie interjected. "A miniature Baltimore album quilt would fit into a cake and still keep her busy until she is out on parole." Dottie moaned, her voice filled with fear. "All those tiny leaves and berries."

Melissa leaned back in her chair and closed her eyes. "I can see it now: a hollow cake filled with fabric, scissors, needles and thread. I can only hope someone will remember to include a package of chocolates. It might not be a bad life. Just think, no decisions about dinner menus, no mud tracked across the kitchen floor, no homework to check." Opening her eyes, she looked at her friends. "Maybe I'll confess, and then I'll have enough time to work on my own projects."

"You're all right." Martha collapsed, laughing, onto her chair. "I didn't do anything to the woman and don't know why I've been acting like such a ninny."

The retreat was moving ahead. Instead of working on her quilt, Theo rolled outside to call Tony. "Hey, lawman." Her voice was cheery. "How are you doing?"

"Tired, beat, exhausted, confused." There was a pause in his litany of weariness followed by a jaw-cracking yawn. "And you?"

Her answering yawn was much quieter. "I thought I'd better tell you a couple of things if you have the time."

Tony finished talking to Theo and stepped out of his office. Most of his meager staff of deputies were doing paperwork. Time for the shift change. Although the talk was general, they were mostly subdued, and the fine lines of tension made them all look hard. Tony glanced at the clock on the wall. He couldn't believe he'd lost track of this entire day. He perched one hip on Ruth Ann's immaculate desk. Luckily for him, she didn't work Saturdays.

"I'm sure you have all heard by now, but Scarlet LaFleur was found dead at The

Lodge early this morning. We do not have an official cause of death but it is a homicide." Leaning forward, he looked from face to face. "Last night, because it was Friday, we had three cars out on patrol. I want each one of you to write down everything that you saw, heard or imagined. In town as well as out. I don't care how trivial you think it might be." Rolling his shoulders didn't relieve any of his tension. Focusing on Sheila and Darren, who normally patrolled the area near The Lodge, he addressed them. "From you two, I want to know what vehicles you saw, what time you saw them, and if you noticed anything missing from anywhere. If you saw people, I want to know who they are and what they were doing. Give me a dead 'possum count." With a yawn, he left the desk and poured himself a cup of coffee. His stomach rolled in protest, but he ignored it. He wondered if the rumor about Art, Claude and Darren's wife would surface.

Tony watched Sheila nod and begin writing. She didn't mention she'd been on duty all day just as most of them had. A lovely and extremely efficient young woman, she had been the first to arrive at The Lodge after Tony and Wade. As usual, her long blond hair was tightly braided and the tail

191

pinned out of the way. Like everything about her, the report would be meticulous, from her elegant handwriting to her phrasing. Tony loved her reports. They were unfailingly coherent and comprehensive.

Seated next to her, Darren Holt, the bantam rooster of the staff, whose patrol should cross her path several times in the early evening but not later, looked at Sheila and suddenly turned pale. He fidgeted with his pen but didn't start writing. In fact, he looked ready to bolt from the room.

Very interesting. Tony thought.

Wade arrived, rumpled and wearing a mustard stain on his brown uniform shirt. Tony noticed Wade's name pin was missing. Tony was sure he didn't look any better.

Practically dragging his feet, Wade made his way to Tony's side, pausing only to greet his fellow officers. "I don't know about you, but I've gotten all kinds of calls from frightened citizens. Portia Osgood knows my number and has called me at least three times to report movement in the bushes around her house." He swung his arms a bit, and Tony heard popping and cracking in his joints.

"Naturally the damned things are moving, the wind is blowing harder and the temperature has started dropping too." Then, more quietly, for Tony's ears only, he said, "I was at Ruby's for lunch. She tells me that her crankiest customers are suddenly being easily satisfied, and a couple of them have even left tips. I tell you what, Sheriff, the diners there are certain someone is killing off the most annoying citizens in Silersville, and the murders have the others looking over their shoulders. No one seems to believe Mr. Beasley died of natural causes, and Ruby says she heard a couple of people talking about forming some kind of citizens' protection group. Since Scarlet LaFleur grew up here, she's classified as a local in many minds."

Tony was sure if he had hair, he would be down to his last strand by now. The last thing he needed was a bunch of panicky cranks running amok in his county. Heaven only knew what kind of trouble they could create. He looked around and saw his officers diligently making notes. Some were checking times in their notebooks. Even as he was filling Wade in about his morning at The Lodge, he noticed Darren's odd behavior. Darren was erasing more than he was writing, and Sheila seemed to be egging him on about something. As Tony approached, Sheila stood and walked to the coffeepot. She indicated with a movement of her head he should follow her. Tony followed. Darren was close on their heels.

"I have to tell you —" Sheila began but was cut off by Darren.

"No, I have to be the one to tell you."

Tony was intrigued. The look Darren gave Sheila was a cross between belligerence and a plea. Then his eyes met Tony's. "Can we talk in your office?" Evidently satisfied, Sheila filled her cup and walked off.

As soon as the door closed behind them, Darren dropped into a chair and covered his face with his hands. "I don't know what came over me, Sheriff. I swear nothing like it ever happened before and if you don't fire me, I swear it will never happen again." His shoulders heaved and a shudder wracked his whole body.

Tony didn't like the way this sounded. "You'd better go ahead and tell me." Darren had never been Tony's favorite officer, but he had never caused any trouble either. Twice divorced from the same woman, he was a reasonably attractive man now married to a different woman. He and the hairstylist, Prudence Sligar, had married only a few months earlier and were parents of a new baby. All the information he'd heard said Darren was a good stepfather to Prudence's brood of fatherless children.

Darren finally lifted his face and met Tony's inquiring gaze. "Sheila is going to report she saw my patrol car parked on the big turnout just below The Lodge." Pressing his lips tightly together, he turned his face away from Tony. His hands were clasping and unclasping as if they had a life of their own. His Adam's apple was bobbing up and down at the same rate.

Arms crossed over his chest, Tony stared at him. He wasn't getting it. Why should parking in the turnout cause so much distress? Unless? "Tell me you're not sleeping on the job."

"Uh," Suddenly Darren's face was brick red, and there was a fine sheen of sweat on his forehead. He shook his head violently from side to side. "Worse." Instead of looking into Tony's eyes, his eyes seemed to be focused on the coffee stain on the carpet. They flickered to Tony's face and fell again. "I swear it was the only time."

"What exactly did you do and who were you doing it with?" Jamie and Chris would have recognized his tone of voice. Even Theo rarely ignored it.

"Sir, I'm sorry." Darren looked more like a teenager who got caught necking in the park than the cocky man he seemed on a normal day. "I was with Prudence. She, um, that is we were, um, you know." Amazingly, his face managed to turn even redder.

Struck speechless for the moment by the mental picture of Darren and Prudence doing the "you know" in the patrol car, Tony blinked several times. His first thought was how much Theo was going to love this story. His momentary flash of amusement was quickly replaced by anger. This man had not been doing his duty to the community paying his salary. What if he could have prevented the death of one of its citizens if he had been on patrol? "Were you in the county car?" Ice was much warmer than his question.

The horrified expression on Darren's face was almost answer enough. "No, sir. We were in her car." His babbling answer seemed to jump from his lips. Then he slammed them together and held them closed while he moaned deep in his throat. Obviously, he was suddenly unsure whether it was worse he had left his car or if it would have been worse if they had stayed in it. "I swear nothing like this has ever happened before. I'm not even sure what happened."

Tony felt his eyebrows shoot up. He leaned forward and snapped, "You're married to her. Couldn't you just go to your own bed? After your shift?"

"Oh, no sir. It was not like that at all. We didn't plan to meet." He sighed. A half smile lifted the corners of his mouth. At least it did until he glanced in Tony's direction. Then he straightened both his face and his spine.

"Heaven help me for asking this, but if you didn't plan to meet there, how did it happen? The turnout isn't exactly on the way to everywhere." In fact, Tony knew, with the encroaching forest, the turnout was practically invisible at night.

"I know." Darren closed his eyes. "I saw Prudence's car parked there. It was well off the road, and there wasn't any flat tire on the side that I could see." His eyes flew open. "She wasn't in the car. Right after I pulled up, she came out of the woods and stopped as soon as she saw me. I got out of the car to talk to her, and I swear I don't know how, but the next thing I knew we were in her car, and . . ." His voice tapered to a stop.

"I know working nights can be a trial for some families, but you were derelict." Tony reached for the antacid bottle instead of Darren's neck. "I'm not sure yet what I intend to do about this." Disciplining an officer for an infraction like this one was nothing he'd ever had to deal with before.

Tony thought a good idea would probably be to buy advice from ex-Sheriff Winston with a six pack, but right now he needed all of his officers, and Darren was reasonably capable. "What else did you see?"

Anxious to atone, Darren began a recitation of events. "There was a bit of traffic early. I saw quite a few cars from out of state and out of county going both ways and parked in the turnoffs as well. I ticketed a couple of out-of-state residents for dumping trash in one and made them clean it up. I didn't recognize most of the cars, parked or moving. But you know, now that I think about it, parked in one of the earlier turnoffs but still within walking distance of The Lodge, was Marmot the Varmint's car/truck."

"Was there any reason for you to stop there?"

"No." Darren gulped air, making his Adam's apple jump. "I don't have a good relationship with Claude." He gulped again. "The vehicle was parked in a safe and legal manner. I assumed that Claude was sleeping inside, which I figured was better than him driving."

"I understand." Tony could visualize the road. It was winding through heavily wooded areas, but there were no hairpin

198

turns. The higher you went, the more turn-offs had been built into the road. The tourists liked to be able to pull off and take pictures without dodging cars, although they preferred the valley side. The road was also popular with couples. Tony flinched away from the mental picture of Darren and Prudence. "When you came back down the road after your, um, encounter with your wife, was Claude's car/truck still parked there?"

"No. It was gone. In fact, all of the turnoffs were empty as I came down." Darren was back in control of himself again.

"So, let me get this straight. You didn't plan to meet Prudence but stopped when you saw her car? What was she doing up there if not waiting for you?"

Darren sat speechless and slowly moved his head back and forth. His eyes were very wide.

Tony sent Darren to finish his written report and considered the chances that Prudence strangled Scarlet. Prudence was taller, younger and, as an arm wrestling champion, much stronger than the victim. Tony didn't believe Prudence was their killer.

# CHAPTER THIRTEEN

Theo was being bombarded with questions. She shook her head to all of them not involved with quilting. Did people think she shared a brain with Tony? The idea made her chuckle, and she relaxed back into her chair. A part of her wondered if there was really any point at all in their staying at The Lodge. Certainly this was not the most relaxing or productive of their retreats. A quick glance around the lobby made her change her mind.

Everyone looked exhausted. The early morning arrival of the sheriff's department, the crime scene unit, and all that was triggered by the discovery of Scarlet's body draped so obscenely in the shrubbery, had taken its toll. Several of the older women had vanished in the late morning for a nap. They were back now and appeared to be greatly refreshed and ready to roll.

"Theo?" Susan waved her hand to attract

her attention. "When do we get the next clue for the mystery quilt?" The circles under her eyes were dark, but her eyes were clear and she was smiling. At her question, every quilter stopped and looked up expectantly.

"Is everyone ready to go on?" Theo didn't want to admit that she had forgotten all about the mystery quilt.

As a resounding chorus of "yes" answered, Theo pulled out the sealed envelope holding the next clue. Passing the sheets around, she watched their faces as they read the next clue. Some of the women looked like they had guessed what was coming next and some looked totally bewildered, but all of the ladies doing the mystery quilt jumped into action. Soon, the room was filled with the sounds of sewing machines and the scent of chocolate.

Theo decided she would take advantage of the moment to slip to her room and take a quick shower. Somehow she had missed getting one earlier in the day. She'd almost reached her door, when upstairs, the sounds of an argument coming from the veranda made her pause. The voices were those of Beth and Art. More precisely, it was Beth telling Art exactly what was on her mind. Her voice was tight and strained, but easy enough to understand.

"I think you had better tell the sheriff what you and Prudence were doing. I am not going to lie for you one more time." There was a pause while Beth blew her nose. "Enough is enough. What am I supposed to believe, anyway? You hated Scarlet. For all I know, maybe you did throw her into the bushes."

"Beth, honey." Art's tone sounded sad and restrained as he pleaded with his wife. The voices were fading as the pair moved along the hallway. "You can't believe that. You know where I was and what I was doing. Surely you can't really doubt me?"

As soon as they were out of sight, Theo wheeled her chair as quickly as she could, going to her room. Before she climbed into the shower, she double-checked her window. It took all of her resolve not to look down into those rhododendrons. Uneasy, she locked the door and put a chair in front of it. "Prudence and Art? No way." She mumbled to herself as she adjusted the water temperature. "I'll call Tony when I get out." Beth had certainly sounded angry, but it was not the kind of anger Theo would expect if she were talking to a cheating spouse. But then again, who ever knew what was really going on in someone else's mind?

"Prudence and Art, with Beth reluctantly covering up for them?" The pieces of the mental picture didn't fit together.

The hot water eased some of the stiffness from Theo's joints. She hadn't realized the effect the day had had on her until now. It was bliss for her as she stayed in the shower longer than her allotted three minutes, luxuriating in the continuous spray of hot water. As much as she loved her house and family, there were days when the promise of enough hot water to go around was merely an unfulfilled dream. Wrapping herself in one of the oversized hotel towels, she hummed a little tune. She wrapped another towel around her head, turban style, and headed for the telephone.

Theo dialed Tony's cellular phone. If he didn't want to be disturbed, he would have it turned off. Knowing Tony, it might be under the seat of the patrol car.

He answered on the first ring.

"Hi, sweetheart." Theo warbled. She grinned at the phone when Tony groaned. "Don't worry, I haven't found any more bodies."

"That's a blessing." There was relief attached to each syllable. "What's up, then? You never call in when you are at a retreat. Did you forget your thread?"

"Hah!" Hearing the concern in his voice, she smiled. "Well," she said, adding a vowel and making it sound like way-ell, "You know, this one has been a bit out of the ordinary, but actually, I just got out of a long and luxurious shower."

"So, what's up?" Amusement replaced Tony's concern.

"I happened to overhear an argument between Art and Beth. It was hard to make out the sense of it, but somehow it involved Art and Prudence, and it sounds like Beth has been covering for them. Does this mean anything to you?"

"Not really, but maybe. At the very least, it gives me an edge. Thanks for the hint. Anything else?"

"I don't think so offhand. It seems like I overheard something I meant to pass on to you but can't place it at all." She yawned and stretched. "You know this is not exactly gossip central. We're all working like slaves."

"Well, you have fun, take lots of showers and I'll see you tomorrow."

As she carefully combed the tangles out of her wet hair, Theo tried to pin down what she had heard, but it was elusive, teasing the corner of her memory, so she shrugged it off and finished getting dressed. The memory would return eventually. Theo just hoped it wouldn't be three o'clock in the morning when it came back.

# CHAPTER FOURTEEN

Tony wasted no time getting Prudence delivered to his office.

She wasted no time calling her attorney, almost as though she was expecting to be interviewed. Through the small window, he could see into the interrogation room where Prudence was deep in conference with her attorney, Mr. Mason. Mason was his real name. Originally from Kentucky, his parents hoped he would be inspired to become a successful lawyer and enjoy a life that did not include mining coal. The ploy had worked like a charm. Driving a gleaming silver sports car, he had arrived from Knoxville in almost record time. On one level, Tony admired Prudence's ability to get her lawyer to Silersville so quickly on a Saturday afternoon, and on another, he wondered why a hairdresser in Silersville would even know the name of a defense attorney, much less have the phone number committed t memory.

Tall, thin and in his early forties, Mr. Mason appeared to be very businesslike, even wearing an expensive gray business suit and spotless white shirt. Although it was a Saturday, the man obviously hadn't come directly from a football game. There wasn't even any orange on his tie. By all appearances, he had been expecting to be in Silersville today, dressed for court. And as he thought about appearances, there was something about the shade of his auburn hair that reminded Tony of Prudence's middle child. Grinning wryly to himself, Tony knew he had settled back into small town life when he started noticing such a detail. Did small town curiosity stem from knowing everyone, or did the door swing in the other direction? Either way, he doubted city people would even be aware the children had different fathers.

What secret could possibly connect Art and Prudence? Had they conspired to kill Mr. Beasley? Or Scarlet? Was Art unwilling to do the deed in his own hotel? If so, Art might have let Prudence inside, but Tony didn't think she was an assassin. Certainly with all her experience arm wrestling, she might be strong enough to do it, but why on earth would she? If Blossom was correct, maybe both Prudence and Art had borrowed money from Mr. Beasley. What else tied them together? Money-lending didn't seem like the right answer. Too bad Theo hadn't been able to hear more of the conversation between Art and Beth.

Mike Ott should return soon with Art. Tony wanted the pair to see each other, but not be able to talk, before he asked a single question. The attorney opened the door and waved to attract Tony's attention. "I understand that you have sent for Art?" Tony nodded. "What about Claude?"

"Claude?" Tony almost swallowed his tongue. "Oh, he'll be here soon." It was a bald faced lie when he said it, but it wouldn't be for long. The second after Mr. Mason closed the door, Tony radioed Sheila. "I want you to swing by and pick up Claude and bring him in. Invite him nicely."

"What if he doesn't want to come?"

"Place him in protective custody, or at the very least sit there and hold his hand, figuratively speaking of course." Surely it was static that made it sound like she was laughing. "I want him in your car now, and I want him here pronto."

"Okay." The radio made a hissing sound. "Does this concern what Pops Ogle was talking about with the highway department truck?"

"Just do it." Tony didn't have an answer. After he disconnected, he mumbled to himself, "That's the jackpot question. What could Prudence, Art and Claude have in common? Besides being represented by the same lawyer. Think, man. They'll all be here soon."

His focus moved to the bulletin board where photographs showed Mr. Beasley's office. Neither anything in the photographs nor any of the forensic details pointed to there being three incredibly disparate people involved with his death. How and why would a trash hauler, a hairdresser/fortune teller and a hotel owner conspire to kill Mr. Beasley? It was impossible. The old guy had died of a medication overdose. Tony believed it was more likely suicide than homicide.

What little he knew about Scarlet's death didn't point to a group action either. Were there members of some underground organization eliminating some of the less popular citizens of Silersville? Maybe they drew straws for the assignment? Although he'd heard it was an idea being passed around at Ruby's, Tony dismissed it. If that were the case, he'd bet Nellie Pearl Prigmore and Angus Farquhar would have been the first victims. Scarlet hadn't lived here in years, and Mr. Beasley wasn't awful.

Killing time, Tony flipped through the reports on his desk. In addition to Roscoe's report of the shooting at the trailer court, there were the normal complaints of shoplifting, vandalism and petty theft, domestic violence and public intoxication. A bar fight resulted in two arrests.

Tony concentrated on the vandalism report for a moment, thinking there could be a connection with the shots fired at Roscoe's trailer. Then he remembered Mrs. Smith and the red tube top. How could he have forgotten — there had been a lot more of the woman than there had been fabric. A report claimed someone had shot a mailbox multiple times with a small caliber gun, probably a .22. The highway department reported someone had broken into several trucks near the ongoing road construction. The details were sketchy, since the crime fell into the jurisdiction of the state and not the county, but it sounded like whatever his little trio might have been doing. Frank Thomas of Thomas Brothers' Garage said someone had taken a toolbox, coveralls and some miscellaneous items, including a heavy duty jack, from his business. Toilet paper was the artist's medium of choice used to decorate the front yard of the middle school principal's house. It had been a quiet school year so far. This was only the second time since classes began that such guerilla tactics had been used on this particular house. The previous year students used a record amount of paper on a roll. Tony's particular favorite report merely said that a caller reported someone picking up stuff along the highway.

Glancing up, he saw Deputy Mike Ott arriving with Art Trimble. Since the time Tony had talked to him earlier in the day, the innkeeper had developed a particularly unpleasant greenish-gray skin tone, and there was no bounce in his step. Tony said, "Take him through the tunnel and into courtroom one," and thought thank goodness, on Saturday, court was not in session. He really wasn't set up for this kind of day. The Park County Law Enforcement Center was bulging at the seams.

Moments later, Sheila arrived with Claude in tow. She handed him a cup of coffee and pointed him to a chair. He grasped the container with all of the fervor of a drowning man clinging to a lifejacket. Instead of drinking any of it, however, he simply held it between his palms and stared at the floor.

Mr. Mason, the attorney, left Prudence

after talking with her for about a half hour. He took one look at Claude and crisply informed Tony the man was not to be questioned without him being present. Tony merely nodded his agreement before leading the attorney to visit his third client. Sitting in the front of the courtroom, Art looked like he was relieved to be in custody. Just to be on the safe side, Tony made sure he read Art his rights in front of Mason, then he left the room. "Let me know when you are through chatting with your clients and we can proceed."

Tony and Mike and Wade and Sheila held a quick conference in Tony's office. After offering his deputies the antacid bottle, Tony began munching its contents. "Does anyone have a clue what these three have been up to?"

Shaking his head slowly, Mike said, "Art just sat in the back seat with his hands pressed between his knees. He didn't look out the window, and he didn't say a thing. It was odd, but he acted like I should already know all about what he had done."

Sheila glanced through the open door at Claude. The coffee cup sat on the floor next to Claude's foot. The man was sound asleep with his forehead resting on the edge of a trashcan. Air released in soft snores ruffled the plastic liner. "What little Claude said was in the same vein. He said he'd been expecting to be arrested, and he knew he would never get away with it and would I tell Katti he will love her forever," she whispered. "He sounded pretty tragic."

Tony groaned. "So all we have to do is figure out what *it* is." Fatigue was not enhancing his thought processes. He could use a nap.

Theo had her hands full at the retreat.

Beth Trimble was sobbing inconsolably at the front desk. Everyone in the lobby had seen Art leaving with Deputy Mike Ott, and while he hadn't been handcuffed, the general consensus was Art remaining at the hotel had not been an option. The chatter in the lobby was focused on the drama. One elderly woman, not one of the quilters, was moaning and complaining that no one was safe in "the hotel of death."

The woman's traveling companion was openly irritated. "For heaven's sake, shut up. This is not a hotel of death. Although," she said, as she looked right at Beth and smiled encouragingly, "I'm sure we would all feel better if we had some information. Or maybe you would prefer it if we just checked out."

"No." At that, Beth raised her still damp and swollen face. "Please don't leave. If you are worried about what happened to Scarlet, this . . ." She waved to indicate Art's departure. "This had nothing at all to do with her death. I promise."

"What then?" Martha stepped to the forefront. "I know all about being suspected of wrongdoing, and it is most unpleasant. Maybe there is some way we can help."

The small bit of sympathy sent Beth into more spasms of grief. "Y-you don't understand." She blew her nose several times on the same worn tissue. "He is guilty." Beth looked into Theo's face. "But not of murder."

Shocked, Theo barely heard Beth's last words which were all but drowned out by the swell of discussions around them. The increased volume of chatter was deafening. It was turning into chaos.

Theo slipped her fingers into her mouth and blew. The shriek of the whistle brought all eyes around to her and stopped all conversation. Jamie and Chris would have been impressed. Theo spoke loudly enough for all to hear. "I understood you to say that Art is not guilty of murder, didn't you?" Beth nodded and Theo continued, "So, Beth, do you want us to stay or go?"

"St-stay." She was rubbing the ear nearest Theo. It had taken the full force of Theo's whistle. "In spite of what you might think, Art would never hurt anyone. He is totally nonviolent."

Still insanely curious herself, Theo turned on her little group. "Stay or go? If you say stay, then we will respect Beth's privacy, okay?" The flock nodded. "We will have a show of hands then. Who wants to stay?"

All hands reached for the ceiling. Beth wiped her face. "Thank you, ladies." She attempted a smile. "I think we need some nachos. My treat." With that she headed for the kitchen.

Dottie, the oldest of the quilters, called to her retreating back. "You know, a beer or some wine would go well with nachos." Almost all of the women looked like they were in agreement. Even the staunchest of the Baptists seemed interested.

Theo worked on her quilting for a few minutes before slipping off to her room to call Tony again. Most days she thoroughly despised the cell phone phenomenon, but today she loved it. Within seconds Tony was talking to her. "Whatever is going on, Tony? Mike Ott came for Art, and now Beth is weeping buckets and swears his arrest has nothing to do with Scarlet but won't tell us anything more."

"Search me." Tony's voice was muffled. "I've got an attorney from Knoxville and three suspects who look like they are getting ready to confess. The only problem is I have no idea what they've done."

Theo recognized the familiar sound of his chewing antacids.

"I have an officer who needs to be disciplined, but I'm already shorthanded. There's an unsolved homicide, and Edith is cooking dinner because I don't have time. The boys are threatening mutiny."

Theo smiled at the phone. It sounded like his plate was full to overflowing, but he hadn't lost his sense of humor. "You did make the scouts happy, though, on Friday night." She gasped. "Was it only last night?"

"That, my dear, was the highlight of my career. I was fabulous. All the boys even said so."

"I'm so glad. You seemed a bit reluctant. If you order pizza before Edith gets too creative, our boys will give you a medal." Without warning, Theo remembered the idea she'd forgotten earlier. "I had a flash about Scarlet. Could she have been robbed? Like violently? I thought of it because nobody else I know ever wore cashmere and jewels to a quilt retreat before."

"Jewels? Wait a minute." Tony broke in. Theo heard papers being shuffled. "The only jewelry she was wearing when we arrived was a large gold ring set with a red stone, possibly a ruby, and a watch. Expensive. Are you saying she was wearing more jewelry last night?" His voice sharpened. His interest was definitely aroused.

"Oh, yes. Scarlet was positively festooned." Theo closed her eyes and tried to visualize the scene. Color was always what she could remember best. "She had on a creamy cashmere sweater. Maybe it was oatmeal. No, there was a definite tinge of yellow in it."

Her husband let her ramble through her thoughts without interrupting. Theo knew he'd wait patiently letting her work through her memory.

"Hanging over the neckline of the sweater was a woven gold necklace. It was longer than a choker, but it didn't come much below her collarbone. It was flat and maybe a half-inch wide. Hanging down from the center was a single large ruby. I mean a really big ruby. I remember thinking it was a lot of necklace to wear around a group that tends toward sweatpants and loose threads."

A choking sound that might have been

laughter came from Tony. Theo smiled and went on. "I'm pretty sure she was wearing matching earrings but her hair covered her ears. I'm sure she had on a bracelet matching the necklace. At first she wore it on her right wrist but it kept catching on her thread as she did her embroidery, so she made a big production of putting it onto her left wrist. She acted like it was new, but no one would dream of asking her about it."

"So she had her watch and her bracelet on the left wrist?"

"Yes, for a while anyway."

"Did she change clothes during the evening? Maybe she took it off."

"No. She didn't change clothes. I'm sure she still had it on when I last saw her before she went upstairs. You searched her room, didn't you?" Almost against her will, Theo was drawn to the window, and she looked down to where the body had been. Maybe the gold would be visible if it had fallen to the ground. Only the dark green of the rhododendrons and the browns of the season met her eyes. There was no flash of gold.

"Of course we did. And you are right. No one found any extra jewelry. Not in her room or anywhere around the scene." After a silence, Tony's voice was quiet. "Was she killed to steal them, or were they taken after the fact? Uh-oh, it looks like Mason is ready for me. I'll talk to you later."

# CHAPTER FIFTEEN

Tony saw Mr. Mason standing in front of his office doorway talking to Sheila. Tony was shocked to see the attorney looked like he had aged ten years since his arrival at the Park County Law Enforcement Center. There were lines of strain creasing his face. His auburn hair was no longer neatly combed. Now it was standing in tufts as if he had been repeatedly running his hands through it. His tie was askew. Even his suit had developed a wrinkle. Just one, but it was a real wrinkle.

Lined up in chairs behind him sat his clients, Prudence and Art. His third client, Claude, was still propped up against the wall where he had more or less collapsed.

Tony finally comprehended everyone was waiting for him. He stood and tucked in the loose end of his shirttail. Smoothing his scalp as if it were still covered with hair, he left his office. Tony attempted a glare at the culprits. "I hope this is not going to take long. I am running out of patience, but we can wait for the county attorney if you like." He addressed Mason. "Archie Campbell is probably at the football game in Knoxville. What would you like to do?"

Tony observed as Mason looked at his clients. Claude looked like roadkill. Prudence sat with one leg crossed over the over. Except for the constant swinging of her foot, she looked composed. Art's hands were being crushed between his knees, and his color had deteriorated. In spite of the pleasant temperature in the room, he was perspiring heavily. Under his armpits, his shirt was soaked to the waist.

As one, they shook their heads.

"I'm afraid this may not fall into Archie's jurisdiction. We will let you decide who to call." Mason didn't look like he agreed with his clients' decision but sank onto the chair someone had found for him and attempted to smooth the wrinkle out of his suit pants with his fingers. "I would prefer to limit this information to as few people as necessary."

Fascinated, Tony and Wade and Mike and Sheila dragged chairs out for themselves and waited for the confession. There was more than enough confusion to go around. Tony was delighted he wasn't the only one in the dark.

Unable to stay seated, Mason lunged to his feet and addressed them like they were members of the jury. Maybe even the Supreme Court. "I'd like to preface this by saying my clients had the best interest of the community in mind. Truly, like other heroes, they didn't enter into this lightly, and neither did they ever expect to be absolved. They —" Interrupted by the tones of the "William Tell Overture" blasting from Tony's pocket, he stopped and smiled in spite of the serious nature of their meeting. Mason waved for Tony to answer his phone.

Under ordinary circumstances, Tony might have been embarrassed he had not switched off the sound, but the medical examiner in Knoxville was on the line. "I have some very preliminary results that might help you, Tony. Grab a pencil."

Tony went into his office and closed the door. "What's up, Doc?" He wasn't smiling when he said it.

Doctor Blake, the pathologist, coughed a couple of times before he started speaking. "Sorry about that. I got some coffee down the wrong pipe. Your victim was attacked from behind. Her neck had a thin wire wrapped around it. Twice. I'd say she died quickly, but not immediately. Someone wearing knit navy blue nylon gloves had a hand over her nose and mouth at the time she died. We were able to find some of the fibers. We passed them on to the wizards. They will do their best with them, but they don't expect they can be traced. Too generic. If you find a pair of blue nylon gloves in your investigation, they might be able to make a match." There was a pause for more coughing and then the sounds of a cigarette being lit. "The metal wire, the murder weapon, is a string for a musical instrument — a dulcimer, to be precise."

Tony remembered Theo's description of Scarlet's jewelry. "Any signs that a necklace or other jewelry might have been involved?" He passed along Theo's description.

"A necklace? You mean like scratches or bruising? No. If she was wearing something, it wasn't caught between the killer and the victim or there would be clear marks on the skin. It must have been removed with some care because there weren't any scratches anywhere on her neck. Maybe she took it off herself. It certainly wasn't caught under the wire." There was a pause. "I know there was something else I wanted to tell you, though."

Tony lifted his pen from the notepad. He

waited while the doctor searched for something in his file, coughing and wheezing the whole time.

"Here it is. I presume you'll hear it from them, too, but Forensics told me that the smudges of grease your deputy found on her back are definitely dirty motor oil stains. Either she was rolling around under a car or her killer had been. He didn't have to be extremely large, but he was probably quite strong. And yes, before you ask, it could have been a strong woman."

Tony was mentally reassessing the possibility that Art had conspired with Prudence. He had a passkey, and she was certainly strong enough to do the deed, but how would Claude be involved? Claude would be more likely than Prudence to have motor oil on his clothes. But if it was Claude, what would be Prudence's role?

"Can you estimate the time of death?"

"I would say she died between eleven and midnight. Here's what's really weird though. She wasn't moved outside until much later." He was interrupted by the sound of another phone ringing in the background. "Damn, it's busy here today. Anyway, she was outside probably only for ten to fifteen minutes before your wife found her. I make it half an hour, max. Until then, she was in a relatively warm, dry place. Do you want to hear all of the technical stuff?" It sounded like he was lighting another cigarette.

"Put it in your report." Tony had heard enough for the time being. "Where are the clothes now?"

"Forensics is keeping them. They aren't doing anything else with them today, but you know eventually the lab rat squad will be able to tell you the brand of motor oil and probably what kind of vehicle it came from. You know, just between you and me, I think those guys are kind of spooky. Bye."

Left holding the silent receiver, Tony personally thought that the medical examiner was a bit spooky himself, but he didn't say so. He looked at his notes. The death had occurred at eleven-thirty or so in the evening and then at about three in the morning, the killer, he presumed, dropped the victim over the rail. Why the delay? Why not leave her in her room where she wouldn't be found until morning or even afternoon? Or was the killer not the one who dropped the body? Should they be looking for a co-conspirator? Tony felt a monster headache working its way up from his spine, but he left his notes on his desk and headed for the group confession. Maybe this would answer all of his questions, and he could take a handful of aspirin and just go home and eat pizza with his kids. In the meantime, he munched on yet another handful of antacid tablets. He wasn't sure if he preferred the fruity ones to the minty ones, but he guessed he was going to have plenty of occasions for a full taste test study this weekend.

Prudence, Art and Claude didn't look any better than they had when he'd left the room. Mason looked even worse than he had. Mike, Wade and Sheila looked as if they were torn between committing a little police brutality and taking a long nap. Tony ignored the conspirators and addressed Mason. "This had better be good. My mood is not improving as the afternoon wears on." He crossed his arms over his chest and stood as tall as he could and stared at the lawyer.

"Well . . ." Mr. Mason looked uneasy but began, speaking to everyone in a well modulated, professional voice.

Tony thought the attorney could have a career on the radio.

Mr. Mason said, "We belong to a small group of concerned citizens. As you know, the recent highway construction has been the source of hot debates all over the area. It has fueled arguments about everything from disturbing ancient burial grounds to the ozone." Passion took over, and he strode back and forth as he expounded on the subject. "The environmental concerns have extended not only across the state, but also nationally. Certainly, the proximity of the national park has given rise to a large number of persons and groups concerned by pollution."

From his position against the wall, Claude interrupted. "It's killing the fish." The expression on his attorney's face stopped him cold. His lips slammed together as he blanched and returned his head to its place.

"As Mr. Marmot so aptly remarked, it is killing the fish as well as affecting the native plants and the entire ecology of the area. It is also interfering with the normal business activities in the area, particularly those connected with tourism." Art nodded in agreement as Mr. Mason adjusted his tie. The attorney's tongue was obviously warmed up now, and he appeared to be preparing for a good long speech.

Tony raised his hand, palm forward, fingers up. "Stop right there." He looked at the threesome. "It sounds like a group of vigilantes but I am not the judge. Just give me the facts. Spell out, in small words, just what they did. I don't need to hear any of their wacko reasons now."

Mason looked offended but stepped forward. "They broke into some highway department vehicles parked not far from Mr. Trimble's business. With no regard for their personal safety, they slipped pieces of catfish into every spot, slot and pipe big enough to hold one." He couldn't suppress a grin. "One of them even managed to insert a chunk between the seat and the backrest in the supervisor's vehicle." He stepped back into his spot. Mason smiled as if he had won the lottery.

In his wildest thoughts, Tony had never imagined this. He'd been half-expecting a murder confession, not catfish guerillas. Covering a grin with his handkerchief, he coughed into it. It would take all of his concentration to keep from laughing. With the handkerchief still near his mouth, he managed to ask, "And are you all sorry?"

As one, they all nodded their assent, but they didn't really look contrite.

Claude whispered, but the sound traveled well. "Yeah, we're real sorry we didn't think of it while the weather was still hot."

Mason frowned at his clients, all of whom were in trouble up to their eyebrows, and said, "Their actions were impromptu and ill-advised." Behind him, three heads bobbed. "In the heat of the moment, common sense died."

Mentioning the dead made Tony think of hot, rotting catfish in the cab of a truck. He bolted into his office where he could close the door and enjoy the laugh. His deputies were right on his heels. "Can you imagine how bad that will smell?" He couldn't seem to stop laughing, even though it wasn't funny. "It's the shock after suspecting all or some of them of murder." He moaned. It took several minutes before he could pull himself together. When he finally returned to the confessors, followed by his staff, nobody had moved, but they did appear to be more relaxed.

Tony stared at them. "I have no idea what the state's attorneys will decide to do about this matter. It really is not my decision. It is vandalism, major vandalism, of several state-owned vehicles. The highway department will not be happy and I don't blame them. I cannot estimate the cost involved in cleaning it up. I will, of course, be obligated to send them a detailed report."

"We'll pay to have the trucks cleaned." Prudence's voice filled the room. The others nodded. "And whatever fine they impose."

Tony wasn't sure he'd ever seen a sorrier

group than the hairdresser, hotel owner and garbage guru — not to mention their attorney, who seemed to be up to his neck in the conspiracy. "You can go on back to Knoxville for the time being, Mr. Mason. As for your clients, I'm going to send them home, for now. I imagine we can find them again without any trouble when we need to." As he looked at each of them, they nodded their agreement. "I have some cases needing to take precedence over this, so I'm not going to lock you up. Today."

The guerillas stood to leave.

"Prudence, please stay." Tony waved the others away.

The guilty parties and the lawyer charged for the door and fought to be the first outside. It wasn't much of a fight because they let Claude win. Mason cut in front of Art. No one looked back. Still smiling, Tony turned to his deputies. They were busily studying the arrangement of the furniture. "You, Sheila, take them home, now."

Sheila was laughing as she trotted behind them.

"Prudence, I want you in my office." Tony held the door for her. "I am not forgetting you were partially responsible for one of my deputies being derelict in his duty. The guilt is his and the punishment will be too."

The hairdresser's face flushed bright red. "I didn't plan that, but when I came out of the woods to my car, suddenly there he was. I didn't want to tell him what I'd been doing and wanted to distract him. It worked."

Tony believed the leading grease experts in Park County had to be the Thomas brothers. If their coveralls were any indication, the garage owners wallowed in the stuff. When he pulled into the parking area, the first thing he saw was Theo's minivan. It didn't run. The brothers couldn't fix it. So luckily, at least for now, Theo couldn't drive.

Wiping his greasy hands on an even greasier red rag, Frank Thomas ambled out of the open service bay and walked around to the driver's door. Tony lowered the window. "Hey there, Sheriff."

"Frank." Tony studied the man's dark blue coverall. Sure enough, it was coated with grease and dirt. There was no logo of any kind on it. "What's the word on the van?"

Frank cleared his throat and spat on the ground behind him. "I'll haul it to the dump for free. It looks bad sitting on my property."

"Sell it for parts." Tony doubted it would bring in fifty dollars. "Keep an eye out for a good car for Theo, would you?"

"Sure thing. How many seats?"

Tony paused, momentarily superstitious. "Six. Two will be car seats."

Frank seemed to be doing math in his head. "Twins?"

"Yes."

"Well, congratulations!" Frank leaned against the Blazer's door.

Tony could smell grease. "I do have a question." Frank's eyebrows rose. "It's about your coveralls."

The eyebrows went higher. Frank glanced down at his outfit. "What?"

"Tell me about them. Do you have a single pair for each of you? Do you rent them?"

"Funny you should ask." Frank looked down at the Blazer's door, pulled out his rag and polished away a smudge left by his coveralls. "Someone stole one of ours."

"When was this?"

"Hmm, maybe Thursday, Friday. It was gone before we opened this morning. We filed a report."

Tony felt like a coon dog finding the scent. "Are they usually locked up?"

"Nossir." Frank chuckled. "We, me and Joe anyways, we're kinda messy except when it comes to the tools. These count as tools. We don't need them as much as we do the stolen jack." He ran a hand down his chest, studied it and wiped it on the dirty rag.

"Anyhow, on Saturdays at noon when we close for the day, officially, we take them all from the greasy box and give them to Missus Ogle. She collects the coveralls and the rags, washes them and brings them back first thing Monday. We was one short this morning."

"Any idea what happened to it?"

"Nope." Frank shrugged. "Ain't never had anyone steal dirty coveralls before. Kinda freaky, don't you think?"

Tony did think it was freaky. He also thought it showed clear premeditation as well as a certain familiarity with the garage and maybe its owners.

# CHAPTER SIXTEEN

On Sunday, Tony came for Theo about noon. He'd missed her. He'd even missed her nagging, a little bit. He parked in the driveway and pushed her out to the Blazer in her shiny new wheelchair. "Nice wheels, lady."

Theo caressed the armrests. "I hate to admit it, but it really is more comfortable than standing for any period of time. I'll probably go crazy locked in the house."

Tony wondered what she was talking about. "Who said we're going to lock you up?"

"Well, you can't carry me everywhere there are stairs. How's Jamie's birthday so far?" Theo felt bad about missing any of his special day. "You didn't give him his present yet?"

"No. But I think he thinks I did."

"Why?" Theo couldn't imagine what he was talking about, and he wasn't giving her any more information.

They made small talk as they drove down the mountain. Tony explained his progress, or rather the lack of progress, on the death of Scarlet. "There just doesn't seem to be a motive. The murder weapon sure didn't provide a clue as to the motive."

"What did kill her?"

"She was strangled with a dulcimer string." The corners of Tony's mouth compressed. "It's not exactly rare but not something most of us carry in our pockets."

They turned the corner onto their short street. In the space between their sidewalk and the park across the street were three pickups lined up side by side clogging the street. The biggest, cleanest one was Gus's white work truck with its built-in tool boxes on both sides of the bed. The next one, black with decorative flames, she knew belonged to Quentin. The third one she didn't recognize. It was bright red and bore temporary license plates.

Tony parked behind Gus's truck, trotted to the back of the Blazer and retrieved her wheelchair. Once she was settled in it, he pushed her to the sidewalk and managed to get her onto the pavement without dumping her in the dirt. "Not as easy as it looks."

Theo wasn't listening to Tony. She was

listening to the sounds of skateboards and Chris and Jamie laughing. Seconds later she saw them. Her heart almost stopped, an expression she'd heard all of her life and was experiencing now. Gus, Quentin and Kenny stood lined up next to a brand new wooden ramp extending from the top of their porch to the sidewalk. The three men were cheering. Chris and Jamie were sailing down the ramp on their skateboards, not stopping at the sidewalk but in the middle of the street.

"Mom! Mom!" Jamie jumped off his skateboard and ran to give her a big hug. "This is the *best* birthday present ever! Wow!" He dashed away as quickly as he arrived.

"Helmets?" Theo croaked. She knew better than to expect them to not play on their skateboards. "Kneepads? Elbow pads?"

"Theo, try this out!" Gus waved toward the ramp. Somehow he managed to look both proud and embarrassed. "It's just makeshift."

Tony muttered under his breath. "With Gus, makeshift means it will only last a couple of hundred years instead of eternity. Let's give it a whirl."

Theo found enough air to laugh. Tony was right. Gus couldn't build anything temporary. The ramp looked sturdy, had a hand rail, and even looked like it had been given a coat of white paint. It was a gradual slope. "I'm sure I'll adjust to the skateboards."

"I'm sure the boys will adjust to helmets and pads," Tony muttered.

They made it up the ramp with no effort at all and warmly congratulated and thanked Gus and his crew for giving up their weekend to build Theo a ramp. Or, more precisely, to build Tony a ramp so he didn't have to carry Theo up and down the stairs.

Gus's wife Catherine stood in the doorway, holding the discarded helmets. "I tried."

"I know you did," Theo said.

Tony took the helmets from his sister-in-law and headed down the ramp again.

Theo gave Catherine a hug. "They'd better listen to Tony, or he'll take the wheels off."

"Blossom came by with Jamie's birthday cake. It looks like a baseball field." Catherine moved to let Theo roll into the house. "It looked like she had two men with her."

Since Catherine and Gus didn't live in Silersville, they wouldn't have seen the trio out and about. "Yes, Blossom's developed two ardent admirers. I think it's wonderful, but the two of them are making Tony nervous."

"Tony?" Catherine said. Her expression showed an element of doubt.

"Oh, but it's true." Theo started laughing. "I'll admit it took me a little while to come to terms with him having such a devoted admirer. Now he's concerned — what if her boyfriends object to her baking for him all the time?"

Catherine's eyes went wide. "I guess they'd find the sheriff hard to deal with. I don't see your husband giving up his pies and cookies without a fight."

# CHAPTER SEVENTEEN

Monday morning, Theo barely managed to get the boys off to school and get dressed before the doctor arrived at the front door. She guessed Tony would have gone to his office early if she hadn't needed help with the indoor stairs. He had been on the telephone for a couple of hours.

"As promised, I found you a caretaker," said Doc Nash. He walked past Theo and stood in the entryway of the small front room. The shabby couch near the front window was Daisy's favorite daytime spot. The golden retriever opened her eyes and stared at him. "This can be your bedroom. I'll have a hospital bed delivered."

Theo stared at him. "You're serious?"

"Yep." He strolled back to where Theo sat in her new wheelchair. "I doubt even the oversized lout you're married to can carry you up and down the stairs all the time."

"Not this oversized lout." Tony came to

239

stand next to her. "I got you up and down the stairs last night and this morning, but I can't always be here."

Theo knew he was right. Still, she felt outnumbered and outmaneuvered. Theo looked up at the doctor. "Who's my caretaker?"

"Ekaterina Marmot."

"Katti's a nurse?"

"No. You don't need a skilled nurse as much as you need a go-fer. I talked to her, and she's excited to be your assistant and hopes you'll teach her how to quilt."

Theo considered her options. There really weren't any. The way the doctor and Tony had arranged the next two months of her life without consulting her rankled only a little, and she felt far more gratitude than irritation. She didn't know much about Katti other than she was from Russia and was Claude's mail-order bride. And liked pink, the brighter the better.

As if she had been waiting for her cue, Katti rolled up to the curb in a vintage, baby pink Cadillac. She trotted up the ramp, ignoring the stairs. The bright pink ends on her dark hair bounced with each step. Every piece of clothing from her pink athletic shoes to her pink and black polka dot pants to an oversize sweater was a different shade, pale to dark, subtle to bright. When she came through the doorway, Theo realized she even wore pink eye shadow.

Katti swooped toward Theo. Although there was a hint of nervousness around her eyes, her smile was wide, and she extended her arms for a hug. "Is good?"

With a laugh, Theo opened her arms. Katti's exuberance made her enjoy the prospect of spending lots of time with her. "Is good."

"I strong." Katti struck a bodybuilder pose. "I sew. I clean. I push you around. Carry for you." She patted Theo's shoulder. "You sit and grow big babies. I bring you food."

The surge of relief was as strong as it was unexpected and tears welled in Theo's eyes. "Thank you, Katti."

"What you eats?" Pretending she had not seen the tears, Katti began investigating the kitchen. "No borsht. Only thing Katti not cook."

"That's good. I don't like it either." From the corner of her eye, Theo saw Tony and the doctor ease out the front door.

"See, we good friends now. Lots we are the same." Katti looked into the old wood burning stove. "You cook here?"

"Sometimes." Theo waved to the newer electric range. "We use this now."

241

"All is good." Katti checked drawers and cabinets.

"What did you do in Russia?" Theo rolled past her. "I mean, did you have a job?"

"I work factory build cars." She frowned. "And I slave to bad man."

"Slave?" Theo wondered if language might be a problem.

"Married bad man." Katti nodded vigorously. "He die. I free. I poor. I lonely. I wear black. Here." She waved her arms encompassing more than Theo and the room. "Here is color. Nice house. Nice husband. Nice. Wear pink. Wedding present pink car."

"Very nice pink car." Theo laughed and gestured toward the front door. "Will you take me to work?"

Katti drove with the top town. "Is beautiful day."

Agreeing wholeheartedly, Theo gave her instructions guiding her to the shop.

They entered the shop like a whirlwind. Katti said she was excited to learn about quilting and fabrics. When Zoë, the office cat, peeked around the open door of Theo's upstairs studio, Theo saw Katti fall in love.

"What precious!" Katti sat on the steps and held her hand out to Zoë.

As if meeting a long lost friend, Zoë lunged into Katti's lap and meowed, kneading her toes on Katti's arm.

"I think you nice cat."

Delighted Zoë had a new friend, Theo said, "I'm not allowed to clean her litter box. Will you do it for me?"

"Yes, yes. Me and cat, we clean."

Katti's huge smile made Theo wonder if she understood the job. Cleaning a litter box didn't generally make anyone so happy. She watched from the corner of her eye. Katti did know the job and took care of it efficiently and with good humor. All the time, Zoë was nestled under one arm purring loudly.

Theo rolled to her new workspace, which was a part of the classroom. Tony had carried downstairs everything she'd packed and set it in a corner near a couple of banquet length tables. "Katti?"

Katti and the cat trotted in together. "We come."

"You don't have to run." Theo pointed to her sewing machine sitting on the floor. "Will you put it here?" Theo patted the table.

"Yes, yes." Katti carefully placed the machine in the exact requested spot and dove under the table to plug it in. Following Theo's instructions, the woman soon had Theo's sewing area set up. Sewing machine, cutting mat, lights and supplies. Still, she never set the cat down.

"Thank you, Katti." Theo was eager to start designing a new pattern. "Why don't you go explore in the shop? See if there is a fabric that sings to you like Zoë does."

"Zoë?" Katti looked baffled. "What is Zoë?"

"The cat's name."

Katti laughed as she trotted into the rows of fabrics. "Come Zoë, we make quilt."

Watching them, Theo relaxed. Zoë had a new friend, and Theo felt like she would enjoy having a quilting slave, at least this one. Katti's enthusiasm was refreshing and contagious.

Tony took a side trip to Mr. Beasley's house before going to his office. Although it had been searched after the man's overdose was discovered, Tony believed there was something else to find. The calls to Blossom, the hints and rumors, while hardly evidence, did make him think of the connection between smoke and fire.

Was Mr. Beasley the town's loan shark? It wasn't the first time the rumor had been attached to his name. Rumors weren't proof. No one ever filed an official complaint about the man. There had never been a suggestion of him taking a baseball bat to a delinquent borrower. Maybe he was charging lower interest rates than credit card companies which would have angered them, not his customers. Tony opened the desk drawer again and stared at the contents.

Nothing had changed. They were still virtually empty.

The telephone rang, startling him. He checked the screen on the handset, hoping a name would show up. "Out of Area." Tony waited for the machine to answer. After a series of beeps and the outgoing message, a woman's voice said, "Mr. Beasley, we received your check."

Tony lifted the receiver. "Mr. Beasley can't come to the phone. This is Sheriff Tony Abernathy. May I ask your name?"

"I'm Elise Cantrell. I work for Children's Hospital." She cleared her throat before continuing. "Mr. Beasley sent us a large check for a donation, and I called to thank him for it. Is there a problem?"

Tony guessed what she was asking was if the check was a phony or stolen money. "I don't think so, Ms. Cantrell. Mr. Beasley is deceased."

"Oh, no." Ms Cantrell moaned like she was in pain.

Tony was curious. "Can you tell me when

245

the check was written and the postmark on the envelope?"

"Yes, surely." After a brief pause, she said, "The date on the check is October nineteenth. That was last week."

Tony sighed. Relief washed through him. He guessed Mr. Beasley had put his affairs in order before overdosing himself. "And the postmark?"

"The same." Ms. Cantrell's voice was subdued. "Is the check no good?"

"I would guess it is just fine. Would you please fax a copy of the check and the envelope to my office?" Tony leaned back in the chair. "Was there a note or a donation form of any nature with it?"

"Yes, a little handwritten note saying he hoped it would help."

"Excellent. In your fax, please send a copy of the note and all your contact information." Tony suddenly couldn't wait to get to his office, pick up the fax and visit the doctor. "I'll be in touch later today."

"Thank you, Sheriff."

"No, thank you." If this settled the business with Mr. Beasley, he could concentrate on the obvious homicide of Scarlet LaFleur without trying to connect the two deaths. He felt like tap dancing down the sidewalk.

■ ■ ■ ■

Theo looked up from the sewing machine, surprised at how quickly time passed. With Katti trotting around doing the leg work, Theo had solved problems, met with the sales representatives from two fabric manufacturers and eaten when she was supposed to.

After lunch she managed to read a whole chapter of a novel, taking a mental break from her designing. Lethargy struck about the same time as the chapter break, and she locked the brakes on her chair, propped her feet up and found a comfortable position. She slept for about an hour and a half.

Waking up refreshed, she cut fabric and had Katti arrange the geometric pieces on the flannel design wall.

"How it stay?" Katti seemed fascinated by the way there was no need for pins to keep the bits of cotton fabric in place.

"I really don't know. It has something to do with flannel being fuzzy." Theo pointed to the fabrics in the upper left corner. "Will you switch those two?"

Katti did and stepped back.

Theo handed her a stack of squares. "You can use these to fill in the holes. It doesn't matter where you put them." While Katti was busy with the project, Theo began straightening up her mess a bit. In place of the book she'd been reading, a six inch tall, green porcelain frog stared at her. It sat on its own lily pad. Theo studied it. The frog wore a crown that looked like real gold and was set with jewels, emeralds and sapphires. "Katti?"

"I come."

Theo pointed to the frog.

"Oooh, is pretty." Katti gently touched the crown with one finger. "Where you get?"

"I was hoping you might tell me."

"Never see before." Katti frowned. "You asleep. I go eat."

Theo thought Katti looked worried. "It's okay. I think I can guess. Did you see a little old woman in the shop?"

"Yes, yes." Katti held her hand at chest level. "Very small. I see her go out door."

Miss Flossie. Theo explained the elderly woman's exchange policy. "I guess I get to keep the frog until Sunday. By the time I get my book back, I may have to start reading it all over."

Carl Lee Cashdollar arrived in Tony's office minutes after Tony himself. The tall, thin attorney was the mayor's nephew. Not a particularly handsome man, Carl Lee looked somewhat the worse for wear this morning. Bloodshot eyes and a general appearance of fatigue were emphasized by the man's fresh tan.

"Welcome back." Tony waved to the visitor's chair. "How was Hawaii?"

"It was lovely." Yawning, Carl Lee covered his mouth with his hand. "But the time zone changes about ate me alive. I don't know whether to eat or sleep. I feel like crawling under my desk and taking a nap." He reached into the leather case at his feet and extracted a large manila envelope marked with stamps and postal stickers. "This is for you."

Tony took the envelope and examined it. From Mr. Beasley to Carl Lee. The envelope was mailed over a week prior, like the hospital donation. This envelope was fat and had required Carl Lee's signature. Tony dumped the contents on his desk. A separate small envelope addressed to him fell out, along with a copy of Mr. Beasley's will. Tony lifted it and looked at Carl Lee. "Tell me."

"There's a large bequest to Blossom." Carl Lee's smile was genuine. "She gets his house, the furniture, the car and a sizeable chunk of money."

Tony thought it sounded fair. She deserved it. "And the rest? Blossom's been getting cranky calls from the relatives."

"They won't like it, but the will's totally iron clad." Carl Lee clasped his hands together. "His creditors, if you will, have their loans forgiven. The list is in my office. The folk museum gets a chunk of cash." He hesitated. "And there's one more."

Tony mentally braced himself. Carl Lee's expression was unreadable. Why was the man acting so weird? "What?"

A slight smile appeared on the attorney's face. "He bought a new vehicle for your wife."

"No way." Tony would never have guessed. "Why?"

The last of Carl Lee's composure cracked, and he starting laughing. "He said something about it being a way to irritate you at the same time he paid her back for what he called 'her many kindnesses.' He said every time you see it, you'll think of him."

"I'm sure he's right about that." Tony sliced open the small, sealed envelope. It detailed Beasley's plan to end his life. He handed it to Carl Lee. "Did you know what he'd planned?"

"No. I knew his health was failing, but he never indicated anything like this." Carl Lee read through the note. "I think he timed it to arrive while I was out of the office."

# Big As a Mountain Mystery Quilt

## THIRD SET OF CLUES

**Block C** — The initial cutting for this step included an extra strip of each fabric. You may or may not need any part of them. It depends on your fabric's actual width. Use them to make extra partial segments if you need them.

Place a 2 3/8″ strip of fabric #1 right side together with a 2 3/8″ strip of fabric #2. Sew together along one long edge. Repeat with 3 more sets. Press to fabric #2. Cut into 72 — 2 3/8″ wide 2 patch units. Label #1+2.

Sew together 2 sets by the same method as above, using 2 3/8″ strips of fabric #1 and fabric #3. Press to fabric #3. Cut into 36 — 2 3/8″ wide 2 patch units. Label #1+3.

Sew together 2 sets, again by the same method, 2 3/8″ strips of fabric #3 and fabric #4. Press to fabric #3. Cut into 36 — 2 3/8″ wide 2 patch units. Label #3+4.

Combine the 72 2 patch units #1+2s — turning one opposite in each set. Sew into 36 four patches. Stack all in same direction and press seam to one side. Repeat process combining #1+3s and #3+4s, making 36 four patches with 3s on diagonal. with 1 and 3 touching on diagonal. Press seam to #3+4.

Lay out the four patches with fabric #2 in upper left corner, and #4 in upper right corner. Sew together. Make 36. Press seam to #3+4. Make two stacks, turning to line up #2 on diagonal and sew together. Make 18 checkerboard blocks.

Cut the 6 1/4" squares of fabric #1, once on the diagonal making 72 generous triangles. Sew onto checkerboard blocks, first sewing opposing corners — fold long edge of a triangle and finger press to make center. Line up with center of checkerboard. Sew. Press away from center. Sew remaining corners. Press.
Trim to 11". Label these — Block C.

# CHAPTER EIGHTEEN

"Isn't a Tuesday afternoon a strange day and time for a wedding?" Tony buttoned the collar on his dress shirt, getting ready to add a tie. He was not going to wear his uniform to this event. With any luck, there wouldn't be a single crime committed on Mike and Ruby's wedding day. Tuesday or not.

"No stranger than having it on the back porch of Ruby's Café." Theo fastened her necklace, then checked her appearance in a hand mirror. "Hey, it's Ruby's wedding, and she can have it anywhere she wants." She fluffed her hair. "I have it on good authority it's so Dammit can be best man — or should I call him best dog?"

"You don't think she's marrying Mike so she gets half ownership of his monster bloodhound, do you?" Tony loved to tease Mike and Ruby about the dog. In fact, he himself was one of the dog's biggest fans.

Dammit was always welcome in his office, drool and all.

Theo shook her head, but laughed softly. "As much as I'm looking forward to seeing the big dog dressed for a wedding, I'm even more excited to meet, even though unofficially, Ruby's little girl, Angelina."

"I agree." Tony knew what Theo's "unofficial" part meant. The girl had only been told part of the story. She didn't need to know, as least not yet, that Ruby was her birth mother. Or that her father stole her from Ruby and gave her to his family and told them to give her away. She didn't even need to know Ruby had named her Anna, not Angelina. One thing at a time. At least, according to Mike, the girl and her family were becoming friends with Ruby and him.

"Have you met the adoptive parents?" Theo hadn't and was intensely curious.

"Briefly," said Tony. "Mike gave the whole family a tour of the station, including my office. They carried a few papers to be signed and notarized, so Ruth Ann and I obliged. Mike and Ruby are willing to make the adoption absolutely legal."

"What did the family use before, like when they signed her up for kindergarten?"

"Don't forget, sweetheart, the family thought it was already legal. They were told the old lady had the right to find the girl a new home and family. The birth certificate was real."

"And the rest of the documents?"

"Forgeries. Good ones."

Theo sat watching Ruby finish dressing for her wedding. The women had taken over the café storeroom, even hanging a full length mirror, turning it into a proper dressing room. The café closed shortly after the noon rush and friends and members of Mike's extended family quickly began decorating, spreading tablecloths, tying bows on the chairs, setting bowls of flowers on the tables. Gus and Tony were busy installing a redwood archway with Gus doing the work and Tony just supplying some extra muscle.

Outdoor heaters on the patio would make it a beautiful place to sit, overlooking the mountains. Not even Ruby, as much as she adored the bloodhound, was willing to let the dog into her café.

Delicious smells wafted from the kitchen where Blossom and her sister Daffodil worked together on the wedding feast. Theo's stomach rumbled.

Theo thought Ruby, legally Maria Costello, was easily the most beautiful woman in East Tennessee. Ruby, while preparing for this wedding, did everything the way she wanted it to be done. The dress she chose was a peachy brown silk sheath with a jacket. Her high heeled shoes were bronze leather and totally gorgeous. They almost matched the color of the best dog.

Ruby poked another hairpin into the wreath of creamy roses on her head. "After the wedding, Mike and I are going to have my name changed. I'll be legally Ruby Ott. I'm not interested in tradition, Theo, and I don't want to hold on to anything from my old life except my little girl."

"She's a beauty, just like you, inside and out." Theo reached for Ruby's hand. "I can't tell you how happy I am she has been loved and raised by such a nice couple."

"Yes." Ruby's smile was undimmed by tears. "They are her parents, truly, and I am happy to be their friend. Mike and I will have children together, and they will grow up knowing her as a friend, not a sister."

"Your decision?"

"Absolutely, yes." Ruby laughed. "Today, for her birthday, I get to throw a grand party and share a cake with her. This morning she opened a present from me, not the last she'll get, but the first."

"Then I wish you nothing but joy." Theo

plucked at her silky blue jumper, grateful Lila had picked it out for her. It was perfect. "You, Ruby, my dear friend and non-traditionalist, are getting married with one attendant sitting in a wheelchair wearing a tarp, and the other attendant is a blood-hound. You deserve nothing but the best."

"Thank you," Ruby said as she placed a wreath of peach roses on Theo's hair. "Did I mention, it's a lovely tarp?"

Tony thought the wedding was brief but elegant. The weather cooperated and the afternoon was warm and sunny. The glorious view from the sheltered deck was of the Smoky Mountains wearing a patchwork of autumn colors and their characteristic blue haze. Folding chairs were decorated with white covers and big peach-colored silk bows. Most of the citizens of Silersville either sat on the porch or stood surrounding the back of the café. Everyone was invited. Extra tables and a dance floor were in the parking lot.

Wade stood next to Mike, holding Dammit's leash in one hand, the rings in the other. Dammit had a peach satin bow tie clipped to his collar.

Theo sat, of course, holding Ruby's flowers. Tony thought she was as pretty as the bride.

While his mom sat next to him, with Chris and Jamie, Tony was surprised to see his Aunt Martha sitting with a man. A man he didn't recognize. He leaned close to his mom, "Who is Martha's date?"

"Oh, his name is Orlando Espinoza." Jane craned around until she could see her sister and her date. "He's been spending a lot of time at the museum. Claims he's working on a book about the area."

"You don't believe him?" Tony thought Mr. Espinoza resembled an old-fashioned melodrama villain with his slicked back hair and pencil mustache.

"Maybe." Jane smiled. "I'm just surprised she invited him to the wedding."

Tony looked across the aisle at Blossom. She sat between Kenny Baines and Du-Wayne Cozzens, one man per hand. Tony had watched her set up the wedding cake. Then she vanished and came back wearing a ruffled lavender dress. It made her magnificent proportions appear even greater. If the expressions on her suitors' faces meant anything, they were delighted by the situation. There was enough to share.

Tony was especially happy to see Ruth Ann sitting with her husband, Walter. After months of physical therapy, he was doing quite well. He'd overheard her say she thought her mother-in-law could go home any time and leave them to lead their own lives.

He was a bit distracted when Claude and Katti Marmot arrived. Claude was clean and shaved and wearing slacks and a starched shirt. And a tie. Tony couldn't decide if the man was strangling or not, but he was smiling at his brightly-dressed new wife. For her part, Katti was a festival of pinks.

And Sheila. Tony hoped she didn't get called in to work. He was so accustomed to seeing her in uniform with her hair in a tight braid, he almost hadn't recognized her with her hair down in loose curls, wearing a dress. She had a date, but it looked like a line was forming with guys vying for her attention.

Doctor and Mrs. Nash sat near the front, right across the aisle from Tony. With them was a young woman. She wasn't one of the Nash girls. In fact, she was totally unfamiliar to him. He liked to think he could remember faces if not names.

The woman laughed at something the doctor said as she smoothed a strand of windblown hair away from her face. On her left hand ring finger, a sapphire ring twinkled in the sunlight.

After the vows, the party began.

The bride and groom, leaving Dammit sitting next to Theo's wheelchair, waltzed together on the makeshift dance floor surrounded by portable heaters and colored lights. Wade might have been chosen to be the best man, but Tony had the honor of dancing with the bride, standing in for the father she had never known. Mike and his mom made their way around the dance floor, laughing at something only they knew about. The line of men waiting to dance with Ruby stretched around the café.

Then Mike danced with many other partners including his unofficial step-daughter, Angelina. The little girl grinned and tossed her head in an uncanny echo of one of Ruby's expressions.

Tony's Aunt Martha and her exotic date made a bit of a stir. A good ten years older than Martha, Mr. Espinoza navigated her across the dance floor. He had fantastic footwork.

"He could give lessons," Tony said.

"I heard he and his former partner won big prizes on the ballroom dance circuit." A woman's voice traveled to him. He recognized it belonged to Eleanor Liston. "He's good enough to make Martha look like a dancer."

Another voice whispered. "He's from Miami."

Blossom and her beaus stepped onto the dance floor and the three of them danced together. They managed so well, Tony guessed it wasn't the first time they'd done it.

Theo found herself consumed by curiosity. The woman dancing with Wade had been sitting with the doctor. Glancing up, she saw Ruby watching too. "Who is she?"

Ruby's eyes widened. "You don't know?" A delighted grin flashed across her face. "Maybe Tony doesn't know either."

Theo shook her head.

"She's Wade's fiancée."

Theo's jaw dropped.

"Her name is Grace O'Hara," Ruby whispered. "She's a doctor."

"Wade sure can keep a secret."

Ruby nodded. "And she's sweet. And, when she finishes her residency, she'll be a pediatrician."

"No kidding." Theo rubbed her belly with an elbow. "No wonder Doc Nash is becoming such a fan of Wade's." Theo studied the young woman. She wasn't sure what color hair Grace had. It was a blend of browns, red, and blond — shiny and it bounced when she moved her head. As Theo watched, she guessed only Grace and she saw the wink from Wade that added extra color to her cheeks. "Do you think she'll want to stay here?"

"Yes," said Ruby, just as her new husband swept her onto the dance floor.

Theo watched Wade and Tony walk toward her wheelchair. When Wade smiled over his shoulder at Grace and nodded, Theo thought the incredibly attractive deputy's appearance surpassed description.

"Oh dear," she muttered quietly. "We'll have to make another wedding quilt."

Grace, following Wade's silent invitation, joined the Abernathys. "Congratulations to you both," said Theo.

Tony thought Grace was attractive in a pleasant way, if not drop-dead gorgeous like Wade. She was not tall and not tiny, but she had a fabulous, warm smile. He said, "You're the best kept secret in Park County."

Grace extended her hand. "Wade admires you very much."

"Wade's a good man." Tony liked her handshake. A glance showed Theo smiling up at Wade, talking to him. "When's the wedding?"

"Um . . ." Grace stared into his shoulder. "We're still talking about it."

Something in her expression told Tony everything he needed to know. He gave her a gentle pat on the shoulder. She looked up, meeting his eyes. He said, "Tell Wade he has to give Ruth Ann the information about when you two got married, if for no other reason than to make you his beneficiary. Being in law enforcement . . ." His words trailed off.

"If it makes you feel better," said Grace, giving him a little wink, "we haven't told anyone in Atlanta."

"I can understand why Wade didn't want to date in a fishbowl, but why the big secret now?"

She flashed him a glorious smile. "As of now, the secret's over."

Tony led Grace nearer to Theo.

Wade had pulled a chair close to Theo and sat to talk so Theo didn't have to look up. He reached into his shirt pocket and retrieved a wedding band and slipped it on. "I'm a lucky man," he said, looking at his bride.

He glanced up at Tony. "When Miss Flossie took my name pin, I was afraid for a moment she'd gotten the ring too."

"So, when was the wedding?" Theo reached to give Wade a hug. And then Grace got one.

"Two weeks ago in my hometown." Grace answered. "It was small, only my folks and Wade's because we didn't want to do the huge wedding thing, and there seemed to be no middle ground."

"And Doc Nash?" Tony guessed the idea of another doctor in town had a lot to do with the overworked doctor's new attitude toward Wade.

"We did have to let him in on our plans," said Wade.

"But not on the wedding itself," Grace broke in. "I needed to know what my options were about my medical practice."

"And they're good here?" Suddenly concerned, Tony realized if her options were not good, Wade would leave.

"Yes," said Grace. "Although Doc Nash did suggest I learn more about the dead. He says you're a body magnet."

Tony shook his head. "I think it's Wade. He's always in the neighborhood too." He gave Wade a slap on the back. "And did the doctor mention your husband's habit when he sees one?"

Before Grace could ask more, Wade swept her off to the dance floor.

# CHAPTER NINETEEN

The wedding reception was in full swing. Tony was enjoying talking football with Patrick MacLeod, whose own wedding was set for Friday. The young football coach had no delusions about the quality of his new team, but he liked the boys and claimed they were working hard. As badly as the team played when he started his job, the only way to go was up. He'd already seen a fair amount of improvement.

Tony glanced across the dance floor to see how Theo was doing. Now in charge of her favorite bloodhound, she held Dammit's leash and was laughing at something Nina was saying. Evidently, not even jet lag caused by her return from Paris was enough to keep Nina at home.

"That's not good." Next to him, Patrick's voice sounded like the voice of doom. "Really not good."

Curious, Tony turned to see him staring

at a candy apple red touring bus gliding to a stop in the overflow parking lot behind Ruby's Café.

Tony studied the million-dollar motor home. He knew the price because he'd seen it featured on some television program designed to make average people feel bad about their finances. Although no name was painted on the side of the vehicle, a mural of beautiful lilies painted in transparent white and gold adorned the exterior. Tony had seen it often as it passed through town on the way to the mansion.

Elf, also known as Easter Lily Flowers, had arrived.

The aroma of diesel exhaust wafted toward them, and Tony wondered if brimstone smelled the same.

The driver, a tall young man wearing jeans, boots and a leather vest, but no shirt, climbed down from the bus. A few strands of long, blond hair escaped his thick ponytail. Tony thought he looked like a model for the cover on a paperback romance. Very handsome and very aware of it, he unlatched a door, lowered the stairs and stood at attention. The only thing missing was a trumpet fanfare.

When the door opened and a woman stepped into the doorway, Patrick sighed deeply. "That is really, really not good." His eyes met Tony's. "She promised she couldn't come. She has a full concert schedule and to be honest, we double checked it before picking our wedding date. We hoped she'd be singing someplace as far away as Australia."

Elf continued to stand at the top of the steps, posing for photographs, before she descended, waving to the wedding guests like they were gathered to greet her. The tiny woman with pixie-like facial features and large, winsome brown eyes was easy to identify. Her picture was on music albums, billboards and frequently on the internet. Gossip clung to her like the emerald green dress she'd obviously painted on.

Tony'd had dealings with her before, not all pleasant ones. He walked over to Mike and Ruby. "I can get rid of her for you. She's got no right to crash your wedding party."

Ruby said, "It's all right. Everyone else in the county is here. Why not Elf?"

And Mike added, "How much trouble can she stir up here?"

Elf swooped through the crowd until she found Patrick, shoved aside his fiancée and flung her arms around his waist. Sobbing, she rested her face against his chest. "I had to come."

To his credit, Patrick gave her a quick hug, set her aside and locked his arms around his fiancée, holding her in front of him like a shield.

"You've met my birth mother," Patrick said loud enough to qualify as an introduction to the gathering in general.

Tony heard him whisper into Celeste's hair. "Stay, love. It's just part of her diva display. She'll move on. She's not really interested in us."

Celeste nodded and leaned back against Patrick before she extended her hand. "I'm sorry about your sister's death."

Ignoring the hand, as well as the younger woman, Elf's wide smile did not seem grief laden. The tears of a moment earlier could have been a mirage. "Well, it did give me a reason to use the fabulous loophole in my contract." She caressed Patrick's cheek. "I came for the funeral, but I get to stay for your wedding. Isn't it marvelous!"

Tony guessed the couple might not have chosen the same word to describe their feelings.

Theo watched the local musician known as Dan-the-Dulcimer Man edge through the crowd, his eyes fixed on Elf.

When he was about ten feet away, the muscular bus driver stepped into his path, blocking the way. "Stay back. This is a family moment."

Next to Theo, Pops Ogle growled. "Like Dan's not part of her family."

Obeying the driver's command, the rangy, weather-beaten man stopped, waiting, his eyes focused only on the petite singer.

"He's in love with her." Nina moved closer to Theo.

Theo grinned. "I'm glad you aren't too jet-lagged to see the obvious."

"Is he Patrick's father?"

"That's certainly been one of the more persistent rumors in town." Theo studied the two men. Patrick was the taller of the two. The dulcimer man was somewhere between his late fifties and late sixties, but looked older, mainly because of his shaggy gray hair and beard stubble. Every autumn he let his beard grow out and shaved again in the spring. He lived in a small cabin above The Lodge. He kept to himself. He made dulcimers and old-fashioned wooden puzzles and toys, all by hand, and sold them to tourists and musicians.

Theo whispered. "I think Elf was about fourteen or fifteen when Patrick was born. Dan wasn't a young man. He'd been in the

Army a long time before he ever moved here. Don't you remember the excitement when she gave the baby away?"

"Yes," Nina agreed. "It was the talk of the town for months."

"He's lived in the same cabin since he arrived. He doesn't make trouble."

Nina looked from Dan to Patrick. "They don't resemble each other."

"That's true, but genetics can be funny." Theo waved at her brother-in-law. "Gus and Tony and are obviously related, but neither of them look anything like their brother Tiberius."

"And Elf is just a little older than we are," said Nina. "Can you imagine having a son as old as Patrick?"

"Not exactly." Theo patted her belly. "I'm not sure I'm old enough to be the mother of little ones."

The stand-off between Elf's driver and the dulcimer man ended when Elf herself dashed between them and stopped, facing Dan. She smiled almost shyly at him. He opened his arms, and she gave a little jump and wrapped her arms around Dan's neck. His arms closed around her, holding her until the driver turned and left, anger contorting his attractive face.

"Well, I guess she showed him who's her

favorite." Nina began pushing Theo's wheel-chair away from the couple.

"I just hope Dan isn't being used to make the driver jealous." Theo glanced at the couple again. Elf was back on her own feet. "He's a nice man and deserves better."

Martha and Jane moved over to chat with Theo and Nina. "What if Elf stops the wedding on Friday?"

The pair seethed with worry and excitement. Theo understood. The grand unveiling of their museum was taking place in less than a week as part of the wedding reception. The two of them had battled termites, weather, a little murder, not to mention some assorted squabbles with donors and supporters.

They had begged and borrowed to get funding and family treasures to display, acquiring both trash and treasures. Martha and Jane considered the bride-to-be, Celeste, their best find. Celeste Durand grew up in Lexington, Kentucky, the daughter of wealth and privilege, and began visiting the world's finest museums when she was a child. She majored in art history and restoration at an Ivy League university, did graduate work at the Sorbonne and finally determined she wanted to be a museum curator. She especially loved preservation and display.

Theo first met Celeste when the Kentucky native came to Silersville to complete work on her master's degree in museum organization. Celeste rented a room in Martha's house. It hadn't taken long before she was dating Patrick, who had years earlier been Celeste's older brother's college roommate. Actually his presence answered a few unspoken questions about why she chose this town's small folk museum over some more prestigious museum's offer.

They chose, after only a couple of months, to marry and make Silersville their permanent home.

Not only to marry but to combine their wedding with the grand opening of the museum. Two buildings were completely ready. Or close enough to get by.

The main museum building, constructed by Tony's brother Gus and his crew, housed the quilt display, including their locally famous "murder quilt," as well as bits and pieces of the area memorabilia and artifacts. Cradles, medical instruments, garden tools, butter churns — if it had survived hard usage, it was left on the museum doorstep.

The women worked long and hard setting the museum in order. They dusted and labeled and catalogued for countless hours. The second building was a reconstructed barn with one of the original advertisements painted on the roof. "See Rock City." The dismantling, preserving and reassembling had entertained Gus and his construction crew for weeks.

On Friday, the wedding vows would be exchanged in the Methodist Church for a limited number of guests. The reception, however, would be in the museum barn on a fresh plywood floor, part of which was currently being used at Ruby and Mike's reception. The main museum display building would be open for the guests to visit. Food, drinks and dancing would stay in the barn. Besides every resident in Park County, a huge contingent was expected from Kentucky. Every motel room and guest cabin in the area was reserved. The Lodge was staying open until the first of November, just to accommodate the wedding guests.

Everything was set. The caterer from Knoxville had been contracted to supply a kitchen trailer complete with ovens, burners and refrigerator with all the food and beverages, tables, chairs, tablecloths, napkins, china and glassware.

Silersville's local florist, Queen Doreen, put out the call to her extra workers to be ready to go to work when the huge shipment of flowers arrived. They would be making giant swags of greenery, roses, carnations and an assortment of berries, dried flowers and acres of baby's breath. The hope was to make the decorations last so they'd still be beautiful at Christmas, two months away.

The bride's parents were prepared with credit cards and a checkbook with a high starting balance.

Theo had been consulted on issues involving community protocol.

As part of the decorations, Theo had been asked to special order sixty full bolts of white tulle. Either they would be able to decorate the barn in style or the local dance teacher could make enough costumes for a production of Swan Lake, including dressing the audience.

Theo first met the mother of the bride on one of her excursions from Lexington to Silersville on fact-finding missions. Theo thought she was lovely and gracious. She also thought the mother-of-the-bride has a difficult job in many weddings. On her shoulders are wings borrowed from fairy godmothers. She is there to help her daughter achieve the wedding of her dreams. At the same time, she is supposed to protect the father-of-the-bride from bankruptcy. A difficult balancing act at times. Add in keeping the bride from nervous fits, pacifying cantankerous family members, losing that stubborn twenty pounds and finding a dress that is flattering.

Now Elf's untimely arrival and the tragedy of Scarlet's death threatened their grand plan. Theo was almost positive not even Elf could derail the wedding, but stranger things had happened.

Like Tony telling her Mr. Beasley had ordered a car for her. And paid for it. Theo couldn't believe it. Or at least she wouldn't believe it until she saw it.

Suddenly fatigued, she signaled for Tony to take her home. The sight of Blossom dancing with her two suitors made her smile. What would Blossom do with a house and plenty of money of her own? Would she still cook and do housekeeping, or would her life take a completely different direction?

# CHAPTER TWENTY

Patrick's adoptive parents, the MacLeods, arrived on Wednesday morning, perhaps twelve hours behind Elf's dramatic intrusion on Ruby and Mike's wedding. Tony knew because his mom called to complain about Elf. While Celeste had been giving her parents a private tour of the museums and explaining what she and Patrick planned for the reception, Elf arrived at the museum with her driver.

"Can't you come out here and get rid of her?" said Jane.

"Her who, Mom?" Tony really hoped she wouldn't say Elf.

"Easter Lily, of course." Jane rattled something into the earpiece. It sounded like thunder. "She has no business being here."

"What is Celeste doing about it?"

"Nothing." Jane sniffed. "I don't know what is wrong with the girl. I thought she'd have a bit more spine."

"She's probably trying to keep peace with one of her mothers-in-law to be." Not for the first time, Tony wondered how different his life would be if Theo's parents hadn't died when Theo was just a baby. He'd never had to deal with in-laws. "You ought to call Patrick's folks and have them join you all. As I understand it, the MacLeods are staying with her mother. She lives just down wind of Nellie Pearl. I'm sure they'd welcome a reason to get away from the smell of camphor."

"Ha, ha, ha."

Before Tony could think of something else to irritate his mother with, she whispered into the phone, "Never mind. Not only are the MacLeods here, but your wife and Katti just arrived."

Katti coasted up to the handicapped space, hung the blue wheelchair tag on the rear-view mirror and jumped out of the pink Cadillac. She pointed a finger at Theo. "You stay. I find peoples."

Theo laughed and saluted. Katti was born to lead. She was going to organize herself and Claude and probably the whole dump before Christmas. She and Theo had come to check on the quilts designated for display and find appropriate storage for the rest. To celebrate Celeste's wedding, they wanted to have as many wedding quilts as possible hanging for viewing during the reception. Theo had been surprised at the number that had been donated. Families were proud to have something in the museum. Some of the quilts were little more than worn out rags, and some looked pristine, like the couple had never used them.

Theo's personal favorites were the ones so worn that it was difficult to identify many of the fabrics. They were well-loved quilts.

Katti trotted back from her fact-finding mission and opened the trunk to retrieve Theo's wheelchair. "Here too is all the parents." She grinned. "Fighting is in barn. We go there?"

Tamping down the nosy side of her nature took a bit of work. Theo finally shook her head. "No. We are going into the museum."

"Too bad." Katti helped Theo out of the car with natural expertise. "More fun where yelling is."

Katti needn't have worried about missing the family battle, Theo thought when the group consisting of the bride and her parents, the groom's parents and the groom's birth mother burst into the museum building. Everyone was talking. No one was listening. The six people created enough sound to drown out what Theo was saying to Jane.

Her mother-in-law's eyes filled with tears. "I don't think this is going to work out." She sniffled. "What if Celeste quits?"

"Where do you get these ideas?" Theo patted Jane's shoulder. "Celeste might do away with a couple of Patrick's relatives, but she's not leaving the museum. She loves it here. I've seen her face when she is setting up an exhibit. She can't stop smiling."

Jane's reply was drowned out by a scream coming from the doorway.

"I am his mother, and you will do as I say!" Elf stormed across the gift shop toward the quilt display. As if reading Theo's mind, Katti stepped into Elf's path, sending the irate woman in another direction. "It needs more flowers. I'll order them myself. It still looks like a barn!" Leaving a trail of perfume almost visible in the air, Elf charged past Katti, a cell phone pressed to her ear.

Theo heard the door slam. Then silence. Finally, Celeste's voice could be heard. She sounded calm and gracious. "I want you all to meet my friend Theo. She's our museum's quilt expert."

Five people gathered near Theo's worktable. "Hello." Theo studied their faces. The bride was still smiling. Always a good sign.

The couple she didn't know was introduced as Celeste's parents, the Durands. Their smiles looked a bit strained. The Mac-Leods, she remembered from when they lived in the area. The MacLeods weren't smiling at all.

Theo didn't blame them. The wedding was only two days away and Elf as a surprise guest had its drawbacks. Theo suspected the area florists were about to get a lot of business.

Tony stared at the reports on his desk. It was a tall stack, almost burying his new super-jumbo sized jar of antacids. He wondered when he would be able to order them in a fifty-gallon barrel. It would save a lot of time, and hopefully money, if he could trot into the storeroom with a gallon pickle jar and a scoop each morning and get his day's supply.

Okay, so he was stalling. The reports had to be read, and he guessed if any of them had a little sticky note with the words "Here's your killer" on it, Ruth Ann would have put it on the top. He peeked at the edges of the files. Nope. Not a single one. Whoever had strangled Scarlet LaFleur with a wire around her neck and dropped her in the shrubbery had gotten away with it. So far.

He started with the file on the top, mostly because it was the skinniest. The phantom with the .22 had been shooting again. Sheila's notes were legible and concise. He wondered why everyone couldn't be so capable.

According to Sheila, sometime during the past week, a shooter or shooters had destroyed stop signs and road signs. Shots had gone through Roscoe Morris's trailer home, which he knew about. Tony didn't know someone had apparently killed a garden gnome. One of the shots had barely missed hitting the unpopular game warden, Harrison Ragsdale. Another had barely missed hitting Nem, the elderly egg man, while he was selling boiled peanuts. A sticky note from Sheila indicated she was checking with his competitor, Old Man Ferguson. Evidently she'd heard rumors of a boiled peanut feud.

A sign near the elementary school had been victimized. Sheila had been called out to the Shady Nest, a monstrosity of a project, high on the mountain overlooking the town. According to Sheila, the front door screen on the foreman's trailer had no fewer than ten holes in it.

The shooting near the school caught his full attention. The crackpot was getting more dangerous each day. The incidents were getting more frequent and were now all over the county and in town.

Sheila reported collecting shell casings — properly bagged, tagged and sent off to be analyzed — she'd found while digging in vegetation. She lined up the shots as best she could, but her technique lacked what she referred to as "finesse and total scientific ability." There were many more holes in things than she had found the brass for.

She had a tip from an unknown source, indicating she should talk to the person shooting a rifle near the Shady Rest. Knowing the shooter was Angus Farquhar, she respectfully requested one of the male deputies check it out. If none were available or willing, she would do it herself, but not alone.

Frowning, Tony considered Sheila's request. She was not an alarmist. She was competent, clever and a fine shot. He'd never heard of her asking to be removed from any case because of her gender. He'd check this out for himself. No one was allowed to intimidate one of his staff.

The Shady Rest was the community's

nickname for the Shady Nest, which was only a marginally better name for the housing development. The plan, or so he'd been told, had been to build quality patio homes for retirees or anyone who wanted to live in a beautiful mountain setting in a maintenance-free home. The homeowner dues covered snow removal, trash, exterior painting and even such items as plumbing emergencies, light bulb changing, and landscape work.

Tony had heard a different story from his brother. Admittedly, Gus couldn't build anything substandard. Theo's wheelchair ramp was ample proof, but Tony had heard a fair amount of grumbling and had served the management of Shady Nest with legal papers from several homeowners. In short, management was being sued for everything from misrepresentation to fraud to endangerment.

As he drove up the winding mountain road, he couldn't help but notice the beauty of his surroundings. The mountains were spectacular. This was one of the most beautiful autumns in memory. He lowered his window to enjoy the scents of the season.

Then he heard it. The crack of sound only a rifle could produce. Either someone was hunting, or vandals were taking pot shots again. The sound was more in line with a .22 than with a higher caliber gun, something for deer.

He drove around the turn below Shady Nest and heard it again. *Ka-boom.* Following the sound, he turned off the road and onto a pair of ruts winding through tall grass and shrubs. *Ka-boom.* He stopped in a clearing near a cabin. Angus Farquhar sat on a ladder-back chair, on his own front porch, shooting his own pickup truck. Surrounding him was an arsenal of rifles and handguns, and next to him was a bottle of scotch, two-thirds empty.

He was wearing nothing but his unwashed underwear and lace up boots. No wonder Sheila refused to come up. The man really was a pig. He even looked like a pig. His big pink body was sparsely decorated with gray hairs, and his nose sort of turned up like a snout. He wasn't as smart as pig, though, or as fastidious about his personal grooming.

Angus had a long history of petty crimes. He also had a long history of public intoxication. It was not illegal to get drunk on your own porch or to shoot your own truck. He wasn't anywhere near the city limits.

"Angus." Tony wanted to be sure the man

knew he was not alone. "It's Sheriff Abernathy."

Angus lifted his bottle and took a big swig. He swallowed a fair amount, then spat the excess back into the bottle before offering it to Tony. "Join me?"

"Thank you, but no. I'm on duty." Tony could think of a few things he'd like less than sharing a bottle with Angus, but not many.

Angus shrugged. He lifted an old rifle and took aim at his truck. *Ka-boom.*

"Why are you shooting your truck?" Tony saw the multitude of holes in the radiator and all the antifreeze on the ground. The only thing left in the windshield was a few glass fragments. "It can't have been that much trouble."

"It ain't the truck I'm shooting." Angus glared. "It's the pack rats."

"Pack rats are causing more damage than your arsenal?"

Angus narrowed his little pink piggy eyes and spat, just missing Tony's feet. "Any of your business?"

Tony thought he could get away with killing the man. There were no witnesses. He could claim self-defense. He doubted anyone in the county would object. Someone might suggest a parade in his honor. Too bad he was saddled with a conscience.

"Are you shooting at the Shady Nest buildings?"

"Nope."

"Have you hit any of the Shady Nest buildings?"

"Nope." Angus took another swig of whiskey. "They claiming I have?"

"I'm claiming your aim could be better. It can't be over fifteen feet to the front bumper of your pickup, and I'd say you've missed more than you've hit or there would be pack rat carcasses all over the ground."

Angus spat in Tony's direction. "I want you off my land."

"I'm leaving now, Angus." Tony didn't turn his back to the pig. "But I'll come back with a warrant if I have to and drag you down the mountain, handcuffed to my bumper."

Tony noticed the days were getting shorter. Darkness came before a lot of workers made it home for the night. A fair number of 'possums, raccoons and other small creatures failed to safely cross the highway. It wasn't unusual to have several deer a night become victims of their own poor judgment and timing. The odd thing was the road kill seemed to be vanishing. He hadn't noticed there being more carrion eaters in the area. The last person he'd ask would be Harrison Ragsdale, the local game warden.

Nicknamed Hairy Rags, the man set Tony's teeth on edge. He carried a maple wood cane, shaped like a shepherd's crook, but not because he needed help walking. He carried it crook down, and he walked a fair amount, always swinging the cane back and forth, ready to hit anything in his path. The man hated animals. All kinds. He didn't like people either. Tony thought it made his choice of profession beyond curious.

Tony had tried discussing the issue of the man and his job with his supervisor. Sighs and apologies meant the man's job was safe. No one liked him. No one thought he did his job exactly as described on the spec sheets. No one was prepared to go through all the hoops required to fire him. The man would eventually retire.

In the late afternoon, Roscoe showed up at the doorway of Tony's office, dragging a highly intoxicated Quentin. "I can't take him home like this." Releasing Quentin for a moment, Roscoe's arms swung in wide circles. "He'll fall out of the truck."

The pair of them were regular visitors. Tony rose to his feet. He tried to herd the two men in the direction of the jail side of the building where Quentin could safely sleep off the alcohol. Tony looked at Roscoe. "Can't you just buckle him in and lock the door and take him home?"

"Not with Baby. He can't ride inside with my Baby." Roscoe's eyes widened when seemed to remember where he was and who he was talking to. "I mean, er, uh, that is, er, Quentin don't like my driving."

Tony's sluggish brain caught up, and he understood. Roscoe knew he couldn't legally keep the bear cub. As a rule, he walked within the law and he had been warned to not keep the bear as a pet. Tony glanced out the front window into the parking lot. Roscoe's pickup sat under one of the myriad lights, and he saw a dark figure sitting in the passenger seat, wearing an orange vest and a wide brimmed orange hat. The arm extending from the cab looked dark and furry. Even from this distance, Tony could see long claws drumming on the outside of the door.

As Tony watched, entertained by Roscoe's ursine passenger, Hairy Rags drove in, parked next to Roscoe's truck, emerged without looking at the glossy furry arm and strode toward the station. He was swinging the cane double time. He charged through the front door and at a nod from Tony, the desk officer unlocked the door into Tony's wing of the building.

Roscoe made a whining sound and Quentin staggered, almost falling. Tony grabbed Quentin's arm and steadied them all. He glared at Roscoe. "You've got to release the bear into the wild." Not waiting for a response, Tony led his little group toward the game warden. "Good evening."

Pointing at Roscoe with his cane, the warden said, "Arrest that man."

"For what?" Tony kept moving forward.

Quentin began singing. "Oh, love —"

Roscoe's eyes filled with tears and he tried to get behind Tony.

"He's got a bear."

Irritated by everything about Hairy Rags, Tony just stared. "This is Quentin Mize, not a bear, and he's going to the drunk tank for a while."

Angered by Tony's attitude, the warden made a jabbing motion with the tip of his cane, almost striking Roscoe. That was too much for Tony. He dropped Quentin's arm and grabbed the cane in the middle of its long side and gave it a good jerk.

Hairy fell forward, releasing the cane so he could break his fall. "It's mine."

Tony placed one foot on the man's shoulders, shoved Quentin and Roscoe toward the front desk where Flavio Weems sat, eyes wide. "Lock up the drunk one — let the other go."

Flavio leapt into action.

Tony watched Roscoe almost fly back to his pickup, his skinny arms and legs churning. Tony waited until he saw the headlights come on before he stepped back. "You can get up."

"Give me my cane." Hairy didn't budge.

"No." Still incensed that the man had the gall to practically assault him in his office, Tony wasn't about to back down. "No."

Hairy's eyes narrowed and his lip curled up over his teeth. "I'll have you arrested."

"Try." Tony felt like slamming a fist into the man's jaw, but didn't.

"He's stealing road kill to feed a bear. Do you know how many laws he's breaking?"

Ignoring part of the man's question, Tony snapped back. "Do you have any proof?"

"You're helping him. That makes you as guilty as he is."

"I'll tell you what I'm doing." Tony reached down and lifted the man to his feet but didn't hand over the cane. "I'm trying to determine who murdered a woman. Do you think your road kill issue is more important?"

"No, but . . ." Hairy Rags narrowed his eyes until they were mere slits. "They're breaking the law, and you're an accessory."

"Just no." Tony handed the cane to him. "You stay out of my way, and I'll tell you if I learn anything I think you need to know."

Hairy wrapped his hand around the crook. "If I catch Roscoe with that bear, I'll arrest him."

"What about the bear?"

"You don't need to know." Hairy's mouth turned down into a repulsive expression.

It sealed the deal. Tony decided he would help Roscoe feed the bear if he had to collect road kill himself. This hate-filled man planned to execute it, whether it was his job or not.

The funeral of Scarlet LaFleur was a quiet family affair. Sort of. Theo saw many members of the Flowers clan arrive to pay their respects and have a family reunion of sorts. Interestingly, the relatives of Autumn Flowers, including Blossom, sat on the opposite side of the aisle from Scarlet's father, Summer. Added to the mixture were some of Elf's fans, who seized the opportunity to sit near their idol. There were semi-professional mourners who attended every funeral in Park County. And then there were a few, like Theo, who weren't sure they should be there, but didn't feel right not attending.

Theo sat near the middle in her wheelchair with Katti on the pew next to her. Only because she was watching for him did she see Tony arrive late and stand in a corner in the very back of the church.

"Why no one cries?" Katti was dressed in a festival of pinks again, but this time each had a black background.

"I don't know. Maybe no one's sad." Theo couldn't think of a better explanation. "Scarlet turned her back on the Flowers family and changed her name."

"She not love family?"

"Maybe. Maybe not," Theo whispered. "I think the biggest argument was between Scarlet and Elf."

"What is this Elf?"

"Remember her from the museum?" Theo pointed out the woman in question, draped in acres of black chiffon, sitting with her son, and explained. "It's been years since the sisters had a big public argument and Scarlet moved away. Later she got married and changed her name. I was surprised Scarlet planned to attend Patrick's wedding."

"She not like sister's son either?" Katti wiggled on the pew, trying to see the family members sitting in the front.

Theo considered the question. Scarlet and her sister seemed to have a rift, but the embroidery expert had said she cancelled classes under contract for over a year in order to attend the wedding. Not only to attend, but to spend over a week before the event in Silersville.

Maybe there was no feud.

Or maybe Scarlet hadn't been feuding with Elf.

# Chapter Twenty-One

Thursday morning, Tony measured the pile of folders stacked on his desk. Two and a half feet and rising. Reports continued to arrive. The toxicology report on Scarlet was complete. The woman had nothing extra in her system. No drugs of any kind. No exotic poison.

Why not leave the body in the room? Or, why wait so long to move it? Was there a killer and an accomplice?

He considered the list of hotel guests and employees. Only a few looked strong enough to snap the woman's neck, although strength wasn't really required; it was more a matter of finesse.

And why hadn't the person left anything but an oil stain behind? Was it too much to hope for a witness to be out strolling in the woods and look up in time to see the killer? As long as Art was skulking around in the woods, couldn't he have helped out?

His frustration mounting, Tony spent the day at his desk, digging through file folders.

Theo and Tony were invited to the wedding rehearsal and the dinner following it because of Theo's friendship with Celeste and the work they were doing together at the museum. The dinner would be in the private dining room of the River View Motel.

Saving her blue jumper for the wedding, Theo dressed in her prettiest top and a skirt with an elastic waistband. Since she'd be sitting in her chair, it wouldn't matter how lumpy it looked. She combed her unruly hair and even put on some makeup.

Tony came downstairs wearing slacks and a nice shirt. He was carrying a couple of ties and waved them in her direction. "Do I need to wear a tie tonight?"

"I don't think so." Theo made a show of displaying her own costume, including the wheelchair. "I'd hate for you to be way dressier than I am. If you wear a tie, I'll have to weave crepe paper in my wheels."

"Sold." Tony tossed the ties onto Theo's new bed and grabbed the handles of the wheelchair. "Let's roll."

The boys barely glanced up as they said goodnight. Their teenaged babysitter, Karissa Sligar, was beating them at their own video game. It looked to Theo like they might still be playing when they returned. Theo hoped they remembered to blink occasionally. "Don't forget it's a school night." Only Karissa looked up. She nodded.

Tony rolled Theo down the new ramp to the Blazer and helped her in. "So, how do you like your wheels?"

"I love them. It's amazing how much better I feel when I'm not standing." Theo relaxed into the car seat. "Speaking of new wheels, when do you suppose I'll get the vehicle Mr. Beasley ordered?"

"I just hope it's not the twin to your hopeless minivan." Tony frowned. "Knowing Mr. Beasley, he probably ordered something you'll fit in and I won't."

Theo thought the idea was hysterically funny and envisioned a tiny clown car, one barely big enough for her and the children.

She was still laughing when they rolled into the church. The wedding party was gathered at the altar, and the guests not participating in the ceremony were sort of clumped together in the back to watch and chat. She and Tony fell into the latter group.

The sanctuary was a mess. Scaffolds were set up around the perimeter, and the distinctive aroma of paint wafted in the air. The carpet was gone — not that the worn, stained, once-blue carpet would be missed. Workmen mingled with the wedding party, each group trying not to get in the way of the other and still get their work done before the ceremony.

The wedding planner called the mother of the bride and mother of the groom to come and pretend to light a single candle together. It was their only assignment and took place at the beginning of the service. Dutifully, the women walked forward, climbed the steps and stood self-consciously pretending to light a candle. The two looked well matched in similar slacks and lightweight sweaters.

"Wait!" Elf ran up the aisle in a cloud of perfume and red chiffon. "What about me? Don't I get to light a candle?"

"Who are you?" The wedding planner glanced down at her clipboard.

"I'm the groom's mother." She twirled, making the beads twinkle on her flame red cocktail dress.

The planner turned to the women standing frozen in place near the candle.

Before she had a chance to ask another question, Patrick stepped forward. "She's my birth mother and welcome guest. But . . ." He made eye contact with Elf. "She is *not* part of the ceremony."

"Noooo, Patrick, baby." Elf's wail bounced off the walls of the church.

Theo stared, admiring the way Patrick didn't break stride or appear to have heard her. He gently but firmly led her to a pew and pressed her shoulder until she sat. He whispered something only Elf could hear and returned to the rehearsal.

Theo wouldn't say Elf behaved for the rest of the time. She frowned. She sighed. She tapped her foot. Her fingers flew over the buttons on her cell phone, making Theo think someone was getting an irate text message.

To Theo, Elf looked younger than she had the last time she'd visited, making Theo wonder if she had a magic elixir or great genes or a really fine plastic surgeon. Elf was only a few years older than Theo herself, but she looked amazing. The hours she kept and the stamina involved in touring and performing did not show on her face or body. It made Theo tired just thinking about her schedule.

Celeste's mother was naturally elegant. She looked like the kind of woman who never spilled coffee on herself — or on anything, for that matter. Theo glanced at the smudge of pizza sauce on her sleeve, disgusted by her own messy approach to life. She must have brushed against the box on the kitchen table.

On the other side of the aisle, Patrick's mother fell somewhere between Theo's mess and the mother of the bride in personal appearance. Theo suspected the lines of tension in her face were directly related to the woman now sitting in the pew behind her. Although they'd all lived in Silersville at the time of Patrick's birth, the family had moved away before Patrick started school.

Theo could imagine if Elf, her sister Scarlet, and their father, Summer Flowers, was the family package attached to the adopted baby, moving all the way to Shanghai to put some distance between them would be very appealing.

Once the fight with Elf ended, the rehearsal went quickly, the service would be traditional. The three bridesmaids and the groom's attendants were on time and learned where to stand and when to move. The wedding planner had everything under control and treated the wedding like a military operation.

After the brief rehearsal, the wedding party and guests were to drive out to the museum for a decorating party. Dinner at the River View Motel, would follow.

The barn where the food service and

dancing would take place was empty. A fresh plywood floor had been laid over the ground. The stalls were framed with fresh boards. The ceiling was open to the hayloft. Theo thought the place smelled fresh and woody.

Elf's perfume preceded her, obliterating the pleasant aroma. "What are we doing here?" Elf's voice whined into Theo's ear.

"Helping decorate for the reception." Theo tried to maneuver her wheelchair away from Elf wondering if the woman swam in the perfume. Theo had been intensely curious about the bride's decorating plan from the moment Celeste came into the quilt shop to order myriad bolts of tulle.

"Really?" Elf sounded stunned.

Theo was sure Elf wasn't feigning surprise. She considered it highly unlikely Elf would be interested in anything not connected with herself. "Yes, it's all part of the event." She pointed to the center of the floor where a large white hoop was surrounded by bolts of fabric and piles of twinkle lights. "Those are for the ceiling."

No sooner had she explained than the small army of volunteers received instructions from the wedding planner. Each of six teams immediately tied the free end of the tulle to the hoop amid much laughter and pushing, everyone vying for space. Once the tulle was set, each team worked to wrap strands of twinkle lights around the fabric, one person unrolling the fabric from the bolt and the other wrapping lights, moving outward from the hoop.

Then came the stepladder brigade. The tallest men, including Tony and Gus, lifted the hoop, climbed the stepladders and attached it to the hayloft. Another group of stepladder workers fastened the free ends of the tulle and light swags to the walls, forming a series of spokes. Each swag was attached to a white extension cord. The effect was lovely when the lights came on.

Theo was helping hang more swags of tulle and lights on the half walls of the stalls when she saw Tony talking into his cell phone. It must have rung immediately after the center was stabilized. Then she saw him talking to his brother, glancing over his shoulder in her direction. She immediately understood. Tony was leaving, and Gus and Catherine would take her to the restaurant if he wasn't back in time.

Tony hoped Sheila's call would mean he would only be gone for a few minutes. Evidently Nellie Pearl Prigmore's daughter in Los Angeles had tried to get her mother on the telephone. Since Nellie Pearl hadn't answered, the daughter called Sheila. Sheila had gone to the house and gotten no answer to her knocks. Sheila knew Nellie Pearl well enough to guess the old woman would shoot anyone besides herself or the sheriff.

Sure enough, when Tony joined her, the business end of a .22 slipped under the sash window and a bullet whizzed past his ear. He jumped behind the Blazer. Sheila joined him.

"What do you want to do?" Sheila whispered.

"Nothing legal." Tony felt adrenaline racing through his system. He thought he heard Sheila chuckle.

"Believe me, since I became her unofficial keeper by default, I've considered several options along those lines." Sheila edged closer to the house. "I'll try talking to her again."

"If she takes a pot shot at you, I *will* shoot her." Tony wished Wade was there because he was a much better shot. "You're worth fifty of her."

"Ms. Prigmore," Sheila yelled. "Your daughter called us. She's worried about you."

The next thing Tony heard was the rifle firing again and then the thud made by a bullet plowing into a tree. He muttered into Sheila's ear. "That's not helping my attitude."

"She's been getting worse each time I come by." Sheila edged back, frowning and shaking her head. "I say at least one of her daughters needs to come deal with it. Maybe we can get her committed on a temporary basis. She's a danger to us and to herself too."

Tony had an idea. "I'll go low and around to the left and come up under the window. The way she has the barrel sticking out, I'll be able grab the end of it. You keep your head down and distract her."

"Sounds good."

Thankfully, Tony's plan worked like a charm. Tony held the barrel tight so Nellie Pearl couldn't take aim. She did fire two more shots, which heated up the metal, but he was not letting go. Sheila slipped up next to him, shoved the window open, and using him for a ladder, climbed inside.

Tony, who had a fair vocabulary of profanity when needed, found himself amazed at the old woman's repertoire. For a moment he actually thought he saw the air turn blue.

Tony returned from Nellie Pearl's in time to drive Theo and himself to dinner. Theo didn't exactly ask him where he'd been. She just studied him quietly, her green gold hazel eyes missing nothing. She grinned.

"You might ask Sheila to wipe her feet if she's going to use you for a ladder."

Tony glanced down at his navy slacks. Sure enough, a dirty footprint, definitely woman-sized, showed where Sheila had stepped. He wiped it with his handkerchief then handed it to Theo and turned his back. "You might want to check my right shoulder blade."

The River View Motel Restaurant and, by extension, the private dining room was the best place to eat in town. Not fun and casual like Ruby's Café, the River View was as close to elegant as Silersville got. Tony thought their prime rib was the best he'd ever eaten and he'd done a fair amount of research over the years.

The wedding party and all the parents, including Elf, were ushered to the large tables closest to the wall of glass separating the dining room from an amazing view of the creek and the Smoky Mountains beyond. Although it was almost completely dark, the last rays of sunshine made the old mountains and forest look huge and mysterious. Suddenly over a hundred strands of tiny lights switched on, and the trees belonging to the motel turned into a fairyland.

Tony guessed there were about fifty guests like them who were not part of the wedding party. It surprised him until he realized the celebration was as much a reunion of family and friends as rehearsal dinner. The MacLeod clan was in full attendance, as well as assorted extras.

Since Theo seemed to be ravenously hungry about twenty hours out of each day, she looked delighted when it was time to move into the River View Motel's private dining room. Tony found a place at a table on the perimeter where it was easy to park Theo's wheelchair and settled onto his own chair.

Tony thought the lines etched into the face of the official mother of the groom were getting deeper. Seated across the table from her was Elf. Tony was close enough to overhear her comments.

"The River View is a dump. You know it and I know it." Elf studied her napkin and her lip curled. "It's cotton. Couldn't you have at least gotten linen?"

To her credit, Mrs. MacLeod refrained from answering. Tony wondered how she managed to stay silent. Maybe she was considering taking up vivisection as a hobby.

"We could use some more candles." Elf

waved her hand at the table decorations. "Maybe something scented."

Mrs. MacLeod stayed silent, but Tony heard Theo's voice. "I don't think I could stand one more floral scent."

Elf fluffed her hair and adjusted, by pulling even lower, the already deep neckline on her red dress before leaning across Mrs. MacLeod to speak to her husband. "I hope the wine's finer than the décor, but maybe you don't think much of the bride."

Tony thought he heard the man say, "I hope you choke on the cork."

As the evening continued, so did the verbal battle between Elf and the MacLeods. After dessert, Theo leaned close and whispered, "I think there might be shooting. Did you wear your body armor?"

"No. Would you feel safer at home?" Tony thought his wife looked tired.

"Yes, but mostly I want to go to bed. It's been a long day."

Tony certainly couldn't argue with her observation. He felt about a hundred and two.

# CHAPTER TWENTY-TWO

Tony promised, even if his day was overfull, to take time away from his job to escort Theo to the wedding and reception. After the tension he'd noticed during the previous evening's rehearsal and the dinner following, he thought a police presence at the wedding might be required. Maybe he should arrange to borrow some officers from neighboring counties. A SWAT team would be a decorative touch. Maybe he could call in the National Guard.

There wasn't much new in their investigation into Scarlet's death. They had contacted the police in San Francisco, where Scarlet lived, asking for any information about her that could possibly be relevant, like threats or complaints by her or about her. Nothing yet.

He got a phone call from the Shady Nest complaining about the shots coming from across the valley. Most likely it was Angus shooting his truck again. Someone, not Sheila, needed to check. Just in case it wasn't Angus.

Mid-morning, Blossom showed up with an apple pie. He felt pathetically grateful she hadn't decided to quit baking for him just because she had a busy social life and an inheritance. "Thanks for the pie." He shifted a stack of papers to make room for it. "What's the occasion?"

When she squeezed into one of the visitor chairs in his office, he realized she was not just sightseeing. Blossom had a mission. She shifted in the chair, not an easy feat because she filled every inch of it, and fluffed the puffy sleeves on her voluminous floral dress. "I was wondering." She stopped speaking and stared, chewing something like a cow with its cud. Then she stopped chewing and sat staring at him with one finger pressed against the dip below her lips. Blossom's deep thinking pose. She sighed. "Is it true it's illegal to have two boyfriends?"

"Two husbands, yes." Tony shook his head. "Two boyfriends, no."

Her eyes widened. "Really?"

"Yes, really." Tony found himself fascinated by her expression. Thoughtful, intrigued and a bit like she'd found out she owned a winning lottery ticket. "Why? Has someone told you something else?"

She nodded but didn't volunteer any additional information. She sat and smiled for a few minutes before hauling herself off the chair.

"Wait a minute, Blossom. Did you talk to Carl Lee?"

Tony knew Doc Wade had signed the death certificate calling Mr. Beasley's death a suicide. The family could squawk all they wanted to. Blossom and the children's hospital would share the bulk of the man's fortune.

"Yes." Blossom gave him her sweetest smile. "I wished I could thank Mr. Beasley. That's the nicest thing anyone's ever done for me."

Theo decided she needed a scarf or shawl to wear to the wedding later in the day. The blue dress looked lovely without a blouse but the evenings were quite chilly. She asked Katti to push her wheelchair across the street to Lila's dress shop. Once they were inside, Theo glanced up at her assistant. "Have you met Lila?"

"No." Katti closed the door behind them. "She like pink too?"

Theo laughed. "I don't know. We'll ask."

Theo quickly realized her timing was not

good. The store was filled with other shoppers, bridesmaids, Miss Flossie and now her wheelchair and Katti. One girl stood in the center of the room, in a stunning taffeta gown, while Lila worked on the back of her dress. It was only hours until the wedding. While the bridesmaid looked panicky, Lila seemed cool and relaxed.

Barely glancing up, Lila said, "Just get what you need, Theo. We'll settle up later."

So, with Katti searching for pink, Theo wheeled around the girls, studying the accessories. Pictures of Lila decorated a wall. Lila with locals. Lila with celebrities, including one with Scarlet's sister Elf and a much younger Gavin, Beth's brother. Lila as a child. One photograph made her laugh because it reminded her of Jamie. Dressed in a martial arts outfit, a very young Lila posed, her hands crossed in front of her. The grin exposed a huge gap where her front teeth were missing.

Theo reached for a silky, silver shawl and slipped it around her shoulders. It felt as insubstantial as a cobweb. She loved it. However, studying the tag, she was not sure about the cost.

Lila walked by and paused to carefully adjust the way it draped. She whispered, "Fifty percent off."

"Sold." Theo smiled, but Lila had moved on.

Katti found a wide pink leather belt with silver studs along the length. "Is pretty?"

"Absolutely," Theo agreed. They left notes on the counter saying what they took and promising to return to pay.

Tony stared at the little man sitting across from him. Where *did* Orvan get his ideas? "What do you think is going on up there?"

Orvan's initial complaint, this visit, was that a stealth bomber had landed in his cousin Otis's tobacco patch. Fifteen minutes into his discussion, his mood changed from indignant to contrite. He shifted his skinny rear end to the front edge of the chair and leaned forward, folding almost in half, and pushed himself onto his feet. Once standing, he straightened.

At attention, he saluted Tony, exposing a band of pale skin between his sleeve and the gnarled, and permanently tanned, hand and wrist.

"I have to tell you what I did."

Tony's heart sank. He'd hoped to get through a whole month without one of Orvan's tales of guilt and remorse. Instead, this was the old guy's second visit in a week. Nevertheless, there was always the hope this was the day Orvan would actually tell him something important. At least Ruth Ann would enjoy the day.

His secretary's dark eyes sparkled when he escorted Orvan toward the greenhouse, their nickname for the interrogation room. Her hand paused, letting pink fingernail polish pool on her thumbnail. In a flash she replaced the brush into the bottle. "Water?"

"Yes." Staring at Ruth Ann, Orvan's eyes went glassy with desire.

Ruth Ann used a tissue to clean up the polish.

Orvan's steps slowed further as he gazed at this goddess. His hands pressed the bib of his good overalls against his heart. "My angel," he whispered.

Ruth Ann's smile widened. "Have you been bad, Mr. Lundy?" She put an extra bounce in her step as she headed for the water.

"Yes ma'am. I have sinned."

As the three of them entered the starkly bare, tiled interrogation room, Wade arrived and set up the video camera.

Tony glanced up the clock. It was ten-thirty in the morning.

Orvan took a sip of his water and looked a bit surprised by its flavor or, more likely, its lack of flavor. He leered at Ruth Ann again.

By noon they had learned little more than before. Finally, bowing to internal pressure created by the three bottles of water he'd sucked down, Orvan leaned forward, lacing his fingers together, officially ending his social visit.

"You know them three families what live in the holler on the far side of McKee's land?"

Tony nodded.

"What they don't know is I've been awatchin' them."

A faint trickle of alarm slipped down Tony's spine. The ATF was watching them too. "Why?"

"Well, 'cause I seen them climb out of a what-you-call-it? A flying saucer."

"A flying saucer like the one on Miss Freddie's lawn?" Ruth Ann suggested. "Or Mr. Ferguson's?"

Tony guessed Miss Freddie had crossed the Atlantic on the Mayflower. The tiny woman looked too frail to lift a tea cup, but she loved to build lawn artwork from cast-offs. All bore definite signs of inspiration from old science fiction movies. Space craft of all shapes and sizes, robots, and aliens were visible from the road. She and old man

Ferguson seemed to be competing in a lawn art contest for two.

Orvan flapped his hands and shook his head. "No. Real."

"Are you confessing to spying on someone?" Tony growled in frustration. "Is this your crime?"

"No, no." Orvan stopped, holding his palms out. "I stole something from them, and I'm scared they'll kill me to get it back."

Tony tamped down the temptation to say "Good" or "I'll help them," and managed to ask, "What?"

"Dynamite." Orvan's voice shook. "There's a guy who saw me take it, and he coulda shot me but didn't. This other even meaner lookin' guy didn't see me but was staring at the one guy. You know, the one what let me take it."

"Uh-oh." Tony knew what he had to do. He stood abruptly and walked to the door. He punched a number in his cell phone as he turned and pointed at the old man. "Orvan, go home and stay there."

"I can get your man out." Tony didn't bother with pleasantries. "Send me a warrant, and a photo, and I'll drag him down the mountain like any other piece of trash. Better yet, send me details on one of your co-conspirators, too."

"What's happened?"

"One of my county's habitual idiots has been up there spying on the group. He's stolen some dynamite. *Your* man didn't shoot him." Tony hoped he wasn't over-reacting. "I have a bad feeling."

"Thank you, Tony. I'll owe you a big one."

Behind him, Tony heard the fax machine printing. He called Rex, who was thankfully in charge of dispatch. "You tell Wade and Sheila to get their rifles and tree climbing gear."

Within minutes, the three of them headed into the higher elevations and separated. When Tony learned his two snipers were in position, he drove into the heart of the terrorists. He considered them nothing but a bunch of whiny, lazy losers. Very dangerous ones.

Standing behind his open door, he called out, "Sheriff." He waved his warrants. "I'm here to arrest William Baxter and Daniel Swinborne."

A tall man dressed in full camouflage stepped around the edge of a house. He cradled an assault rifle in his arms. "You and what army?"

Tony recognized him as the leader of this group. The man had grown up around here and knew most of the members of the Sheriff's Department. Good. "Me and Wade and Sheila."

"I only see you."

"Exactly." Tony smiled. "I've got them covering me. I believe you know how effective they are with rifles." He wished the man wasn't wearing mirrored sunglasses.

"How do I know you're telling the truth?"

"Well, for starters, I can have one of them shoot you in the foot if you want proof. You won't be able to walk." Tony stopped smiling. "Give me Baxter and Swinborne and we'll all go home."

No more than two minutes after they got back to the law enforcement center and locked Swinborne in a cell and put Baxter in the drunk tank with Quentin, Rex called Tony. In his normal, unflappable voice, Rex said, "The Volunteer Fire Department went to check on a chimney fire up at the Shady Nest when they came upon a vehicle partially blocking the road. They couldn't see a driver."

"And?" Tony squeezed the receiver. It wasn't like Rex to tiptoe around something.

"They said music is blaring through the open pickup truck window. How could the driver not be deafened by it? Surely no one in the truck could hear the emergency siren or their horn. Actually, they said it didn't sound as much like music as a series of thumps, thuds and screaming that could disguise the sound of a gunshot. And it had."

"Don't tell me this." Tony thought about sticking his fingers into his ears and humming. "I don't have the time or the resources."

"Yes, sir, I do know that, but *you* need to call in the TBI if you want them to help."

"Okay, okay. Where's the pickup? I'd better go up there first."

When he, Wade and Doc Nash arrived, the radio was still blaring. The pickup sat on one of the narrow roads leading from town to the housing development on the side of the mountain. As expected, the truck sat empty.

Tony looked toward the nearest house. Smoke billowed out of the chimney and through the surrounding roof. The building was surrounded by firemen with hoses, axes and big boots. The chief waved them forward and pointed at one of the front windows.

A neat hole pierced the screen.

Tony looked inside. The main door was ajar. Even from this distance Tony could see a very similar sized hole had pierced John D. Smith, right between the eyes. The worst building contractor in the history of the profession was very dead.

Tony sighed. His brother, Gus, had suggested something like this would happen. It was only a matter of time. Smith's enemies were legion — but dead, he would never pay them one penny of any legal judgment made against him.

Mr. John Smith and his son-in-law built the units in record time. They hired day labor and paid them slave wages. Of course they got what they paid for: workers with no skills or pride in their work.

Gus had been very outspoken in the community about Smith's workmanship. His complaints were referred to by Smith as "sour grapes," since he and his son-in-law were making money hand over fist and the houses looked good. For a while. It took less than two months after move-in before the first lawsuit was filed. The foundation sank a foot. The house cracked like an egg dropped on a sidewalk. The other nine houses followed suit.

Tony knew the pickup with the obnoxious radio belonged to the son-in-law and wondered where the man had gone. The moment Tony stepped into the house, he saw the man's body. It lay on the floor crumpled in a heap not far from Smith. Tony guessed the shooter had killed the proverbial two birds with one stone, or more precisely, two bullets. The stone in this case was most likely a high powered rifle.

Across the narrow valley from where he stood, Tony could see Angus Farquhar's cabin. He was considering sending someone, or actually several someones, over to collect the man when Rex's voice came through the radio. He received a call from Darren Holt and said it was urgent Tony talk to his deputy.

Still angry at Darren, Tony called him.

"Sir, I've got an apparent suicide in a car up here."

Before Tony could ask where "up here" was, Darren continued talking.

"There's a note on the driver's side window, facing out. It claims he just killed two men up at the Shady Nest. It's addressed to you."

"No kidding." Tony waved for everyone around him to stop moving and be quiet. "Read me the whole thing."

Darren began, " 'To Sheriff Abernathy, I lost everything because of the developer known as John Smith. He cost me every penny I had, my wife and children. My home and my job. No legal means came to me, so I decided, on my own, to rid the earth of this plague. I shot him and his worthless son-in-law. The rifle is locked in the trunk of this car. Tell Nancy I will always love her and the kids, that is, unless you think telling them would make matters worse.' " Darren cleared his throat. "He signed it 'yours truly, Henrik Anderson'. There's also an address and phone number in Michigan."

"What else can you tell me about the scene? Anything?"

"Yessir. Looking through the windshield, it looks like he ate a revolver. It's still in his hand."

Tony rubbed the back of his neck. "The man addressed the letter to me, but I don't recognize the name."

Darren said, "I used to see him around sleeping in the car, but I had no idea he'd invested up at the Nest. He would move the car from place to place." There was a pause. "It has Michigan plates."

"I'll send the doctor up but it sounds pretty clear cut to me." Even though part of Tony was relieved to have the shootings easily solved, he regretted that the man had felt he had no other options.

# CHAPTER TWENTY-THREE

The Methodist Church was resplendent for Patrick and Celeste's wedding. Resplendent was the word of the day on Tony's calendar. He smiled at the apt description. When Tony was just a boy, his father, a Methodist minister, moved his family to Silersville to serve in this church and community. He'd died prematurely in a car accident.

"My dad would have loved seeing it like this," Tony whispered into Theo's ear. "I don't think it has ever looked better."

"Yes, your dad would be proud and no, I don't think it's ever been lovelier," Theo whispered back.

Nina arrived on the arm of one of the ushers. "I told him I wanted to sit with you two." She fluffed her gleaming red hair as she settled next to Tony. She flashed him a wide grin. "You look good in a suit, but I trust you've got a gun handy. I heard this might be a dangerous place today."

Tony groaned but didn't comment.

Nina wasn't fazed. She leaned over him to talk to Theo, parked in the aisle next to him. "The church looks terrific. Did the bride's parents really pay to have it painted and new carpet put in? That's what I heard."

"Yes. They were still hard at work in here during the rehearsal." Tony pointed up at the stained glass window in the front. "And they had the glass mended and completely cleaned."

"With all the gorgeous flowers, I can barely see the fresh paint." Theo shifted in her wheelchair, apparently studying the enormous but tasteful displays of roses and candles. She glanced over her shoulder toward the doors. "Speaking of flowers, Blossom's here with Kenny and DuWayne. They're getting to be quite a threesome."

Tony turned to watch the two men walking with Blossom, each clutching one of her arms. They apparently waved away the official ushers and kept their respective positions. If two escorts were company, three might be considered a crowd.

Tony thought Blossom looked as resplendent as the refurbished church. She was wearing a frothy yellow dress with big orange polka dots. When she saw him and Theo, she waggled her chubby fingers in their direction and her smile widened. After they made it past their pew, he whispered to Theo, "I think the polka dots match Blossom's hair color perfectly. What do you think?"

"I think she looks like a lovely ocean liner with a pair of tugboats guiding her out to sea."

Theo was having a wonderful time. She enjoyed weddings as a rule. When the music began, everyone settled into their pews to enjoy the event. The first notes from the organ made her eyes widen in surprise. She leaned toward Tony. "Did they buy a new organ too?"

"I guess. Or they found a magician to fix the old one."

"Must be nice to have a checkbook without limit." Theo sighed. "It's certainly improved the quality of the music."

Tony reached for her hand. "Are you sorry you didn't marry a rich man?"

Theo felt all warm and gooey inside. "Nope. I got just what I wanted." She glanced over his shoulder at the woman being escorted down the aisle. "Uh-oh. *Not* good."

"What?" Tony didn't turn.

"You'll have to see for yourself. Elf is making quite a statement."

Tony did turn then, his curiosity evidently winning out.

Theo barely heard him groan. She couldn't stop staring at Elf. The singer wore a floor length black sequined gown with the neckline plunging all the way to her waist in the front and even lower in the back. "How does it stay on?"

"She looks like a lounge singer from Las Vegas." Nina sounded shocked.

The youthful usher at Elf's side appeared to stumble against the end of the pew, but he didn't lift his eyes from the exposed cleavage.

Theo glanced to the front of the sanctuary where Patrick and the minister and groomsmen waited. With the exception of the groom, the men appeared frozen. Patrick looked murderous. He took a step forward, his hands clenched into tight fists.

The best man, the bride's older brother, reached forward and touched Patrick's arm, stopping him.

Theo thought it took an eternity before Elf stepped into her appointed spot and sat down. Theo couldn't see her face, but she guessed her expression was triumphant. If being noticed was her goal, Elf achieved it in her unique style. Not in good taste though.

The next usher escorted the official mother of the groom. In her lovely champagne beige dress, she looked happy and relaxed, except for some lines of tension around her mouth. Her husband appeared proud. As he stepped past Elf, he did glance down into Elf's cleavage display, and his cheeks flushed almost purple.

The mother of the bride maintained her elegant demeanor. Her dress of aqua silk made a quiet swishing sound as her escort led her past the other mothers and settled her into place on the other side of the aisle.

Theo held her breath, half expecting an explosion, but all she heard was beautiful music. The clear tones of the much-improved organ rang as the processional continued.

The bridesmaids' gowns, a beautiful shade of deep teal shimmering with overtones of rose, were elegant and flattering. The girls carried a fortune in flowers.

Everyone, except Elf and Theo, stood when the music changed and signaled the approach of the bride and her father. The bride was lovely, of course, and kept her eyes focused on Patrick.

Theo could see Elf, by peeking between

the standing guests. The singer slouched on her pew and crossed her arms over her almost bare bosom. Theo assumed she was not smiling.

The remainder of the ceremony went smoothly although Theo could almost feel the congregation waiting for an explosion. The bride and groom kissed, inspiring a great cheer of joy mixed with relief. The couple turned and led the way down the aisle. Elf managed to jump into the path of the groom's parents, but the MacLeods didn't appear concerned. Their part of the wedding was over. Even Mrs. MacLeod smiled, all tension relieved. The rest of the celebration belonged to the bride's family.

"How would you like to be posing for pictures with the tight-jawed wedding party?" Nina asked as they waited to leave the church.

Theo leaned toward Tony so she could speak softly, "I'm guessing Elf is not going to be in many of them."

"Or the photographer is going to alter the digital pictures and erase her." Nina's distinctive laugh drew attention from other guests.

Theo rolled her eyes and grinned. "At the very least, I'll bet he adds a bit of computer fabric to the front of Elf's dress."

Nina didn't exactly whisper when she said, "If I was in charge, I'd turn it into a turtleneck."

"What's the plan?" Tony shifted on the pew. "Are we supposed to go somewhere now or just sit in here until the fight ends?"

"And listen for the sounds of gunfire?" Nina cupped a hand to her ear.

The jests got worse. Finally Theo held her hands up in surrender. "The plan is for us, all the guests, to go out to the museum and look around and enjoy light snacks. It's supposed to be the guests' entertainment while the wedding party is driven around town in an open, horse-drawn carriage and has a thousand pictures taken."

"And Elf?" said Nina. "Do you suppose she's part of the wedding party?"

"I think she'll be lucky if they don't run her down."

Because of the large guest list and limited parking at the museum, a fleet of small buses that looked like old-fashioned trolley cars, were supplied for shuttle service. Tony opted to drive his vehicle because of Theo's wheelchair. He escorted Theo and Nina into the museum and left them with friends while he went to look for his mother. He found her sitting on one of the display

329

chairs, staring into space, ignoring the sign she had spent so much time working on. The card lay at her feet. "Do not sit here."

"Mom?" Tony didn't know if he should chastise her or not. "Are you okay?"

"Didn't the church look lovely?" Jane lifted her face and her smile was nearly as radiant as Celeste and Patrick's.

"Yes. I'm sure Dad would agree." He leaned against the wall behind him, watching as the wedding guests wandered about the museum, oohing and aahing. "I think he'd like your museum, too."

Jane glanced around and seemed to notice the crowds of people for the first time. "Oh, my." She jumped to her feet and replaced the sign. "I'd better pay attention. I'm supposed to answer questions and hand out brochures."

"I didn't see you at the church and wanted to make sure you and Martha got there for the ceremony."

"We had a lovely time even if we held our breath when Elf sashayed down the aisle in that dress. My goodness, I've never seen such a gown." She fanned herself with a brochure. "How's Theo?"

"The wheelchair is just what she needed." He helped her adjust the sign. "Have you met Katti?"

"Oh, yes. I think she's wonderful." Jane laughed. "I wonder if Claude was prepared to have her take over his life. I can't wait until we all get to go out to the dump for their wedding celebration. It promises to be lots of fun."

Theo watched Elf strut into the museum, clinging to the arm of her driver. If anything, the front of the dress looked like it had dropped even lower. At least the driver's chest was covered today with a white shirt and conservative suit.

Next to her, Nina whispered. "If she's wearing anything under the dress, it's not much. There's just about nothing left to the imagination. My ex-husband would be salivating all over her."

"Not if her bodyguard could help it." Theo studied the man. "Do you think he seems to be more than professionally involved?"

"I'm guessing she hired him as much for his looks as his bus driving talents."

"Speaking of which . . ." Theo leaned closer. "Why do you think she's staying in her touring bus instead of the mansion?"

"Is she really?" Nina looked thoughtful. "How do you know?"

"Someone mentioned it at the shop the

other day. We have our fair share of up-to-date gossip, you know."

"Well, there's certainly been a bit at the high school. The halls have been buzzing."

Since Nina taught where Patrick coached football, Theo was curious. "Don't tell me Elf followed Patrick to the field, or worse, into the locker room."

"It hasn't been quite that bad, but I heard him say if he'd known she was coming, he might have suggested they run away and get married." Nina took a beautifully decorated canapé from a passing waiter. "Mmm, caviar."

Theo selected a puff pastry tidbit filled with salmon mousse. "I don't know whether to feel sorry for Elf or slap her. It would have worked out so much better for everyone, especially the now deceased Scarlet of course, if they could have followed the original plan." Theo craned her neck to keep Elf and the driver in view.

The bride and groom made their grand entrance into the museum amid cheers and applause. The couple posed for more pictures in front of various displays. They included Elf in many photographs, but the photographer appeared quite adept at separating Elf from the other mother of the groom.

Theo guessed it helped, but she still heard an almost constant litany of complaints from Elf. She wasn't interacting with any of the guests, the bride's family or any of her own relatives.

Nina leaned over and whispered in Theo's ear. "If she doesn't quit whining, I vote we shove a sock down her throat."

# CHAPTER TWENTY-FOUR

Tony was visiting with Mr. Durand, the father of the bride, when the caterer imported from Knoxville trotted over to where they stood.

The caterer's face was taut and furious as he pointed toward Elf. "She, she."

The bride's father cut him off. "She's got no authority to do anything here tonight but eat, drink and keep her mouth shut. If she so much as looks like she has more to say, tell me. I'll get rid of her."

Obviously mollified, the caterer headed back to do his job.

Durand glanced at Tony. "She's a menace. You're welcome to keep her." Durand lifted a tumbler of whiskey with a little ice in a quiet salute before taking a sip.

Tony couldn't disagree with the man's assessment of Elf. In all honesty, he could easily live without hearing or seeing the woman again. "I wanted to thank you and your wife for all the improvements you paid for at the church. It's a small congregation and not a wealthy one."

"I don't think you realize how much money it saved me having the wedding here." Durand's gray eyes sparkled under heavy, dark eyebrows. "I'm delighted the church didn't need a new roof or all new plumbing."

"Excuse me?" Tony wondered if he'd missed something. The man had spent a fortune already and the caterer was pouring more of his money into crystal glasses. No limit. Besides the shuttle buses, there was a separate fleet of cars prepared to take over-imbibers directly to their homes. Tony could practically see the dollar signs fly by.

"If Celeste had gotten married in Lexington, her mother would have worn the numbers off at least six credit cards instead of two." He smiled at his wife and raised his glass in a silent toast even as he continued talking. "She'd have given parties. She'd have redone our church, but it's much larger. She would have redecorated the house. I hate to imagine the cost of the new wardrobes she would have purchased for all of us."

A waitress carrying a tray of shrimp and crabmeat treats stopped by and offered it to them. The man paying for everything stacked them high on a small china plate. "I might as well get my money's worth."

Moving away from the happy man, Tony saw the wedding planner nod her head in the direction of the DJ. The torch was passed. The man lifted his cordless microphone and suggested the wedding party and friends make their way from the museum into the barn. The real party was about to begin.

He found Theo and Nina chatting with his mother and aunt. Everyone looked happy. Evidently, Mr. Durand's donation to the museum was more than generous.

"Are you locking up the museum or leaving it open during the reception?" Tony asked.

His mom patted his arm. "We have to leave it open for the restrooms. There aren't any in the barn, dear."

"Let's go eat." Theo pointed to the door. "I'm starving again."

Even though she had helped with the lights, Theo was stunned by the change in the barn. The draped tulle and tiny lights created a fairyland. In the center of the large room, a dance floor was roped off from the tables by garlands of greenery and roses.

Round tables covered with damask held not only silverware, crystal and silver chargers, but bowls of roses and more candles.

Musicians filled the largest stall, making Theo smile. The horses once stabled there wouldn't recognize the place. The wedding cakes were in another stall. The bride's cake consisted of several elegant tiers, cascading the length of the table. The groom's cake had its own table. It looked like a snow covered football field. She whispered to Tony, "I think it's Red Velvet. Blossom made it."

She heard his stomach growl.

The planner held a seating chart and directed traffic.

The DJ requested everyone be seated and offered a formal introduction of the bride and groom. Applause dropped to silence when no one appeared. Theo wondered if the happy couple had run away, leaving the problem of one too many mothers behind.

She wouldn't blame them.

And then, smiling widely, the couple walked in, holding hands. Everyone stood and cheered. Almost everyone. Not Theo or Elf. Elf sat at her designated spot, arms crossed, glaring at everyone. Her handsome escort was on his feet, applauding and cheering. At least Elf's driver was ready to party.

Dinner was delicious. The service impeccable. There were numerous occasions of toasts and jests. The DJ kept everyone to the prearranged timetable.

The groom led his bride onto the dance floor. The music began and the couple performed a well-rehearsed tango. Then Mr. Durand danced a slow waltz with his daughter.

It was time for the groom, Patrick, to dance with his mother, and he led Mrs. MacLeod onto the dance floor. As they began dancing, Elf jumped to her feet, threw her glass of champagne on the floor and stormed out of the barn. Her driver/escort was hot on her heels. She slammed the door in his face.

He calmly opened it and went out, closing it softly behind him.

When everyone in the room started breathing again at the same time, Theo realized she had been holding her breath as well.

The party began in earnest. Wade and Grace danced past her. Near them, Mike and Ruby looked happy to have the evening off. Together, Blossom's escorts led her onto the floor. Theo saw Mr. Durand dancing with Jane. Mr. Espinoza made Martha look like a dancer.

It was lovely.

# CHAPTER TWENTY-FIVE

Tony woke early Saturday morning. Halloween. He groaned into his pillow, already dreading the first complaint about stolen and smashed pumpkins. He yawned and stretched trying to unkink a knot in his back.

Until they discovered who killed Scarlet, or ran into a dead end, he would have to put in at least several hours each day. So this Saturday would be just another work day for him. He couldn't believe it had only been a week since the woman had died. It felt like a year. And, although the killings at the Shady Nest were clear cases of murder/suicide, the paperwork would require two trees.

At least he could be grateful for Katti Marmot. Claude's bride was just the assistant Theo needed. He didn't have to worry about his wife getting herself into trouble.

His cell phone buzzed and he checked the

screen. "Not already." He felt stomach acid begin to eat into his gut and reached for the antacids at the same time he answered.

"Sheriff." Flavio's nasal twang blasted into his ear. "I hate to bother you on a Saturday, but, well sir —"

"Just spit it out."

"I, that is we, just received a call from Elf's driver, and he says she's dead. Claims she was murdered in her fancy touring bus."

"Did you tell him not to touch anything?" Tony reached for his uniform shirt.

"Yessir, I did, and he told me he walked in, found her, ran out and called me."

"And, where are the man and the bus?"

"Parked behind Ruby's."

"Call Wade and Doc Nash and tell them to meet me there. And notify the TBI. Let them know we need their help. Again." He disconnected and finished dressing in record time. Having anyone murdered was a tragedy as well as a mystery. He guessed having a celebrity like Elf murdered would create a media frenzy beyond anything he could truly imagine. He wanted to arrive at the scene before the first newshound, especially Winifred.

When he pulled his Blazer into Ruby's parking lot, he parked to block the entrance into the overflow area where Elf's huge bus

341

sat alone, its lily-decorated paint job gleaming in the first rays of the morning sun. It should have been a lovely sight.

Mike and Dammit walked toward him from the café's back porch. The big dog looked like he suffered from a hangover. It was his usual off-duty expression.

"Don't you get a honeymoon?" Seeing him, Tony felt a sense of relief. They needed every officer they had. His tiny force was simply not equipped for celebrity homicide.

Mike shook his head. "We don't leave for our cruise until next week. Ruby wanted to get married on Anna, er, Angelina's birthday."

"So that's why she picked Tuesday."

"Yep. I'm just lucky we didn't have to go through eleven months of the calendar after finding Angelina." Mike tipped his head toward Elf's driver who sat on the café's deck staring at the bus. "He's pretty shocky."

Wade pulled in next to the Blazer, and Doc Nash parked on the far side. Neither of them smiled as they stood studying the bus. Wade carried a large camera bag and a stack of yellow plastic numbered markers. "You want me to start here or inside?"

"Start here." Tony needed to see the crime scene. "Take some pictures of this whole area for reference." Tony waved his arm to indicate the parking lot, the motor home, and the driver.

Without another word, Wade began systematically photographing the area. He placed a couple of markers as he moved toward the open door but generally focused on the broader view. The doctor was right on his heels, following in his footsteps. So was Tony. Mike and Dammit began setting up barricades and stringing crime scene tape to limit, as much as possible, contamination of the area.

Tony thought Wade's camera clicking sounded amazingly loud in the unnatural silence. Not a dog was barking, nor a bird was chirping anywhere nearby. He climbed into the bus and took more photographs. Tony, watching over Wade's shoulder, knew when he focused on Elf. Wade, prepared for his inevitable reaction, quickly handed Tony the camera and pulled a plastic lined paper bag out of his pocket and threw up into it.

Tony barely noticed. He felt a chill run through him that had nothing to do with the weather. Elf's body lay sprawled in the open space of the living room. No longer dressed in the "black lounge singer gown" she'd worn to her son's wedding, she wore baggy jeans and a well worn oversized gray sweatshirt. Her bare feet looked no bigger than a child's. He'd catalogued her overall appearance quickly but now he stared, feeling queasy in the closed space. Tightly wrapped around her neck, he guessed twice, was a thin steel wire with a loop on one end. A dulcimer string.

On the coffee table was a bottle of wine and two glasses. Both looked untouched. "So she had company or was expecting it."

He glanced into the doctor's face. Doc Nash was shaking his head even as he pulled latex gloves onto his hands. Tony watched him move close to Elf's face.

"Wade, picture." The doctor pointed at the face.

Wade slipped his barf bag into another plastic bag and stuck it into a small pouch hanging on the camera bag. Eyebrows lifted, he followed the doctor's instruction, taking multiple photographs of the face from several angles before following his own protocol for cataloging every inch of the crime scene.

"What is it?" Tony stepped closer to see what drew the doctor's attention.

"Paper in her mouth. That color." Doc pointed to a stack of paper next to a small electronic keyboard on the coffee table.

"There was nothing in Scarlet's mouth or throat."

Wade took a few pictures of the table and paper.

Tony, his hands covered with gloves, slid the paper from the table into an evidence envelope and jotted a note on the outside.

"The wire?" Tony stared into the doctor's face. "Is it the same kind?"

"You'll need a wire expert, but I'd say unofficially 'yes,' and I'd say the wrapping technique is the same as Scarlet's or very similar. I'll let you know after the autopsy if the paper was put there before or after she died." Doc Nash's frown deepened. "But why?"

With a shake of his head, Tony moved his gaze from Elf. He studied the interior of the motor home. A wall of glass cabinets with a mirrored lining flanked the doorway into the next living space. Dulcimers of many sizes and shapes were on display in the cabinet. Most were traditional hourglass shapes, some crudely formed and some with delicate inlays of mother of pearl or multiple colors of wood. One exquisite teardrop-shaped dulcimer had "ELF" inlayed under a heart-shaped sound hole.

"Do you suppose the killer brought the string or used one of hers?" Tony talked to himself. Scarlet didn't have any musical instruments.

The doctor frowned, staring around the space. "Not much seems knocked around. Don't you think she'd kick over a crystal lamp or something?"

Tony thought the same thing. "Unless she died instantly, or maybe she did thrash about and our killer took the time to put everything back."

"I'll dust every surface including the keyboard." Wade gazed around, probably seeing it for the first time without a camera lens. "It wasn't robbery because her purse is right there."

Tony agreed. Without touching it, he could see a stack of money inside.

A horn blaring in the parking lot drew their attention. The TBI's crime scene van had arrived. Reinforcements.

Theo was enjoying Saturday morning home with the boys. They were busy mixing the family recipe for pumpkin cookies. She sat in her wheelchair watching a blob of dough stuck to the ceiling and wondered if it would fall. Even with the energetic stirring, she thought it was in a remarkable location. Tony was the only one who'd be able to reach it.

As if her thoughts conjured him, her cell phone chimed. Tony barely let her answer before he rattled off his request that she and the boys go to the shop, told her Elf was dead, and informed her Katti was on the way to pick them up. Then he disconnected.

Theo put the uncooked dough in the refrigerator. She guessed he wanted her to keep track of the conversations at "gossip central," as Tony liked to refer to her shop. She preferred the term "local news," but whatever called gossip or news, it flowed through the quilting room like water through a sieve.

At the shop, the boys vanished upstairs into her office, where a corner belonged to them. Theo and Katti barely made it into the classroom before a deluge of quilters, seeking information about Elf, struck like a tsunami. She wondered how they heard the news before she did.

Summer Flowers stalked into Theo's classroom, sending the quilters hurrying back into the fabric end of the store. Summer and Autumn Flowers were brothers. They didn't act like brothers. Theo had known them all her life and their differences still came as a surprise. The two men didn't look like brothers. Blossom's father, Autumn, was round of face and body like his daughter and loved to tell corny jokes; Summer, known as Sum, was lean and hard and wore a perpetual expression of gloom and doom on his gaunt face.

Sum Flowers was *not* a nice man. Theo watched him carefully. He stood in her makeshift workroom clasping and unclasping his skeletal fingers and staring at his feet. His heavy boots were shedding dry mud on her clean floor.

Theo felt warmed and relieved when Katti came to stand beside her and, although she said nothing, it was clear Katti wasn't pleased to see him either. Theo couldn't imagine what brought him into her shop. She waited for him to speak.

"She wasn't a good girl." His raspy voice finally broke the silence. His eyes lifted from the floor to give Theo a malevolent stare. "Got what was coming to her."

Theo felt a ripple of fear. She would not want to be alone with the man. Was he talking about Scarlet or Elf? Theo didn't know what she was supposed to say to the man who'd lost both his daughters. What happened to not speaking ill of the dead? She considered asking him to leave.

The man's first wife, the girls' mother, had been an alcoholic who drank herself to death, leaving her daughters to run wild.

His second wife didn't last more than two years with him before she packed a couple of bags and left town with a package delivery man.

"Mr. Flowers?" Theo rolled her chair a bit closer in spite of her distaste for the man. He hadn't been at Scarlet's funeral. "Why did you come here today? Do you need something?"

"Her and her sister both." He seemed to study the room, ignoring her. "Trash, giving birth to more trash."

"Sir?" Theo saw Katti reach for the broom.

"You tell your husband he don't need to strain nothing looking for who rid the world of them girls." He spat on her floor.

"Out." Enraged, Theo pointed to the door. "Get out."

Katti waved the broom and yelled something in Russian.

Sum left.

Stunned, Theo and Katti stared at each other for a moment. Finally, Katti broke the silence. "He come back, Katti fix him. Not good man." She pantomimed slitting her throat.

Theo nodded. The way Sum made her feel, she'd probably help. Even from a wheelchair, she could mop up blood.

■ ■ ■ ■

Tony and Wade attended the autopsy of Easter Lily Flowers. Doc Nash went along with them, more from professional curiosity than necessity. The medical examiner in Knoxville, with the unfortunate name of Gould, had done work for Park County before and welcomed the threesome like he was inviting them into his home for a card game.

"Come in and make yourself to home." He shook hands with everyone before pointing out where he wanted them to stand. He even supplied a bucket for Wade before turning to business. "There's probably already several Internet nuts claiming either responsibility or blaming the extraterrestrials. What say we find out the truth?"

Tony barely nodded before the man launched into his monologue again. The doctor talked non-stop for the rest of the time they were there.

The most important thing they learned was the paper in Elf's throat was a song. She had drawn some music notes and written a fair amount of lyrics on the paper she used when composing. The paper had been folded several times and the creases crimped tightly. The tightly folded paper had been shoved deep into Elf's throat before the wire, a dulcimer string, was wrapped around her throat. She did not die instantly but would have struggled for a while. She suffocated.

Not a good way to die, in Tony's opinion. It was similar to Scarlet's death, but slower.

The sweatshirt and jeans she'd worn were carefully bagged and labeled. "I'm sending these to forensics for you." Dr. Gould looked cheerful. "There's oil and grime of some nature on the back of the sweatshirt."

Wade copied the lyrics from the paper before it was whisked into another bag headed for the lab.

Tony, Wade and Doc Nash stared at each other and waited for Dr. Gould to announce his opinion.

"Cause of death is clearly suffocation." Dr. Gould began signing his forms. "Manner of death is homicide. And I'd say by the same person as killed her sister." He chuckled. "Of course, that last bit is just my personal opinion."

Tony wanted to talk with Elf's driver. With Wade by his side, he found the man sitting at a table by the window in Ruby's Café. He stared at the motor home. A half-eaten sandwich was on a plate near, but not in front of, him. It looked like he'd lost his appetite and pushed it away.

Ruby whispered that he'd been in the café all day, in the same pose.

Tony and Wade slid onto the chairs facing the man.

Before either of them could ask a question, the driver looked up, his eyes red, but dry. "What happened to her?" A shudder worked through his whole body.

"Actually, we hoped you might be able to shed a bit of light on what happened last night." Tony didn't think the driver killed Elf, but thinking something didn't make it so. "You were her escort to the reception but didn't sit with her at the wedding."

"No." His eyes flickered away from the motor home and back.

"Because?"

"She wanted to be the center of attention." He frowned and played with his fork. "As much as I liked her, most of the time, she had these spells of pure crazy. I learned fast not to argue with her then. It was like she became a whole different person."

"Could you start with your full name?" Wade put his notebook on the table.

"Pericles Antonopoulos." He spelled it for Wade. "It's Greek."

Tony managed not to blurt out "No kidding" and concentrated on his questions. "Were you in the church for the wedding?"

"Yes. I sat in the back."

"How did the two of you get out to the museum for the reception? I didn't see you in the shuttle bus line." Tony glanced at the motor home parked behind miles of yellow tape. "You don't tow a car."

"No. We rented a car from the guys at the garage." Pericles sagged in his chair. "It ran. It was clean. And Elf chewed my ear from one end of this hick town to the other about it. She wanted a limo."

"Doesn't she have a fleet of cars out at the mansion?" Wade waved his pen in the air. "Including a limo?"

"It *was* weird." Pericles straightened. "The whole trip was weird. She didn't want to go out there, and usually she can't wait to get into the house and play with the ATVs and drive one of her little sports cars." He rubbed his forehead. "I thought maybe Scarlet's death scrambled her brains, but the truth is, she was acting weird before."

"Did you know Scarlet?"

"Oh, yeah. She visited Elf a lot. They was really good friends but acted otherwise when they got within fifty miles of this place." He shook his head. "I have no idea why or what was going on."

"How long have you been with her?" Wade said.

"About three years now." Pericles poked at his sandwich. "Before me was a guy named Gavin."

Tony decided it was time to get back on track. "So, you drove her back to the motor home from the museum. And then?"

"She said she had to work on a song and I should sleep in my bunk. I have a private space between her living area and the front seats."

"Was that unusual?" Wade looked up from his notepad.

"No. In fact, it was the most normal thing about this trip. I stretched out on my bunk and watched movies on my DVD player."

"Did you hear anything? See anything?"

"Nothing but the sound of the movie coming through the headset. I fell asleep with it on." An expression of horror tightened his face. "I slept through her murder."

Tony sat in silence thinking about the man's story. He couldn't stop wondering why Elf hadn't wanted to go to her house. As soon as he and Wade were through at the diner, he voted for a drive. He glanced at Pericles. "When did you find her?"

"I cook her breakfast every morning. It's

354

part of my job." Pericles blew his nose on a napkin. "I let myself in with my key. The door was locked but it's automatic." He gulped air like a beached fish. "She was . . . was staring at me with those big, dead eyes."

"Can you think of anything else weird happening recently?"

Pericles stared at the motor home for a long time. "She thought she had an overly interested fan."

"Like a stalker?" said Wade. "Or an admirer?"

"Stalker, I'd say. She complained about little items missing from the motor home. But it's locked all the time, and I keep my eye on things." He cleared his throat. "You know really, I think she lost or mislaid things and then blamed it on this mysterious person. This all started when she began working on her life story. It made her nervous."

"She was writing a memoir." Tony guessed.

"No, she was telling the story of her life." Pericles gave Tony the "how dumb can you be" look. "I think she was really dishing the dirt though."

"How many people knew?"

"I dunno." Pericles studied his hands. "We didn't talk much about it."

# CHAPTER TWENTY-SIX

Tony was almost in the Blazer when Nellie Pearl accosted him.

For as long as he'd known Nellie Pearl, which was nearly thirty years now, she had been in the habit of dressing without paying any attention to the constraints of fashion. It was not unusual to see her wearing jeans and a shabby flannel shirt, even in church. She always wore steel-toed work boots.

He dimly recalled seeing her in a dress — it might have been at his father's funeral. In his memory, the toes of those worn boots peeked out from under the crooked hem on her baggy, overlong dress.

He stared at the apparition before him.

Nellie Pearl stared back. Her expression belligerent, her arms crossed over the layers of plaid flannel covering her chest. Even from this distance, Tony could identify three different shirts worn together. The buttoning was uneven, some pieces of shirt sticking above the collar of the next, and one side of the tails hanging lower. Her jeans were unbuttoned. It looked like this pair was covering another pair. They were zipped.

He found his gaze riveted to her feet. Exposed by the too-short pants, her customary boots were gone. Feet that looked like weathered wood, gray and rough, were stuffed into bubble gum pink high-heeled sandals. A leather daisy drooped against the largest, longest, thickest and most yellow toenail he'd seen in his life.

A wave of nausea took him by surprise.

He called Sheila, begged her to come deal with Nellie Pearl and climbed into the Blazer. He knew he was running away like a weasel and called himself names.

In the passenger seat, Wade made no comment.

Tony glanced at Wade just before he turned into the driveway of Elf's mansion. "We'd better get someone out here to keep uninvited guests out. Surely we can bill the estate."

Wade radioed dispatch. "Hey, Rex, the sheriff needs someone to watch Elf's mansion."

Tony nodded his approval. "Thank goodness it's Rex back on duty now instead of Flavio. There's no one better in an emergency or with the press."

Wade didn't respond. All his attention was on the view. He was staring straight ahead. "Oh, my."

A half-second later, Tony realized what Wade saw — or rather what he didn't see. "The house is gone?" He stopped the Blazer in the driveway and climbed out. Sure enough, as he walked forward he saw a massive hole where the mansion had been.

"When's the last time anyone was out here?" Wade frowned.

"What did they do with the rubble?" Tony was flabbergasted. The house had been a huge three story juxtaposition of Victorian gingerbread and traditional farm house. "There's not even a board left."

"The garage and cars are gone." Wade removed his sunglasses and blinked in the bright sun. "Elf must have known. That's why she stayed in town."

Tony felt like his head was bouncing on a spring. "Why not tell Pericles?"

"Why tear down a million-dollar house?"

"And who did it?" Tony could think of several contractors, including Gus, who could do the job. "Were they sworn to silence, or did we just not hear about it?"

As if conjured by Tony's question, Gus's big pickup came up the drive and parked behind the Blazer. He had a huge grin on his face. "Quite a hole, isn't it?"

"You did this?" Tony was shocked by Gus's cavalier attitude. He was angry. Gus's expression went from jovial to wary in a heartbeat.

"Don't tell me she changed her mind and called you in."

"Who?"

"Elf." Gus looked to Wade as if searching for answers. "Who else?"

And then Tony realized his brother had no idea Elf was dead. Had they managed to keep her murder from the media? "You listen to the radio today?"

Gus shook his head. "Book on CD."

"Elf's dead."

"No way." Gus held his hands up.

"Oh, put your hands down. I know you didn't do it." Tony gestured to the site of the former home. "What's this all about?"

"Elf decided to level the house and give the acreage, with a check, to the newlyweds. She hired me to do the demolition."

Wade stared down the driveway. "Does Patrick know?"

"About the house or his mother?"

"Mother."

Tony nodded. "Only by chance, I happened to know where the couple is spending their weekend honeymoon. I called the sheriff over there and asked him to relay the news."

"Doesn't seem like a good weekend for honeymoons. First Mike and Ruby didn't get one, and now Patrick and Celeste are probably on their way back from theirs." Wade continued, "At least Grace and I got an entire day together."

Gus said, "I guess I'll go home. I just came by to make sure we got everything cleaned up."

Tony looked at Wade. "Let's go talk to the out-of-town relatives before they escape. Call Rex back and cancel the guards. No one's stealing a hole."

They found the MacLeods and Durands eating a leisurely brunch together at the River View Motel. Four smiling faces looked up when Tony and Wade walked in. "Join us?"

Tony hoped a bit of coffee would snap his brain into high gear. A waitress wearing a cat costume came to take his order and reminded him it was Halloween. The prospects for a good night's sleep vanished. "Better make it strong."

He told the two couples the news about Elf and then excused himself from the table and called Theo.

"You've reached the insane asylum." Theo's voice sounded chirpy but not happy.

"Theo, honey."

"Oh, no. Any time you start a call with 'Theo, honey,' it's a disaster. I don't have time for this."

The sound of myriad women talking in the background made him groan. "I guess your customers heard the news about Elf?"

"You're a bad man. Why didn't you tell me why you wanted me at the shop? You said she was dead, not that she was murdered, I thought she'd been in an accident. I could have used a bit of warning," Theo hissed. "I was blindsided by about twenty customers this morning. Each one them had a different story to tell, but I gather the main fact is accurate. Elf really was murdered?"

"Yes. There's no way her death could have been accidental."

"One of my ladies claims there is a curse on the Flowers women," Theo fumed. "And I'm standing there, er sitting, with my mouth open because I didn't know anything about it."

Tony thought a little change of subject

361

might help settle her down. "Today's Halloween."

"What?" Theo caught up with him. "Oh, no. I'd almost forgotten. We were working on the cookies when you sent us into the madhouse."

"I doubt I'll be home to take the boys trick or treating. They won't want to stay home, and I don't want you wheeling around in the dark either."

"I have to say, neither of those sounds very pleasant to me either."

"Maybe Nina will take them with her merry band."

Tony heard Theo sigh.

"I'll call later." He hung up and returned to the parents, who were now discussing Elf in hushed tones.

"I seem to have lost my appetite." Mrs. MacLeod placed her napkin on the table. "I didn't always get along with Elf, but I never stopped thanking her for Patrick. He is a wonderful son."

"She put on quite a display of temper last night." Mr. MacLeod reached for his wife's hand. "Frankly, I was surprised. When we talked a couple of weeks ago, she was all sweetness and light, and she said if she was able to attend, she would just sit back and enjoy the party."

Mrs. MacLeod nodded. "I think that's why we were so irritated. She promised one thing, and the next thing we know Elf's dancing down the aisle in that red cocktail dress at the rehearsal. Her behavior was terrible."

"Not to mention wearing black to the wedding," Tony added. "Her dress was not the usual wedding attire."

"I thought Celeste and Patrick handled it very well." Mrs. Durand jumped into the conversation. "I'd say she looked like she'd just come from singing in a bar. We met her for the first time at the rehearsal." Her expression conveyed a combination of displeasure and unwillingness to speak ill of the dead.

Minutes after the boys left to trick or treat with Nina and her kids, Theo knew it was a great decision. For a while, she considered leaving a bowl of candy on the front step and taking the boys herself. She enjoyed trick or treating with the boys as a rule, but rolling her wheelchair in the dark held no appeal.

While the boys were away, the doorbell never stopped ringing. Only half of the people on her doorstep were children. The adults weren't looking for candy — they wanted gossip, and Theo knew less than they did.

Theo finally parked her wheelchair on the porch and sat wrapped up in an old orange fleece blanket from her college days. She had to look like a huge pumpkin. She wished she had a green hat to wear like a stem. What she did have was a small digital recorder tucked inside the blanket. She turned it on to help her keep track of the comments and questions right after old man Ferguson hobbled up the sidewalk to ask if it was true Elf left a million dollars to every resident in the county.

Theo said something in response about how she doubted it but thought it sounded like a lovely gesture.

Out of candy, she was about to head inside when Patrick and Celeste walked up, having returned from their half-day honeymoon. They expected to find Tony at home. Disappointed, they perked up when she offered them a place to hide — her kitchen — while she called Tony. "I've got the honeymooners stashed in front of the television. What do you want me to do with them?"

"Hide them from the press, I guess. I'll be home as soon as I can." His jaw cracked nosily when he yawned. "Do you think I should I come in through the kitchen?"

"Yes, absolutely, but don't park here." Theo glanced outside and saw a small horde of people standing in the park across the street. "Unless you want to get mobbed by more nuts than you'd find at a squirrel convention. It's been a madhouse. We've been out of candy for an hour." Theo felt like a big baby complaining. It wasn't as if Tony was off having fun. At least she managed not to sniffle. "Even turning off the porch light hasn't stopped the parade. I've had children, grumps, greedy souls and reporters. Enough is enough."

# CHAPTER TWENTY-SEVEN

The media frenzy was even worse than Tony had anticipated. By the time he dragged himself home at close to one in the morning, he'd been subjected to national reporters, state, local, television and print, entertainment reporters and a psychic with no credentials. Paperwork was usually the bane of his existence. Dealing with the media eclipsed it and made him want to impose not only a news blackout but actually have none of the press allowed within the boundaries of Park County.

The first one he'd toss out personally: Winifred Thornby representing the *Silersville Gazette.* The woman was not winning any points with him. First she'd printed a list of the women going to the quilting retreat, practically begging petty thieves to help themselves. No. He shook his head. First she'd stalked him in high school. Their relationship had not improved.

This evening, Winifred had arrived in the front row of the first wave of the press, trying to push through the locked doors of the law enforcement center. Even the unflappable Rex almost lost his temper. He sent them all to the conference room at the courthouse with vague promises about someone coming soon to give them details and updates.

Unfortunately, Tony was "the someone."

Fortunately, he arrived with sandwiches and coffee and made his escape while the starving members of the press were too busy fighting for a meal to realize he'd slipped away. They'd find him soon enough.

In the meantime, he was met at the kitchen door by Daisy. Awakened from a nap by him deviating from his normal behavior, the big golden retriever alerted the room with a "woo, woo" instead of her normal bark.

Tony saw the newlywed couple cozily ensconced on the sofa in the kitchen, near the fireplace. Theo was curled up on his recliner, wrapped in a quilt, sound asleep.

"We tried to get her to go to bed." Patrick started to stand, but settled back when Tony motioned him down. "But she insisted."

Not surprised by her behavior, Tony picked up his wife, quilt and all. "And Chris and Jamie?"

Celeste laughed. "They sorted and counted their candy, taught us how to play a new video game and went to bed hours ago."

"Let me put Theo to bed," Tony whispered. He took one step away and turned back. "That sofa opens into a fairly comfortable bed. I'm too beat to think or talk, and there are reporters sitting in every bush and shrub, waiting to pounce on you like a duck on a bug."

Patrick glanced at his new wife who nodded. "Thank you. We'd love to stay."

"I'll be right back with some sheets and stuff."

Tony managed to get Theo tucked into her bed without waking her. He found a couple of unused emergency toothbrushes, clean sheets and a down comforter for the couple. They looked as tired as he felt.

Five minutes later, he was upstairs in his own bed, sound asleep.

Halloween ended officially at midnight. At two minutes past two in the morning, the telephone rang in Tony's ear. He croaked a greeting into the receiver, sounding more like a bullfrog than a human. He didn't feel human either.

"Sheriff?" J.B. Lewis was the one deputy who enjoyed night duty.

A thirty-year veteran of the sheriff's department, he was both unambitious and unflappable. J.B. would never call Tony unless something extraordinary had occurred. He didn't sound happy.

Instantly alert, Tony sat up. "What's up, J.B.?" He moved the receiver away from his ear. Why wasn't J.B. talking to dispatch? Had the army of reporters marched on the law enforcement center and taken over the building?

As expected, J.B.'s voice boomed into the room. "I thought I'd call you direct because I thought you'd want to know this. Dispatch alerted me. A caller said we ought to check for someone in the cemetery digging up Mr. Beasley."

"That's ridiculous! Why would someone steal his body? He's been buried for over a week." Tony's bare feet hit the cold floor and he shivered, realizing the temperature was dropping. "Are you sure the phone call isn't a Halloween prank?"

"I don't know, Sheriff. I'm almost to the cemetery now, and there does appear to be a faint light and some movement in there about where Beasley's planted." There was a burst of static. "It's probably kids, but it

369

doesn't feel like it."

As close as his house was to the cemetery, Tony could probably reach it faster than any of the patrol cars. "Park by the side and turn out your lights. I'll meet you there in five minutes." He decided not to wear his uniform, but grabbed jeans, his vest and a sweatshirt with the department logo embroidered on it. Grave digging was a dirty business.

Tony pulled the sweatshirt over his head as he trotted down the stairs. After retrieving his gun from the safe, he glanced into Theo's makeshift room. She lay, wide-eyed, watching him finish dressing. He didn't know what to say so he just kissed her and left. At least he'd had almost a full hour of sleep.

The fog was back. Rising from the ground, it swirled in the headlights. At least he was hidden from prowling reporters. Half smiling, half concerned, Tony glanced around, his eyes searching for grave robbers or vampires flying about looking for dinner. At this hour, there should be a wolf howling somewhere in the distance to complete the spooky movie scenario. Illuminated by the streetlights, the mist made it look like things were changing shapes. Surely that was all that J.B. was seeing, he thought, and immediately dismissed the idea as ludicrous. J.B. was not given to hallucinations. The man simply did not have an imagination.

Tony's Blazer rolled up behind the patrol car, and as he climbed out, he saw J.B. standing by the driver's door, staring into the cemetery. J.B.'s voice came to him, as soft as the fog. "There is definitely something going on in there, but I can't tell what it might be. Could be drug dealers hiding their stuff."

Nodding his agreement, Tony joined J.B. and they headed toward the light, carrying their heavy flashlights but leaving them switched off. They picked their way through the hedge hiding the cemetery fence. The gates would be locked at this hour, so they climbed the chain link fence. The mayor, also the town undertaker, lived out of town a few miles. He had the key to the gates, but neither police officer wanted Calvin Cashdollar flapping around like a buzzard. Luckily the fence was only about four feet tall.

Once over the fence, the going was slow. Uneven ground, vegetation and fog conspired against them. Tony stubbed his toe on a flat tombstone but managed to swallow his curse. The same heavy air that muffled some of the sounds of digging made it possible for Tony and J.B. to walk up to the gravesite without betraying their presence. A chill breeze teased the back of his neck as he and J.B. freed their weapons from the holsters.

The muted, wavering light J.B. had spotted was held in the palsied hands of an elderly woman. It was lighting a new hole in the dirt covering a fresh grave. Another elderly woman was laboriously digging in the loose dirt.

Tony's mouth dropped open. He would have been less surprised to find a hunchback named Igor collecting body parts for his demented master than to find the Bainbridge sisters, both of whom were in their eighties, digging in an occupied grave. A glance at J.B.'s face in the wavering light showed the same dumbfounded expression. Tony slid his gun back into its holster and cleared his throat.

Neither of the old women heard him. Tony didn't want to scare them to death. He tried again, slightly louder.

Finally the one doing the digging stopped and looked around, her eyes wide and fearful. "Is someone there?" she asked softly. Her hands looked blue as they quivered, and her voice shook. Whether it was more from fear or from cold would be hard to tell.

Tony made an effort to keep his voice soft and soothing. "Yes, Miss Bainbridge, its Tony Abernathy and J.B. Lewis."

Her shoulders sagged, and she let the shovel fall at her feet.

The woman with the flashlight leaned forward. "What's the matter, Muriel? Do you want me to dig for a while now?"

"No, Letty. It is over. We have been found out." She pointed toward the men.

Startled, Letty jumped and swung around, momentarily blinding the men with her flashlight. "Oh, no." Her eyes filled with tears, and even though they overflowed, she made no effort to wipe them away, obviously defeated. "Oh, no."

Fearful for their fragile health, Tony didn't move. "You two ladies are the last ones I'd suspect of grave robbing." He wasn't smiling. "Why don't you come down to the station with us? We can have a little coffee and a chat."

"Do you have tea?" Letty asked. "I really don't much care for coffee, but a cup of hot tea would be most welcome."

"I believe there are still some tea bags down there." Tony stepped forward to assist the women.

Muriel whispered something into her sister's ear. Whatever it was, it made the last vestige of color disappear from her faded face. "Oh, no, we can't, I forgot about Emery."

"Is Emery here too?" J.B. flicked his flashlight over the shrubs and tombstones sending a bright light over the area. "I don't see your brother."

Tony didn't see the old gentleman either but expected to. He escorted his sisters everywhere.

Muriel pointed at an old quilt rolled up under a tree. J.B. began unrolling the quilt but stopped as soon as he realized it was Emery's shroud. Startled, an oath escaped him. "I apologize for my language ladies, but I didn't expect to find a corpse."

"Neither did we, J.B., but these things do happen." Muriel wrapped an arm around her sister and turned to Tony. "Do you suppose we might sit in your car until we go for tea? It has been a long evening, and it's very cold out tonight."

Tony led the way. He half expected to see a mummy strolling out of the bushes. It wouldn't be as peculiar as what was actually going on here tonight. "I'll get the ladies settled and call Doc Nash and be back as soon as I can," he told J.B.

"I appreciate that, Sheriff. I can't say I relish the idea of staying out here in the fog with a fresh stiff and a partially open grave."

Tony lifted the ladies, one at a time, over the fence. He wondered how they had gotten into the cemetery with Emery's body, but at the moment, they were clearly not up to answering any questions. When he had them settled in the back seat of his Blazer and covered with a blanket, he phoned the doctor and returned to the gravesite.

It didn't take long for Dr. Nash to arrive. By the light of their combined flashlights, he was able to make a preliminary examination of the body. "I'll bet he just up and died of old age, Tony. I'll do an autopsy tomorrow, but it's probably just a formality. One thing for sure. He didn't die here, and he has been dead for at least twelve hours, I'd say." He pulled the quilt back over Emery's face and stepped away. "You'd better go to the old ladies and get them home as soon as possible, or you'll have two more deaths."

"I'm taking them to the station now, so why don't you drop by after you get Emery moved?" Tony turned toward the fence. "I doubt they've eaten much, if anything, all day. I'm going to fill them up with something warm and ask them a couple of gentle

375

questions before I take them home. Sheila's on her way to the station. It might not hurt to have you check them out, healthwise."

Doc Nash yawned widely without covering his mouth. "Since I'm up and wide awake, I might as well."

No one spoke in the Blazer. The ladies still huddled together under the blanket, but Tony could see them shaking. Their fright didn't make him feel good, but he thought he had a fair idea what they'd been up to tonight, and it certainly wasn't stashing drugs.

Sheila met them at the station and helped the ladies out of the back seat. As soon as they were seated at the table in the lunchroom, she covered each of them with more blankets.

It didn't Tony long to make some strong, hot tea and several cheese sandwiches and heat some soup. Silently blessing Marigold Flowers, who fed the jail inmates, for keeping the big refrigerators stocked with home-made soups and sandwich fixings, he wrote her a note detailing what he'd taken and dropped it in a jar on the counter. Like her sister Blossom, Marigold cooked well. Members of the department often enjoyed the bounty, paying on the honor system.

The way the ladies devoured the simple

repast made Tony wonder when they had last eaten. By the time they were warm and full, Doc Nash was standing in the hallway, watching with professional intensity. Tony knew that he would call a halt to his questions if he had any concern about the way they were being treated.

Tony, Sheila and Doc Nash shared the table with them. "We need to know what happened tonight. Are you ladies up to answering some questions now?" They nodded their assent and clutched the cups more tightly, highlighting the blue veins in their almost fleshless hands. Tony sat near them, sipping his own tea. "I guess the first thing that I need to know is about what time did Emery die?"

After an exchange of meaningful looks with her sister, Muriel answered. "It was during his nap after lunch." Letty bobbed her head in agreement. "We ate lunch about eleven-thirty or so and he stretched out on the sofa as usual, but he didn't wake up."

"The three of you shared the house and expenses?"

"Yes," said Letty. "Ever since Mama died."

"Well, not exactly," said Muriel. "Emery was the only one with a steady income. I'd have to say that he did all the sharing. Letty and I sometimes made a little on the sale of our preserves or a quilt, but nothing consistent."

Tony laced his fingers and rested them on his knee as he leaned forward. Deliberately making his tone as gentle as possible, he said, "By any chance does Emery's steady income get deposited into your bank account?"

Two sets of red-rimmed eyes looked back at him. The ladies nodded.

"So you decided if you didn't tell anyone about Emery's death, the money would continue being deposited?"

They nodded again but more slowly, as if wary of what would happen if they did.

"Why bury him in Mr. Beasley's grave? Emery hated the man."

Muriel straightened to her full height. "We know." She patted her sister's shoulder. "We hate to admit it, of course, but Letty and I are not as strong as we used to be. We thought that it would be easier to dig in a fairly fresh grave. It was harder than we expected it to be. The dirt was loose, but there was so much of it, and we were going to put poor Emery on the top of Mr. Beasley's casket and cover them back up." She seemed to wilt and grow smaller. "We just hadn't counted on there being so much dirt. It was so heavy." Without warning, fat tears streamed through the dirt on her cheeks. "That's why we were still there when you came by."

Letty hugged her sister. Defeated, she pleaded with her eyes. "We couldn't get him buried, and we couldn't just leave him either." Both of the sisters started sobbing.

"I've heard enough." Tony addressed Doc Nash. "I'm taking the ladies home. Do you want to come along?"

"Sure thing. Let me grab my bag." He shot to his feet.

"You're taking us home? We don't have to sleep in the jail?" Letty clutched Tony's arm. She was so frail that he could barely feel her touch.

"For now. I don't see how keeping you two here will further the law in any way." He gently patted her back as he helped her stand. "Tomorrow we might have to talk some more, but I don't see jail in your future."

Muriel looked so much livelier at the news Tony decided he could ask one more question. "Just how did you all get over the fence? And with Emery too?"

Her giggle was almost girlish. "Living as close to the cemetery as we do, we've seen teenagers sneaking under the fence for years. We know where all of the good spots are." She patted his big hand. "We waited until it was dark, and then we just dragged Emery over there on the quilt." She batted her eyes at him. "That was the easy part."

Theo didn't know what time Tony had gotten home. She remembered him mumbling something about needing more insurance, but nothing making any sense, before he trudged up the stairs again.

Her wheelchair fit nicely under the pull out cutting board in the kitchen. Her eyes still half closed, she had just started fixing coffee when the boys flew into the kitchen. It looked like they were ready to launch into an argument. She pointed to the sofa where Patrick and Celeste appeared to still be sleeping.

"Hush." She gave them the "mom glare," and they climbed up onto their stools and waited like little angels for her to start a pot of coffee and get them cereal and juice.

"Are they homeless?" Jamie's whisper was slightly quieter than a fighter jet.

"Can we watch cartoons?"

"No to both of you." She paused, hearing water running above them. "Sounds like your dad is up. When you finish eating, I want you to play in your room or in the front room until further notice."

Surprisingly, both boys nodded and started shoveling milk and cereal into their mouths. It looked like a race.

Tony appeared seconds after the boys bolted from the kitchen. "What are they up to?"

"Honestly? I'm not sure." Theo handed him a cup of coffee. "Did you get any sleep at all last night?"

"I'll probably crash later, but I slept like a rock for the first hour." He glanced over his shoulder at the couple on the couch before wheeling her into the front room.

"You haven't mentioned last night. What happened?"

Tony's broad shoulders sagged. "It was awful, and I still don't know what will happen." Theo wrapped her arms around his waist and waited in silence. "There we were, J.B. and I, creeping through the foggy cemetery at midnight, or close enough to it for me, and we found a pair of grave diggers, strictly amateurs."

Theo could tell from his expression that the attempt at humor was forced. "Who were they?"

"Misses Muriel and Letitia Bainbridge."

"No! I don't believe it. Where was Emery? He doesn't let them go anywhere without him." She visualized the threesome as they were so often, walking home from the store, Emery pulling a rusty wagon filled with their groceries.

"He was there, but he was wrapped in an old quilt for burial. The old gent died of old age, and the ladies were going to bury him and then pretend he was still alive so they would get his Social Security deposit."

"Those poor old ladies." There were tears glistening in Theo's eyes. "What will happen to them?"

"I'm not sure. I have a meeting this morning with Doc Nash and Archie Campbell. I doubt there will be any charges filed, but we have to find a way to help them live." He touched her cheek. "I certainly don't want word of this to get around. It would be devastating to those old dears."

Theo agreed. This was *not* a topic for the quilt shop gossip. "What about our little honeymoon couple?" She tipped her head toward the kitchen.

Tony lifted his coffee mug in a silent toast. "I'll shake them out of bed when I finish this."

# CHAPTER TWENTY-EIGHT

"The last time I saw my mother, she threw her champagne, glass and all, on the ground and stomped out. You saw her. No one could reason with her." Patrick sighed. "I didn't plan for her to be there. I considered keeping my marriage quiet until after the wedding." He held his empty hands palm up. "I did have to tell her I was getting married, didn't I?"

Tony remained quiet, notebook in hand.

Patrick gazed, apparently unseeing, at his breakfast. "She needed adoring fans or staff to make it through the day. For as long as I can remember, she craved the sound of applause, the flash of cameras and I knew I had to stay out of sight."

"She's not much older than I am." Tony eyed the groom. He looked like he was in his mid to late twenties.

"No." Patrick twisted the brand new shiny gold band on his finger. "She just turned forty-two. I'm twenty-seven."

"And your biological father? Where is he?" Tony didn't follow the lives of entertainment figures, except some baseball players. Maybe the life story of Elf was public information and he was expected to know all about this family.

"I don't know who he is."

"Where did you grow up?" Tony really wanted to know how he had turned out to be a decent, level-headed young man.

Patrick didn't dodge the question. "I spent most of my time with Mom and Dad and only occasionally my mother." A grim expression replaced his smile. Unshed tears magnified his eyes. "Elf never had much time for me, but when she did we were pals. When I was a little boy, she was still in her early twenties. She'd take me up in the hills. I can remember us running together, barefoot, laughing like crazy. Or we'd get all dressed up and go out to dinner or a concert. Amusement parks. We had lots of fun together."

"Was this in Nashville?"

Patrick looked confused. "It was always someplace different."

Tony thought he was getting the idea. It was probably whatever town she was performing in. "How did she get on with your parents?"

"Generally, she was fine. The only real fight I can recall was the year I turned sixteen. I wanted a car, of course, and my folks thought I should get a job and buy an old beater."

"So, you told your wealthy mother, and what did you get?"

"An Italian sports car. Silver." Patrick's eyes sparkled as he remembered. "I loved that car. It was fast and sleek and could hit a hundred miles an hour in fourth gear."

"How long did it last?" Tony guessed a month.

"Two weeks. Then I wrapped it around a bridge support and broke an arm and a leg. And sliced up a lot of me." He pointed to one shoulder.

Tony could see a series of scars where Patrick's sweatshirt with the cut-off sleeves and missing neckband exposed lots of skin and a small heart-shaped birthmark. He groaned in sympathy. "So, you were surprised by everything that happened at the wedding?"

"We weren't expecting her to come." Patrick twisted the ring again. "She had a gig in Dallas and sent an extravagant wedding present with her regrets."

"When did you learn she was coming?"

"When she arrived." Patrick glanced up. "It's not like she sneaks into town in her touring home. She told me because her sister died, she could walk away from the gig."

Tony felt his eyes widen. "She could? What about contracts?"

Patrick shrugged. "She pretty much did anything she wanted to. You know: the runaway bus approach to life. I guess the Dallas gig was different anyway — not part of a real tour. She said it was an informal arrangement and no tickets were sold specifically to see her appear. It was a charity deal and she was one of many. But . . ."

"Yes." Tony could read the young man's expression. "I imagine someone was angry she didn't come straight back after the funeral."

"I'd say you're the master of understatement." Patrick stared at the floor.

"Can you think of anything else?"

"She has been different lately, more manic. I'm not sure how to describe it." He waved a hand. "She asked me not long ago if I minded not knowing who my real dad is. I told her no. I've got a great dad. Then she got kind of snippy and said I might find out anyway."

"Do you think she was writing some kind

of tell-all book or something like that?"

"Maybe."

Theo didn't mind the company. Having Patrick and Celeste stay at the house was the only reasonable place any of them could come up with. Evidently a horde of reporters was camped in front of Patrick's small house. Another group learned Celeste had been living at Martha's house before the wedding and patrolled her neighborhood.

Tony was on his way out when his phone chirped. "I'm going to bury this thing in the backyard if it rings one more time." He glanced at the screen. "Hey, Doc."

Theo watched and tried to listen, but got no information. Whatever the doctor was telling Tony made his head shake. He wasn't smiling when he disconnected.

"Leukemia." Tony glanced past her. "According to the doctor, she has . . . er, had, leukemia."

"So she might have been putting her house in order, so to speak? Could it be treated?"

Tony shrugged. "Should I tell Patrick?"

Theo considered what she would want if she was in his situation. "How would it help?"

"It might explain her recent behavior."

"Then go for it." Theo hoped it was good advice. "The honeymooners are playing video games with the boys."

Tony, with Wade, drove up past The Lodge. From the road they could see yellow crime scene tape still fluttering from the balcony and surrounding the shrubbery where Scarlet was found. Tony found it hard to believe it had only been a week since Theo's discovery and call. He felt at least twenty years older.

"Do you suspect Dan?"

Wade's question snapped Tony back into the present. It was a fair question. "I don't think he killed either one of them. Not really. I am hoping he can fill in some of the blanks or identify the dulcimer strings." He glanced at his deputy. "What about you?"

"I'd say no," said Wade. "But, I think he's less of a recluse than most people think."

"How so?"

"To start with, he runs an internet business. He sells dulcimers and supplies." Wade paused. "So he could have sold the strings to someone he'd never seen."

Tony glanced at Wade. "How do you know this?"

"My cousin drives a delivery truck. One

day he mentioned his best customer is Dan."

Before Tony could organize his thoughts, he turned on to the road to Dan's home. The home was small, a single story with a covered front porch running the width of the house. The wood had peeling white paint mixed with bare wood weathered to silver gray. There was no sign of life. No dog, car or light. When they climbed out of the Blazer, all they heard was the sigh of wind through the trees. A few birds were sitting on a feeder hanging from the porch cover.

Wade knocked on the front door. Nothing

Together they walked toward the back of the house on a driveway of two ruts. Behind the house was a cabin. Dan sat on the bench of a picnic table, his arms crossed on the table, his face buried in his arms. Great sobs wracked his shoulders, but he didn't make a sound.

"Dan?" Tony called. Nothing. "Dan." He called louder.

Dan lifted his face and looked at them. Tears poured down his face, following the creases in his weathered skin. "She's really dead?"

Tony nodded and walked to the edge of the table. Beyond them, an open door led into Dan's workshop. He could see a partially completed dulcimer on a spotless workbench. "I know you and Elf were close."

"And you came to see if I done her in?" His head jerked from side to side, spraying teardrops in a wide arc. "I loved that little girl, but not like folks think. She was my friend and I was hers."

Tony and Wade eased down onto the bench opposite him. "How'd you meet?"

Dan's eyes closed, and he clasped his hands together, resting them on the table. "I came back from 'Nam and wandered for a while, looking for direction, I guess." He opened his eyes, surprisingly young in his old face. They glistened with still unshed tears. "I bought this land with money I borrowed from my folks in Oklahoma. Then I discovered dulcimers and learned everything I could about them. Years passed, and I found peace up here."

Wade shifted, impatient, and Tony frowned him into stillness.

"One day I was sitting out on the house porch and I looked up, and there was Easter Lily standing down near the road. She wasn't bigger than a mite and was barely more than a kid. I could hear her crying and went over to check on her." He wiped

390

some of his own tears away with the heel of his hand. "She said she was pregnant and her daddy threw her out of the house."

"Did she tell you who the father was?"

"Nope, and I didn't ask." Dan rubbed the back of his neck. "I told her she could visit all she wanted, and I'd teach her to play the dulcimer, but I couldn't have no little girl living in my house, 'specially not one with child."

"So she went home?" Tony guessed she must have left school until after the baby was born because he'd never seen a pregnant girl in school when he was a boy. Nowadays it was, unfortunately, not uncommon.

"She stayed up here all day every day and slept in her daddy's house." A flash of anger hardened his expression even more. "The old tyrant didn't feed her, but I did. For a little girl, she sure could eat."

"And she learned to play the dulcimer?"

He nodded. "When she was close to having the baby, I introduced her to a nice couple I knew who wanted to adopt, so I guess I was a matchmaker of sorts."

"You weren't at Patrick's wedding." Tony made a note to ask the groom's parents how they remember the events leading to Patrick's adoption.

"Nope. I had my visits with Easter Lily and her sister earlier." He glanced at his house and cabin. "I ain't real social."

Wade said, "Were you and Scarlet close too?"

"Not as much. She didn't care for music, but she'd come up sometimes with her sister since she was pregnant at the same time, and no, I don't know who fathered her baby either. I always sort of had the idea it was the same man though." He narrowed his eyes as he rubbed his chin. "Scarlet's was stillborn."

Tony had a feeling the man had something else to get off his chest, so he sat back, relaxing. Birds high in the trees made soft noises. A slight breeze carried the scent of wood smoke.

"I've got no proof." Dan's voice rumbled into the quiet. "But I think the daddy's been paying those girls to keep their secret. And I'd guess it would amount to a pretty penny after all these years."

Not surprising, Tony guessed, but disturbing on another level. One man, impregnating two girls, and then paying for silence. Theirs had not been a case of teenage love or lust, but rather one of an adult abusing children. But why kill them now? Did they threaten to talk? Did they ask for more money? After a more than a quarter of a century, why was it still a secret?

"Let's go." Tony stood and shook hands with Dan.

Wade trotted at his side. "Who would be so destroyed by telling the secret that it's worth killing two people?"

"I don't know." Tony stopped at the Blazer and stood with one hand on the door. "What do we have for a motive? Anger? Fear? Revenge?"

"Neither of the women even lived around here anymore." Wade shoved a hand through his hair. "So has someone been waiting for them to return?"

"As freaky as it sounds, I think that's exactly what happened. What did the pair of them know, or who did the pair of them threaten in some way? Coincidence does happen, but I think both of these deaths were deliberate."

"You mean the grease on their backs?"

"Among other things." Tony searched his pockets for antacids. "The grease is either a direct clue or an attempt to cover up something."

"You mean like point the blame on the Thomas brothers?"

"Sure. Why not? They are well known. Their tow truck or pickup is always on every road. They would be almost invisible to local eyes."

"Hide in plain sight?"

"Exactly."

"So the grease on the backs is either a clue or a red herring?"

"Yes, but our killer, who is either cunning or doesn't want to dirty his clothes, has left something behind."

"What?" Wade stared into Tony's eyes. "Did you find something?"

"The lab will. I'm sure of it. There will be some exchange of hair, skin, blood. The difficult part will be identifying it and its donor."

# Big As a Mountain Mystery Quilt

## PUTTING IT ALL TOGETHER

**Layout —**

Row 1 — Place one of block #A in upper left corner, next block #B, block #C, block #B and block #A.

Sew blocks together. Make two sets.

Row 2 — Place one of block #B in upper left corner, next 3 blocks #C, and end with block #B.

Sew blocks together. Make two sets.

Row 3 — Sew five number 3 blocks together.

Make two sets.

Sew the rows together — 1-2-3-3-2-1.

Measure through center, both length and width.

From 4 1/2 inch strips of fabric number #2, cut 2 to length measurement and 2 to width measurement.

Sew longer strips onto sides. Press to border.

Sew 4 1/2″ square of fabric #1 on each end of remaining strips. Press to fabric #2. Sew one onto top and one on bottom.

Quilt as desired and bind with the remaining 2 1/2″ wide strips of fabric #3.

# CHAPTER TWENTY-NINE

Tony drove up the mountain taking Quentin home. His time in the jail was up, and he said he had no one to call for a ride home. The road was dry and clear, which made the trip at least possible. In bad weather, the road was treacherous at best. Quentin was the sole owner of this section of the mountain. Property rich, but too cash poor to improve it.

Tony made the last turn and stopped next to Quentin's shiny black pickup painted with decorative flames on the front. At the top of the drive, Quentin's mobile home sat to the right. If anything, it was more worn out and miserable than the last time Tony had come up here, but the removal of a crumbling, rusted-out shed improved the appearance of the place. Overall, the property looked better. Tony thought Quentin had also installed a new portable outhouse. The bright blue shed sat slightly downhill of the trailer.

Another new addition caught his attention. To the left sat a camping trailer, quite a bit smaller than a mobile home. The brown and white striped trailer had cinder blocks stacked around the tires, keeping it from shifting position. It hadn't been there the last time Tony made his way up the mountain. "Are you moving, Quentin?"

"No."

"Do you have a tenant?" At Quentin's blank expression, he tried again. "A renter?"

Quentin said he did at the same time Tony saw Roscoe.

At the far side of the new trailer, a patch of vegetation had been mowed down, forming a lawn of sorts. Cinder blocks formed steps to the door. Someone had put together a porch cover using two-by-fours and a blue tarp. Dora, the vending machine, nestled in the shelter. Smoke billowed from a round black barbeque grill, and Tony smelled cooking meat. Roscoe stood next to the grill, ineffectively waving away the smoke with a long fork.

"What's for dinner?" Tony made his way through the weeds.

"Uh . . ." Roscoe's expression dropped from welcoming to furtive. "Uh, nothing."

Watching Roscoe stab the cooking meat

made Tony doubt the man's veracity. He studied the surface of the grill. He'd bet the meat of the day was squirrel. "I prefer mine fried."

"It was already dead, just layin' by the side of the road." Roscoe grinned, his relief palpable. "Don't tell the game warden. He says I can go to prison for this."

Tony was flabbergasted. Hairy Rags was evidently out of his mind. Maybe a fine. Maybe a warning, but prison for a squirrel dinner? Road kill squirrel at that. "Since I'm here, I thought I'd stop by and talk to you and Baby."

"Nossir. Baby's moved on." Roscoe's eyes crossed from his effort to tell a convincing lie.

"She was in your truck the other night." Tony took a relaxed pose against a tree. "She looked quite festive in all her hunter orange."

"Well, yeah, but . . ."

"Where'd she go?"

Roscoe caved in. Tony knew he would. The man just couldn't lie worth spit. He always refereed a fair game, and he wasn't good with secrets and half-truths.

"Why's he after my Baby?" Roscoe wailed like a toddler and fat tears ran down his face. "She's working on her winter sleep

398

home back there."

Baby ran out of the woods toward them, loping on all fours. Ignoring Tony, the young bear stood on her hind legs and licked Roscoe's face; her long pink tongue bore a striking resemblance to a big dog's. With her hunter orange vest and glossy black fur, it was clear she was healthy and well cared for.

"Where's her bear family?"

Roscoe's skinny shoulders rose and fell. He pressed his hands over the bear's ears as if to shield her from unpleasant news. "Her mama was kilt by some of those wackos up past the Old Nest. I seed it myself 'n hid Baby from them. They was going after her too, 'n they're who old Sourpuss ought to be a-chasin'."

"Can you show me on a map?"

Roscoe nodded and clipped a leash on Baby's collar. "She loves squirrel and ain't learned about fire," he said as he led the docile bear to Tony's Blazer.

Tony pulled out a stack of maps and waited as Roscoe studied each one in turn. Just when Tony was ready to abandon the project, Roscoe jabbed a map.

"They was here." He grinned. "Betcha thought I didn't remember."

Tony hadn't doubted the man's memory

as much as his map skills. Roscoe's fingernail rested exactly where Tony suspected it would be. On the county line. Tony smiled. Part of the problem was locked up in his jail. Surely there would be less activity up there at the Nest, at least for awhile.

Tony was sound asleep. After days of trying to keep up with the chaos in the county, he was worn out. He wasn't wild about sleeping alone, but he got to use a lot more of the bed without his overburdened wife. A whisper roused him slightly. The sound of little boys giggling was followed by the vibrations of the two of them climbing onto the mattress. Tony slipped back into his dreams. It was dark as homemade sin when a sound awakened him. His eyelids lifted. Two sets of glow-in-the-dark lime green teeth grinned at him.

Startled, he sat bolt upright.

The little boys laughed and jumped about, making their plastic teeth wiggle and bounce around like fireflies in the room. "Gotcha."

After the past few days, Tony was feeling more than a bit loopy, and his sons' antics struck him as the funniest thing he'd seen in a year. He laughed so loud and hard, he almost didn't hear his cell phone ring on the nightstand.

"What is going on upstairs?" Theo asked, checking up on them.

Tony tried to describe the glowing teeth and his reaction to them, but it failed to really paint the picture. Most likely because he kept laughing like a fool.

"I'm jealous," said Theo and disconnected.

The paper jammed down Elf's throat remained with the coroner. A photocopy of it lay on Tony's desk. It was newly composed music. The paper was designed for the purpose with treble and bass staffs. Hand drawn notes on the lines were barely visible under the string of words written in pencil. "My heart. The little heart."

He felt the sizzle of discovery. He assumed Elf was working on this music, these very words, when her killer arrived. Was she expecting anyone? Whom did she trust, or at least whom did she not fear? He assumed "the heart" was either her lover's or her baby's.

If she was ill and knew it, was she saying farewell to her son? Was she telling him the identity of the fathers of her and Scarlet's babies?

He was still disturbed by the demolition of Elf's house. What about its contents? The furniture? The piles of papers and records and family pictures — where were they? He called Gus.

"Hey, baby brother."

Tony wondered how to get rid of caller ID. "Hail, Caesar." He thought being Marc Antony was better than being Caesar Augustus. The one thing all the Abernathy siblings agreed on was how much trouble their mother's penchant for old Rome caused.

"Okay, we're even." Gus laughed, a great rolling laugh. "Is life better today?"

"No." Tony did feel better just hearing something fun. "It's an ugly business no matter how you look at it."

"Can I help?"

"Maybe. Tell me everything you know about the house you demolished for Elf, like what happened to the furniture and papers."

For awhile, Gus made some humming noise. Then he said, "There was a moving truck, not a big cross country rig, just a truck from some place in Knoxville. I can see the logo in my head. I just don't remember the name offhand. Anyway, they were pulling away when I arrived to see what Elf had in mind."

"And?" Tony wanted to squeeze the information out of his brother.

"Hey, don't get your underwear in a wad. I'm trying to remember the details for you." Gus started humming again. "Okay, the first time I went into the house, there was no furniture, no rugs and nothing hanging on the walls. There was a stack of boxes back in the music room. I assumed they were her gold records and such, but I didn't look into any of them."

"How big was the stack?" Tony had no idea if the information was important or not.

"Oh, maybe ten boxes, the size even you could carry if filled with books."

"Was that it?" Tony ignored the jibe.

"Yep." Gus sounded confused now. "There wasn't another stick of furniture, paper or musical instruments. There wasn't even a can of beans in the kitchen."

"Did you notice any reason she wouldn't want to give the house to Patrick as it was? Were there termites or mold or rot?"

"Nope. She just said she wanted it torn down to the dust or she'd burn it."

Ruth Ann waved a hand in Tony's direction. Either she was drying her fingernails or wanted to attract his attention. The phone pressed to her ear made him think it was the latter.

"Here he is now. I know he'll be happy to talk to you." She extended the receiver and mouthed "Frank Thomas."

Not sure he'd agree to the "happy" part, Tony accepted the phone call. "Frank?"

"You know them coveralls you was as in about?"

"Yes." Tony decided Ruth Ann was ps chic. He was delighted by the call and di even know why.

"Well, the oddest thing happened." Fr coughed into the phone. "They're back found them folded all neat-like this mor ing on the clean stack."

"Have they been washed? Are they cle Had the killer taken the time to do laundry before returning the stolen iten

"Nossir. They's just as dirty as can be.'

"Don't touch them. I'll be right over." Tony tossed the receiver to Ruth Ann and headed for his parking bay. He snapped his fingers. "Wade, come."

It took them maybe three minutes to drive to the garage, where they found Frank and Joe Thomas staring at the stack of coveralls. Sure enough, there was a dirty pair on the top of the stack. Each of the mechanics held clean ones. Tony could feel himself grinning. A stupid move on the part of their killer.

Wade was smiling too. "Not above committing murder, but too honest to steal coveralls?"

"Says a lot, doesn't it?" Tony pulled three large bags from the back of the Blazer. "We need to take the dirty one, the one under it and whichever of those" — he pointed to the ones clutched in grimy hands — "whichever one was on the top."

Joe Thomas placed his coveralls into the bag like he was delivering a holy relic. "How'd whoever it was get in to put the coveralls there?"

"Excellent question, Joe. Any ideas?" Tony glanced around the interior of the garage. Besides the big overhead door, there were three normal doors. One opened into the office. One for the restroom. One on the front of the building, next to the overhead.

Joe just shook his head.

Frank rubbed his chin and glanced up at the ceiling. "Well, we was both gone for a while this morning. Had to haul a big rig out of a ditch up near the national park."

"Don't you lock up?" said Wade.

"We lock the office." Joe glared. "Only at night do we lock it all."

# CHAPTER THIRTY

Concerned by the plight of the Bainbridge sisters, Theo called Tony. The news was good. The ladies had arrived mid-morning, well rested. They had carried with them a packet of Emery's papers, per his instructions to them, which they had forgotten all about in their sorrow and panic. Tony and Doc Nash had sifted through the papers while the ladies sipped tea and charmed Ruth Ann. It turned out that Emery had been a fine, if somewhat overprotective, older brother. He had purchased a life insurance policy on himself large enough to allow the sisters to live extravagantly for the rest of their days. No one was even considering pressing charges against them.

Delighted by the news, Theo signaled for Katti to push her into the shop. She braced herself for the inevitable chaos. She was sure it would get even worse by the time of the funeral. Theo thought if Scarlet's funeral had been sparsely attended, Elf's was going to set a record in the other direction. Rumors had suggested music and motion picture stars were expected to attend. The family members in town for Patrick's wedding were by and large the ones who would come for the funeral. They decided to "have the funeral while we're all still here."

Theo wasn't surprised — or pleased — when Nellie Pearl burst into her shop, carrying with her the aroma of dirt, body odor and menthol. She loved to rub mentholated chest rub on her hair and skin. She was not allowed to touch anything in Theo's shop.

"The funeral's to be at the high school," Nellie Pearl announced. "Can you believe it? Only heathens would hold a funeral there."

Theo preferred churches as well, but the decision to use the high school made sense. The gym held more people than any place except the football field, and the weather was not conducive to outdoor services. "Are you going?" What she wanted to say was, "I heard your daughter is coming to get you, bathe you, and lock you up, you old bat." She didn't.

"Of course. Me and Elf was thick as thieves back in the olden days."

It was improbable, but possible, that they

had been closer many years ago. Theo wasn't about to get into an argument, but maybe she could learn something. "So, were you friends with Scarlet as well?"

"Miss Priss?" The old woman laughed, but there was no humor, only malice, in the sound. "She thought she was special, didn't she? How could anyone ever like her?"

Theo felt the woman's bitter hatred. It poisoned the air around her. "Why not?"

"She tried to steal Easter Lily's man away, didn't she?" Nellie Pearl reached for a pair of scissors, but Gretchen got to them first. "A-course, he was a mighty purty man. The two of them weren't his only conquests." She flashed a coy grin.

"He was pretty?" Theo tried a smile, momentarily wondering what a young Nellie Pearl might have looked like. "Was he young like Elf? Does Patrick resemble him?"

"I don't know you." Nellie Pearl suddenly stopped and stared at Theo. She pointed a finger at Theo and stirred the scent of menthol again. "Get out of my house."

Tony watched the white hearse bearing Elf's body to the high school gym. Someone had arranged an enormous floral display almost covering the entire vehicle, like a float in a parade.

Sitting in the gym, waiting for the cortege to arrive, were the celebrity guests and other mourners lucky enough to draw a number allowing them to attend. The numbers indicated the section of the gym where they could sit.

The fans without tickets lined the road throwing flowers at the passing hearse and the limos carrying the close family members.

Summer Flowers sat alone in the first limo. After Theo's description of the man's attitude about his daughters, Tony was surprised he bothered to attend. Maybe he'd reconsidered his opinion, or maybe he thought it was amusing.

Patrick and Celeste had bowed to the pressure of funeral director and mayor, Calvin Cashdollar. They sat in the back of the second limo, holding hands. Pericles, his face buried in a handkerchief, rode next to the driver.

Blossom, along with her father Autumn Flowers, her mother and the whole garden of girls, their husbands and children, as well as both of Blossom's beaus, arrived in a veritable caravan.

Tony watched the gym fill up, not sure what he expected to see. What he wanted was someone to stand up, holding a sign with an arrow and a confession: "It was me," or "I did it." A simple, tasteful "I'm guilty" would be lovely.

The section of the bleachers directly behind the family held mostly out-of-town musicians, actors, politicians, television personalities. A professional football player was slated to sing. In Tony's opinion, all they needed was a tent and an elephant to complete the circus.

Wade sauntered up to him. "I've been looking for anyone who might look like Patrick."

"Tell me you've found someone." Tony knew he was begging, but dignity wasn't important. "I'd love to talk to Patrick's mysterious father."

"Sorry." Wade held up his camera. "I'm taking lots of pictures, though. Maybe we'll find somebody when we go through them."

"I don't suppose we could run a DNA test on everyone attending?"

Wade shook his head. "Sorry boss. Do you think the killer is here?"

"Yes." Tony was sure. The biggest problem, other than identifying the unknown person, was the huge number of mourners and observers who were not inside the gym. It was impossible to check every face.

At last the funeral service began. Tony was

relieved it was a dignified service and not the media free-for-all he'd imagined. The football star had a beautiful baritone voice. No one shrieked or fainted. No one streaked the event. Although incredibly slow moving because of the hordes of fans tossing flowers at the hearse, the cortege managed to get to the cemetery. Easter Lily Flowers was buried next to her sister Scarlet. Whether friends in life or not, they would share common ground in death.

Tony couldn't help glancing over at Mr. Beasley's grave. After the Halloween grave digging episode, his dirt had been neatly returned to the site. Tony found himself grateful the disturbed plot hadn't been Elf's grave. There would probably be a photographer ready to sell a picture of the old ladies to the tabloids. He could imagine lurid claims of cloning or sales of body parts on the Internet.

With her wheelchair and temporary handicapped tag, Theo was given a spot close to the front in the gym and at the cemetery. She tried to imagine what had brought murder up to her quilt retreat and how the one murder was connected to the death of a very popular entertainer. What secret did the sisters share? Besides Patrick, who wasn't a secret. The identity of his father was. And did the man even know he'd sired a son?

In the midst of people leaving, heading for their cars, Theo overheard a raspy male voice say, "I'm sorry she's dead, but I guess that makes me a free man."

And a woman's voice drowned out by the noises of the crowd had agreed. Theo tried to maneuver the wheelchair to find the source of the voices. It was impossible to do so in the crush of mourners.

"Theo." Martha charged through the crowd and grabbed the wheelchair handles. "What are you doing out here alone? Where's Katti?"

"We got separated." Theo leaned forward, searching for a flash of pink. "I think I'd better wait here for her."

"I'll wait with you."

"Shouldn't you be teaching?" Theo didn't want to admit her sudden unease at being alone in the disorganized crowd.

"Not this afternoon." Martha grabbed the wheelchair and pulled it out of the path of four men walking abreast, deep in conversation. "With the funeral in the gym, the high school students went home at noon. Elementary is still in session."

Theo relaxed. At least she hadn't misplaced her sons. She smiled at Miss Flossie, who was picking her way between the tombstones. The old woman fumbled with the buttons on her coat. The glint of a heavy gold necklace with a single large ruby, winked at Theo and disappeared.

"Hey, Tony." The voice on the phone was one he had heard only a few times and could never forget: the accent was North Dakota meets Appalachia. Today it positively rang with excitement.

"Hey Lars, what did you find?" Tony held his breath. Lars had been given the coveralls to work his magic on.

"I'm still picking bits of evidence off the outside of your coveralls, but I found some really great hairs on the inside."

Tony heard the sound a keyboard clicking before the voice came back. "I have enough hairs to run nine kinds of tests on them and share the extras with you. Who knows, maybe you'll recognize the color and length."

"We're small, but we've got a few people living here."

A laugh like a donkey's bray came through the receiver. "Okay, point taken. Maybe carry them around to your three beauty shops. I'll bet one of them has seen the dye job."

Tony felt like tap dancing down the hall. A real clue. "I'll have someone pick up the hairs in two hours at the latest."

In Silersville, there were actually four full time beauty parlors, as Tony thought of them. Prudence Sligar Holt threatened to throw him into the street when he said something along those lines to her. The champion arm-wrestler and part-time psychic wasn't someone he wanted to antagonize. Although he thought one of the members of the "catfish guerillas" ought to be a bit more gracious to the sheriff.

"I run a salon."

"Fair enough," said Tony. He held the hair sample encased in a plastic sleeve. "Does this hair ring any bells?"

Prudence studied it carefully, holding it up like she was comparing it to hair on a head. Then she picked up a metal ring with gradated color samples, short braids, and picked out one. "Here's your color."

"I'm impressed." Tony stared at the color sample, trying to imagine that shade of hair on anyone he'd seen. He touched the sample ring. "Would everyone using the same dye match exactly?"

"No. The chemical formulas are not identical from brand to brand, but the end result could be too close to call."

"Do you know anyone who might match?"

"Yes, several folks." Prudence began flipping through a notebook and stopped, turning the page to face him. "These women and a man." She watched while Tony made a note of the names. "These are just the ones I do. I'd bet every *stylist*" — she emphasized the word — "has a minimum of three similar. It's a good color, not brassy, and this length" — Prudence waved to Tony's hair sample — "is neither long nor short. It could be a man or woman."

Somewhat crushed, Tony thanked her. He had hoped for a miracle. What he had was a clue and the cause for more questions. The investigation would take a while, but a conclusion would be reached.

# CHAPTER THIRTY-ONE

Tony stood by the side of the highway connecting Park County to the back side of the national park. It was a beautiful road, full of twists and turns, and had no shoulder in areas where the road was cut through stone. At one of the turnoffs, a boiled peanut vendor had set up a makeshift store in the back of his pickup. He recognized Old Nem by the mustard and green sport coat he wore when he was working. It had seen decades of use and still hadn't worn out. Most of the year, Old Nem was simply "the egg man." Today he had his wares arranged neatly, and his mongrel dog and constant companion, Lucy Two, stood next to his cash drawer — a rusty coffee can covered with aluminum foil.

Lucy Two wasn't much of a deterrent to crime. Anytime a person got within five feet of her, she'd roll over onto her back, legs sticking up, and wait to have her belly scratched. If she ever growled at someone, it was time to pay attention. Old Nem wasn't a criminal, in Tony's mind. Tony thought the old guy simply didn't understand the concept of needing permission to park where he wanted and sell his eggs and peanuts.

Writing him a citation would be a waste of time and money. There were few citizens in the county who hadn't eaten eggs or peanuts they'd bought from Nem. He was honest and trustworthy and helped out in the community.

Tony handed him five dollars for some peanuts. "Have you been out here long today?"

"Yep."

"I've been getting reports of signs being shot with a .22." Tony pointed toward the sign behind him. It was so peppered with holes, the black numbers were impossible to discern.

Nem looked over Tony's shoulder at the speed limit sign. "Yep."

"In your travels around the county selling your eggs and peanuts, have you witnessed anyone shooting with a .22?"

"Yep."

"Would you tell me who it is?"

"Yep."

Tony busted out laughing. Old Nem joined in, and Lucy Two yapped and ran in a circle. "So who is it?"

"Man in a black truck."

Tony guessed there were more .22 rifles in Park County than black trucks, but it was a starting place.

"I tell you what made me afeared." Old Nem's voice dropped to a whisper. "That crazy Nellie Pearl carries her rifle down to the road and shoots at them automobiles."

The idea of Nellie Pearl Prigmore shooting at passing cars was serious. The old woman's dementia seemed to worsening rapidly. She wouldn't talk to her daughter. The only person she seemed to trust, at least on alternate Tuesdays, was Sheila Teffeteller, the only female deputy in his department. Nellie Pearl had some respect for his badge and office, if not for him. He was an outsider because he didn't move to Silersville until he was eight.

"Thanks, Nem, I appreciate the help." Tony scratched Lucy Two one more time before climbing in his official vehicle.

Tony left a message with the highway department to have the sign replaced.

With the excitement of the funeral over, Theo remembered she needed to pay Lila for the silver shawl and wheeled herself across the street, leaving Katti to help Gretchen unpack a new shipment of fabric.

Lila was busy with a customer, so Theo rolled toward the photo wall. She saw a picture of herself and Lila at the grand opening of her quilt shop. Had she really ever been that thin? She glanced down at her massive belly and sighed. More photographs celebrated events they had both attended. Lila posed with a variety of men and women, famous and not.

One photograph in particular caught Theo's eye. Why hadn't she noticed it before? The man standing next to Lila was a politician from a neighboring state. What was unusual was the heart-shaped birthmark just below his jaw. It looked just like the one she'd seen on Patrick MacLeod's neck at breakfast.

Lila's customer departed. Positive she knew who'd fathered Elf's baby, Theo rolled past a poster advertising tuxedo rentals and stopped at the cash register. "I'm here to pay for the shawl."

"I almost forgot." Lila opened a drawer and pulled out not only the sales slip for the shawl, but the book missing from Theo's workshop. "Miss Flossie was here."

Theo asked what Flossie had taken from

Lila but only got a slight shrug for an answer.

"You don't know much about women, do you?" Theo stared up at Tony, holding the copy of the music Elf had been composing. "Her baby's heart. Her lover's heart. She couldn't stand it. The jealousy was eating her alive."

"She? You mean Lila?"

"Yes."

"But why? Her boyfriend's affair with Elf ended a quarter of a century ago." He shook his head. "How long does jealousy last?"

"In Lila's case, forever." Theo rubbed her belly. "He had children with his wife. He had children with both of Summer Flowers' girls. Lila probably craved one of her own, and he wouldn't give her one. It wasn't just jealousy, it was also blackmail. Her silence was probably very expensive."

Theo had described the photographs and the man with the heart-shaped birthmark to Tony. Her most convincing information was Miss Flossie's exchange of Theo's book for Scarlet's necklace. "Lila must have been frantic when she saw the necklace was gone."

Tony and Wade sat opposite Lila and her

attorney. Carl Lee tried to get Lila to remain silent, but she wasn't listening to his advice.

"No. I want to explain."

Tony was shocked. He'd known Lila for most of his life. She'd always seemed so nice. Friendly. Normal. "What happened to Scarlet?"

"I knew she was staying up at The Lodge. I drove up and parked in the lot like everyone else. It didn't take much thinking to find her room. I just took a key from the drawer and went up." Lila's fingers mimicked playing with an invisible dulcimer string. "I sat in the bathroom, in the dark, running my fingers over the string. Her sister made a fortune playing music." Her lips curled. "And even with all her money, she made my darling pay and pay."

"Why wait in the bathroom?" Wade leaned forward.

"I figured that the less I moved around, the less likely I would be to leave evidence. I didn't want to take a chance, even though I was wearing those nasty, smelly oil-stained overalls."

"And the dark?" said Tony.

"I was afraid the light might shine under the door and scare her off. The last thing I needed was to have a whole gaggle of women barging in, trapping me in the bathroom."

"Go on." Tony wanted to get through this and go home.

"It felt like I sat in there for days. I almost left, but finally I heard the key in the door. I stood up and caught her from behind the second she was in the room. I wrapped the string around and around her neck and jerked hard. Her neck snapped. She never knew what happened."

Tony felt a chill. Lila was the picture of disappointment, and her voice sounded plaintive.

"I did want her to know I did it. *I* was the one who killed her. She claimed I was weak. I wanted her to see I am not a worm."

"Why did you drop her outside? Why not just leave her in her room?"

"That's where my plan got confused. I thought if I pushed her into the bushes from the balcony, it might look like an accident and then it would be perfect. Just some trash. But every time I wanted to do it, I would hear someone talking in the hall, so I decided that it would be real late before I would be able to leave." She started talking faster and faster. "One time I saw a TV show where the body was kept warm and the time of the death was all confused. I thought it might be better if I had an alibi, you know, just in case. So I wrapped her up and put her near the heat." Sweat was pouring off Lila's face now, and she was gasping for breath. "By the time the hotel got quiet, I was so freaked out I couldn't think straight. I took the jewelry. I figured I could hock it safely the next time I was on a buying trip to some city. I couldn't believe that batty old lady took the necklace. I saw her wearing it at Elf's funeral and knew it was only a matter of time before you found out."

"Did you kill her for the money?" said Wade.

"No." Lila's eyes filled with tears. "She owed me more than money."

"Why?" Tony guessed he was missing something big. Something Theo understood. "What made you hate her and her sister?"

"They tainted my love." Lila looked surprised. "They both tempted him with their bodies. They both carried his children."

"I knew about Elf's baby, of course, but Scarlet's?"

"Oh, hers died." Lila's smile was just short of triumphant. "But even it had the birthmark. I hated them all."

"Blackmail wouldn't have been necessary

if he was a better man." Tony doubted two lonely girls seduced by an adult were anything but victims of another type of criminal. "What happened to Elf?"

Clearly furious, Lila slammed her hands on the table, half rising from her chair. "She promised not to tell."

"And she kept her promise, even from her son."

Lila's head moved sharply from side to side. "She was writing her memoirs, wasn't she? I couldn't trust that she wouldn't tell."

"How did you get into the motor home?"

"I saw her driver go into his space." Lila's expression became dreamy, like she was recalling a pleasant event. "I still had the coveralls in my car, so I pulled them on over my dress. She let me in. Everyone acts like she was something wonderful, but she was stupid. Stupid Elf."

Tony saw Carl Lee try again to silence her. Lila shook her head.

"I'm not stupid like Elf." Lila hissed. "She said she was working on a special song. She was distracted, kind of spacey. When I asked her what it was about, she said it was a song about her baby."

"Patrick?"

"There it was on the table. All about her little heart. No one else would understand, but I did. Elf went to get us some wine. While she was in the kitchen, I took the sheet of paper and folded it up and put it in my pocket." Lila's eyes were wild and spittle flew from her lips. "I pulled out the dulcimer string and waited."

"The music was in her mouth." Tony checked his notes.

"Oh, she plopped down on her chair and poured the wine like we were old friends having a party. Can you imagine?" Lila went quiet.

Carl Lee opened his mouth, but she shook her head.

"I gave her the chance to apologize, to promise to leave him alone."

"And?" Tony prompted.

"And nothing. She yawned like she was bored. Didn't even cover her mouth. I fixed her good — shoved the paper into her open mouth and tied her voice shut. She'll never sing that wretched song."

Tony and Wade walked into the hall, and Tony glanced back. "It's like she doesn't realize what 'dead' means."

A week later, Tony arrived home just as a truck pulled up in front of their home. Sitting proudly on the flatbed trailer was the brightest yellow SUV Tony had ever seen.

425

Painted to resemble quilt blocks was "Theo" in huge block letters, extending the length of the vehicle on both sides.

"It's hideous." Tony murmured into his wife's ear as he rolled her chair down the ramp.

"It's gorgeous!" Theo bounced in her excitement. "I can't wait to drive it, or at least ride in it. Let's take it to the Marmots' party."

So Tony drove, embarrassed by the gaudy car but secretly thrilled by Mr. Beasley's kindness.

When they arrived at the dump for Claude and Katti's wedding celebration, he decided the SUV wasn't too bright for him after all.

At least it wasn't pink.

Pink paper lanterns hung from the Marmots' trees. Pink crepe paper streamers covered the ceiling in the living room. Even the appliances in the kitchen were pink. A huge red velvet cake with bubble gum–pink icing sat on the dining room table surrounded by a stack of pink plates and napkins.

Theo showed him the brand new pink and brown quilt proudly displayed in the bedroom, accented with a pink satin pillow with "Katti" embroidered in brown letters and a brown satin pillow with "Claude" in pink.

It made Theo's yellow car look rather washed out.

# ABOUT THE AUTHOR

**Barbara Graham** has loved mysteries "forever" and wonders what could be more fun than making up people and then killing them off. Legally, that is. She began making up stories in the third grade and immediately quit learning to multiply and divide. Her motto is "Every story needs a dead body and every bed needs a quilt."

An enthusiastic, if dreadful, gardener, she is a prize-winning quilter. Her quilts have been in calendars and magazines, as well as displayed in shows. Her favorite quilts are the well-loved and frayed ones that get hugged every day.

Married to a wonderful man who can do math in his head and the mother of two perfect sons, she has acquired a fabulous daughter-in-law.

Visit her website at www.bgmysteries.com.